The Perfect Blend

"C. Kelly Robinson has created a perfect blend of humor, drama and emotion. Nikki was too real." —Gloria Mallette, bestselling author of *Shades of Jade*, *Promises to Keep*, and *The Honey Well*

"Robinson flaunts his literary skills and spins a tale of love and family that is emotionally riveting and highly entertaining. This is one read you will not want to miss." —Tracy Price-Thompson, bestselling author of *Chocolate Sangria* and *Black Coffee*

"C. Kelly Robinson is a wonderfully talented writer who captured my attention on page one and kept it until the very end." —Kimberla Lawson Roby, author of *Too Much of a Good Thing*

Also by C. Kelly Robinson

No More Mr. Nice Guy

Between Brothers

The
Perfect
Blend

C. Kelly Robinson

NEW AMERICAN LIBRARY

New American Library
Published by New American Library, a division of
Penguin Group (USA) Inc., 375 Hudson Street,
New York, New York 10014, U.S.A.
Penguin Books Ltd, 80 Strand,
London WC2R 0RL, England
Penguin Books Australia Ltd, 250 Camberwell Road,
Camberwell, Victoria 3124, Australia
Penguin Books Canada Ltd, 10 Alcorn Avenue,
Toronto, Ontario, Canada M4V 3B2
Penguin Books (N.Z.) Ltd, Cnr Rosedale and Airborne Roads,
Albany, Auckland 1310, New Zealand

Penguin Books Ltd, Registered Offices:
80 Strand, London WC2R 0RL, England

First published by New American Library,
a division of Penguin Group (USA) Inc.

First Printing, January 2004
10 9 8 7 6 5 4 3 2 1

 REGISTERED TRADEMARK—MARCA REGISTRADA

Library of Congress Cataloging-in-Publication Data:
Robinson, C. Kelly (Chester Kelly), 1970–
   The perfect blend / C. Kelly Robinson.
       p.   cm.
   ISBN 0-451-21036-0
   1. African Americans—Fiction.   2. Illegitimate children—Fiction.
   I. Title.
   PS3568.O2855P47 2004   2003012362
   813'.54—dc21

Set in Garamond BE
Designed by Daniel Lagin

Printed in the United States of America

The
Perfect
Blend

Nikki

I knew it was time to have my husband's baby on Sunday, May 11. I know, it was Mother's Day, but there was more to it than that.

The day didn't start too poorly. I was a newlywed four months into marriage, minding my business and preparing for church with my husband, Mitchell. I was in the kitchen of our new home, cooking some turkey bacon on the electric stove and slicing up a cantaloupe, three apples, and a bunch of grapes for fruit salad. Java simmered in our high-tech Mr. Coffee as I hummed along to a gospel jazz CD I'd bought the week before.

Turning off the bacon, I wiped my brow and checked my watch. If Mitchell didn't get his butt downstairs now, we were about to be late, and I didn't need to hear my mother-in-law's mouth if we walked in after the choir's processional. "Any day now, babe," I yelled over my shoulder.

My words had barely melted into thin air when my husband's hands slid around my waist. I shivered at the tingling sensation of his teeth as they gently locked around my right earlobe. He's a sneaky something when he wants to be.

"I felt your call before you spoke," he whispered playfully. His grip, however, tightened, and I could feel that he was more than happy to see me.

Sliding the bacon from the skillet onto plates—real glass plates, I figured I'd start using paper after our six-month anniversary—I sighed in mock protest. "You don't even care that it's Sunday morning, do you?"

"Uh, well," he said, grinding gently against me, "when God

said be fruitful and multiply, how'd he expect us to do it? Nothing wrong with a little love, is there?"

I turned to face him and cupped his chin, staring into his wide, adorable eyes. "You've had plenty of love these past four months, whenever you've wanted it."

"And I ain't done yet. Now come here and—"

Mitchell's antics were cut short by the purr of the phone. Reluctantly, he let me go and danced across the hardwood floor in his bare feet. He snatched the cordless phone from its wall mount. "Yeah?" He can be rude when he's horny.

The way Mitchell's expression changed suddenly, from annoyed to frightened, I knew it could only be one person. Gina Tatum, my husband's "baby mama."

"Now, hold on," he was saying into the phone, looking at the receiver like it was a person, "you're not making sense, Gina. Last night you said Clay was fine and ready to go with us this morning. He got the flu that quick?"

I stood at our cedar-topped island, our plates of bacon and fruit salad ready, our cups of coffee poured and steaming. As trickles of sweat began to soak the starched collar of his oxford shirt, Mitchell paced from one end of the kitchen to the other. He passed me three times as he waited out Gina's argument.

"Let me come get him," he said when she apparently came up for air. "I swear," he whispered through gritted teeth, looking at me. "Gina, the court order didn't make exceptions for Mother's Day. I let you keep him yesterday to celebrate, but legally I could have picked him up Friday like usual. Just let us come over and—" Mitchell, waiting out another verbal tirade, held up his hand as I walked to him. "Forget it, you enjoy your son on Mother's Day, but tell him Daddy loves him. . . . No, I don't want to talk to him right now because he's sick, remember? Let him get some rest. Bye."

As only she can, Gina left my six-foot, broad-shouldered husband as impotent as Bob Dole without Viagra. We wolfed down breakfast in relative silence, punctuated mainly by Mitchell's hushed profanities, then made the drive to Trinity United Methodist, where we attend as regularly as we can.

It was a beautiful sunny day out, the prime spring temperature at seventy degrees with a nice breeze wafting in and out of my new Infiniti. Our surroundings were beautiful, but the mood inside the car was not so fresh.

"You know," I said, sliding a hand over Mitchell's as he pulled onto I-57, "we can talk about it."

Blowing air through his nostrils, he tugged at his tie and shook his head. "It's moments like these, I know I've let you down."

"Now look, we've done this. I married you knowing I was in for drama. I looked past that. I looked at *you*."

Clay wasn't supposed to be Mitchell's son, you see. Mitchell and Gina hadn't been a real item in the first place. When the little guy was conceived, the two of them were going through bedmates like J.Lo goes through husbands. Granted, I'd had an issue when I first learned Mitchell might have gotten Gina pregnant. He and I weren't exclusive either, but I'd known Gina enough to be disgusted that he'd even swapped fluids with her.

Then came Gina's Act I, where she moved out to Los Angeles and swore there was little chance of Mitchell being the father—she'd been with so many guys during the same time that no one's odds were worth calculating. Eventually, I forgave Mitchell's dalliances and figured Gina would turn out to be right. I mean, I knew it was common, but who really wants a blended family of "hers and his kids" if they can help it?

Wouldn't you know my optimism was not rewarded? Gina returned to Chicago to have the baby, and two months later decided her son should at least know his full genetic history, just in case. I couldn't exactly blame the girl; if I hadn't learned about the long line of heart attacks in my father's family, I'd still be eating fries and burgers every day. Mitchell was one of the guys who contributed a blood sample, and my man was blessed with the luck of the draw.

By the time we arrived at the church, Mitchell had calmed down. "Nik," he said as he put the car into park, "God smiled on me, keeping you in my corner." He leaned over and the smell of his cologne, mixed with the new leather scent of my car seats, set me off. We embraced desperately, suddenly, forgetting where we were as we kissed and groped each other like it was our first date. We cooled it when a playful passerby tapped his horn at us.

Giggling at ourselves, we walked hand in hand into the sanctuary and took a seat in the same pew as Mitchell's mother, as well as my longtime girlfriend Angie and her two little stair steps, Sarah and Milton. Sarah is eighteen months and Milton is eight months. Baby number three is due around Thanksgiving, so yes, Mitchell's big brother, Marvin, has kept Angie busy in the literal sense of the word. She hasn't made it back to her reporter's desk at the *Chicago Tribune* since she said "I do." Today, as usual, Angie was on her own with the little ones while Marvin, a successful attorney and former college-football star, did his duty as a soloist in Trinity's choir. He was on stage in the risers, beaming down at us and giving a thumbs-up. We'd made it just in time to avoid Mrs. Stone's righteous wrath.

The senior church deacons were winding down the morning's devotion, and as the sanctuary hummed to life with the notes of the organ, I held one of Mitchell's hands and peered down the pew at my mother-in-law, who was leaning past little Sarah and Angie while holding baby Milton. "Don't you want one?" she whispered, nodding toward the little bundle in her arms. I smiled back innocently and threw a soft elbow into Mitchell's ribs. I made a mental note. This was three times now Mom Stone had nudged us about starting our own family. Having survived the first few months of marriage, we were now fair game.

I knew Mitchell was probably more annoyed by this than I. I

grudgingly understood where he was coming from. We probably did need time to get settled as a couple before the interruptions of a baby, especially given the instant drama Gina and Clay injected into our marriage. All the same, I'd gladly give birth tomorrow to Mr. Mitchell Stone Jr. or maybe Ms. Ebony Stone (who would be named for my mama).

I'd already geared everything into place. Mitchell had cut down on his meat intake around the time we got married, to keep his weight down. I'd read somewhere that a vegetarian diet could endanger a man's fertility, so I'd started spiking my baby's coffee with a carefully selected zinc supplement, to make sure he came correct when the time was right. I had also convinced him to start sleeping in boxer shorts—roomy boxer shorts—after reading up on the importance of keeping male equipment at room temperature. I even made sure I prepared, or at least bought, all of our meals. As a busy music executive, I don't hardly have the time, but it's been the best way to keep Mitchell's diet free of sperm-blockers like excessive bran or caffeine.

Now don't trip and start talking about me behind my back. You don't know what you would do if you found yourself thirty years old, newly married, and feeling stalked by your past. I mean, I don't just hear the normal biological clock ticking; I have extra issues. When you've had a nameless one-night stand from college give you the gift of a burning pelvis, you realize you can't take having children for granted. Time was when I could push it from my mind, when I gave up on the idea of Mr. Right and was content to focus on my career and the occasional empty dance between the sheets. Mitchell, I have to admit, changed that. After years of dating players and roughnecks who probably reminded me of Gene, the father who barely acknowledged me until the last couple years of his life, I'd finally settled down with a man with whom I could make a home.

So there I was, feeling a little pressed about adding to my family as Pastor Wright announced the morning's Mother's Day tributes. Several children formed a line at the front of the sanctuary and gave glowing praises to their moms, one by one. It was deep, seeing several sisters my age quiver with tearful appreciation as their teenage kids read how their mothers had sacrificed and supported them. Of course, these sisters couldn't have been my age with kids in their teens, right? They probably just looked good for their age; at least that's the story I'm sticking with.

When the choir launched into the congregational hymn, I patted Mitchell's hand and scooted into the hallway to visit the ladies' room. The tributes to moms had been sweet, but given that we wouldn't see my mama until that afternoon and I wasn't a member of the club myself, I felt a little lost. "Easy, girl," I whispered to myself as I stood in front of the cracked rest-room mirror, "you'll get yours. You and Mitchell." I had to give him time, I knew it. Mitchell had been laid off from his most recent job at our company, Empire Records, and to be honest, he's been trying to find himself for the past year. He has a good job as a business manager for O.J. Peters, an up-and-coming deejay, but his heart's not really in it. I knew I had to give him time before pressing him about starting a family. Blinking a tear out of one eye, I hugged myself and did my business, then returned to the lobby.

As the rest-room door closed behind me, I nearly ran over Ms. Gina herself. Tall for a woman, around my height, and not looking like she'd ever carried a baby, Gina Tatum stood there in a dazzling white silk dress, her hair styled attractively as a short, spongy natural. I wish I could say she looked a mess, but truth is truth.

My heart in my throat with shock, I looked down and saw little Clay Stone himself, clinging to his mom's left knee. Styling in a sharp little navy-blue suit, white oxford shirt, and clip-on tie with a sailboat down its middle, he was as adorable as always.

Looking at me with deadpan eyes, Gina tugged at one of Clay's arms. "Tell Nikki hi, sweetie."

Grinning at me mischievously, Clay covered his eyes, then emitted a high-pitched "Hiiiiiii, Nik."

I knew from experience that "Nik" was the best he could do for now. Smiling at him, I knelt down, grabbed him in a big hug, and pinched the little cheeks that reminded me of Mitchell's baby pictures. "Look at you, a week goes by and you're already an inch taller," I teased, tousling the jet-black, fine head of hair Clay got from his daddy.

Standing and balancing in my heels, I cast a sideways glance at Gina. "He's better already, huh?"

Gina gave me another deadpan look, then the sanctuary doors burst open, flooding all three of us with the morning hymn, "Leaning on the Everlasting Arms." Licking my lips, I stood back and let Gina and Clay go down the aisle in front of me as the usher led us up to Mitchell's pew.

That's when everything went off the rails. Heads turned, one row after another, as Gina and Clay made their way down the aisle in all their glory. I saw people pointing, whispering "Mitchell's boy," or "Clay and his mama." Some choir members even stopped singing long enough to point the blessed mother and child out to one another. I realized it had been a few months since we'd brought Clay to church with us, between us being out of town and assorted other excuses Gina found to limit Clay's time with us. For most of the congregation, this was their first time seeing Mitchell's son since he'd passed into the bumbling toddler stage.

Not to mention, Gina was pretty stunning in her own right. Mind you, I was no slouch myself, with my newly styled reddish-brown cornrows, sapphire-blue pull-string skirt with matching top, and a figure pretty close to what it was in high school. Who was I kidding, though? All that was nice, but on Mother's Day it was pretty much irrelevant.

We reached the pew, and before I knew it Gina had plopped her lithe, long frame into my seat, leaving me with no room to scoot in. As I hovered in the aisle feeling homeless, Mitchell shook as if he'd been slapped and stood, motioning for Gina to move down the aisle closer to Angie and her little platoon. Grunting without meeting my piercing gaze, Gina scooted an inch down and acted like that was the best she could do.

Narrowing his eyes, Mitchell turned and motioned at the lady in the pew behind him. She had extra room, so Mitchell scooted out past Gina and we squeezed in there, sitting a few inches from Gina's back. Oblivious to the tension, Clay climbed up over Gina's shoulder and reached for me. I tried not to yank him as I removed him from Gina's grasp and placed him in Mitchell's lap, before giving him another kiss on the cheek. It was hard, loving a little guy whose existence could hurt so much, but there was nothing I wouldn't do for Clay Stone. It was his mother, the one who'd tried to sit there like she was Mitchell's woman, who was angling for a smackdown.

Sensing my mood, Mitchell squeezed my hand and leaned over. "Hey," he whispered, "my boy must have had the one-hour flu, huh?" We shared a conspiratorial wink and chuckled loud enough to make Gina glance over her shoulder.

Mitchell's playful attitude helped me get through the service, but reality came stalking back as we stood in the rear of the sanctuary with his family and the ministers. "This must be your baby," said Sister Jenkins, a sweet older lady who baby-sat for Mitchell, Marvin, and their sister Deniece when they were toddlers. She walked up to Mitchell and held her hands out for Clay. "He look just like you." Mitchell handed Clay over, and the little guy promptly knocked Sister Jenkins' yellow, bejeweled hat from her head.

"Clay, stop, that's not right," Mitchell said, stooping to get the hat and then accepting his giggling son back from Sister Jenkins. "Two years old and already a pistol, I'm afraid."

"He's a baby, you'll raise him right, I know your family," the sister said, smiling wide and pinching Mitchell's cheek as if he was still in grade school. She paused suddenly, looking between me and Gina, who was standing on the other side of Mitchell and Clay. "Now," she said, trying me first, "this your baby, right?"

"Oh, no," I said, clearing my throat, "I love him like a son, though—"

"I'm the mother," Gina purred as she extended her hand. "Nice to meet you."

"Oh, I should have known," Sister Jenkins said, smiling in recognition, "the baby has your nose. You're blessed to have a child with this one," she continued, patting Mitchell on the back. "Good stock, you know."

I stood there and watched in disgust as Sister Jenkins completely ignored me and interviewed Gina like a reporter for *The New York Times,* trading mothering tips along the way. It was the same humiliation I endured any time Gina came around with Clay in tow. It wasn't long before Mrs. Stone, Marvin, Angie, and their kids joined the party as well, tossing Clay around like a toy and feigning interest in Gina's upcoming graduation from Roosevelt University's journalism program. It was Angie, my old friend, who broke away from the pack to come stand by me. Ignoring little Sarah's insistent tug at her leg, she rubbed my back slowly, not saying a word. None was needed.

I guess I've learned there's a moral weight, a certain significance a woman gains the moment she gives birth. She's no longer some female responsible only for herself, no longer just a potential feminist and ladder climber or an easy target for men's lustful affections. No, she's a *mother*—an expected provider, protector, and teacher to a life force that may sink or swim based on her efforts.

There was a time when I didn't need any of that extra weight or moral significance. I felt I had plenty on my own, and I suppose I still do, but the game's changed now. I love Mitchell Stone, and I know he loves me. Problem is, it's clear Gina thinks she can break that bond by dangling her connection to him like a toy prize.

I won't let it happen. Our home will always be open to Clay, and I'm going to be a kick-ass stepmom. But the best way to get Gina to back off is to show her a real, live, tangible product of my love for *my* husband. Whether he knows it or not, Mitchell is going to help the stork make another delivery, ASAP.

2

Mitchell

Life's been quite an adventure for me since little Clay came into the world. The nine-month buildup to his birth was one of the most agonizing, disorienting times I can remember. The real fun began after he was born.

I wasn't there to witness the birth, given that Gina was in her "me against the world" phase, so I spent the first two months of my son's life trying to pretend he didn't exist. What choice did I have—to sit around like a little punk and wring my hands, asking "is he is or is he ain't my baby?" I occupied myself with my courtship of Nikki, pouring my efforts into solidifying a relationship first built on a false façade of my own creation, the "player" persona my friends Tony and Trey helped me create. Peeling away all those layers to reveal the true man beneath was not a simple process.

Nikki and I bonded something fierce during that season of doubt, but when Gina called me out of the blue early one Saturday morning, I was humiliated by the joy that juiced my spirit. As much as I despised her, I'd lived every moment waiting to hear from her, simply so that I could *know*.

That morning, Gina sniffled her way through an invitation to come to Clay's pediatrician's office and take a blood test. I don't know how many other guys she invited, but the day I went in to give my sample I recognized three other faces in the waiting room. We all acted like we didn't see one another.

Once the results confirmed the best or the worst, depending on your point of view, the little guy had me curled around his knobby little fingers. He had to earn his way with my parents, though. You have to understand, they'd had a false alarm before where grandkids were concerned. Marvin's first wife stepped out on him, and let's just say little Marvin III, who Marvin still spends time with on occasion, turned out to be from a different gene pool. Combine that with the embarrassing circumstances surrounding Clay's conception, and my mother was ruthlessly suspicious of this new pretender to the throne.

She and Dad met me in the hallway of the Cook County courts building the day I filed for joint custody and the accompanying obligations. I was flanked by Gina, her mother, and little Clay. Nikki had chosen to stay home.

After some quick greetings, Mom asked if we could step into one of the conference rooms, a meeting place she'd already arranged with a security guard she'd charmed. I looked at Dad for some relief and he shot back a pained look and a shrug.

We filed into the conference room, where Mom smiled wide and waved her hands toward Gina. "Give me that big, beautiful baby."

We passed him over to Mom, and she stood at the conference table, beneath the overhead lamps. Before I could stop her, she held Clay back from her at arm's length. "Oh yes," she said, her eyes narrow with concentration as his little legs kicked in search of safe ground, "that's the Stone nose all right, it flares just so." She gently laid him on the table, cradling his head as she turned to Dad. "Marvin, hand me those pictures, dear."

With a sigh, Dad handed over a bundle of photos, which Mom spread across the table. My stomach lurched when I saw Mom's exhibits: baby pictures of me, Marvin, my father, and all four of my uncles.

"Mmm-hmm," Mom said with tentative satisfaction, "complexion is consistent with the pattern, especially when you account for the males in my family. His eyes," she said, playfully stroking my boy's chubby cheeks, "it's like I'm looking into

Mitchell's soul, that's the home run." She picked Clay back up, turning him around slowly in front of her face. "Those legs, um, have a little more meat on 'em than my boys had at this age." She looked at Gina and her mom accusingly. "Lot of men with fat little legs in your family line?"

Pressing against her mother's forearm, Gina stepped forward and snatched Clay out of her hands. "Look, heifer, are you—"

"No," I said, stepping between them. "We're not doing this, in front of Clay or anywhere else. We're here for him, okay? Mom, he's my son, you can stop the scientific analysis. Gina, if we're going to do this with as little drama as possible, we'll have to respect each other's families. Agreed?"

Well, everyone said all the right things that day, but it turned out to be largely lip service. I'm not perfect myself, mind you, but I couldn't play the type of mind games Gina has mastered. It's literally always something. Her little Mother's Day stunt last week was just the latest, but I could tell it got to Nikki as much as it got to me. Gina keeps this up and my baby will be pushing me to have *another* baby, way before I can handle it. Nikki and I each make a good salary right now, but we've got a new house, obligations to help her mom cover some of her bills, and 401(k) funds that are worth half what they were back during the Roaring Nineties. That's enough pressure without another mouth to feed. There should be time for another baby once I figure out what I'll be when I grow up.

That reasoning led me over to Gina's this rainy morning, on my way to work. It was the best time to go, since I knew Gina would be home studying for finals and I wouldn't have to explain my whereabouts to Nikki. I didn't want her to know I was letting Gina get to me.

I pulled my '99 Accord into the cramped parking lot of Gina's apartment complex, a subsidized development that looks like a renovated Motel 6. Sprinting to the nearest cement staircase to escape the rain, I came to the second-floor landing and rapped at their door. Gina's mom, Djuana, flung it open and greeted me with a bored frown. "Hey, Mitchell," she said, her breath flooding me with stale smoke. "C'mon in," she huffed, finally closing her orange housecoat over her bare chest. She paused as she shut the door behind me. "Gina know you were comin'?"

"Probably not, no. Is she here?"

"Hmmph." Djuana chuckled, scratching at the plaid scarf wrapped around her curlers. "She should be, but she ain't alone. Let's just say Clay spent the night in *my* room."

I took a seat on the plastic-covered plaid couch in their front room, my heart sinking as Djuana yelled for Gina and trudged back into her bedroom, shutting the door. I worked day in and day out to respect my son's mother, despite the fact I'd never really liked her as a person. I'd dropped my idea of suing the maker of Trojan condoms the first day I held Clay in my arms, but even my love for him couldn't blind me to Gina's contradictions. Here she was, admirably earning a degree and trying to make a better living for herself, but still letting her boyfriends spend the night, in front of Clay. How hard was it to slip out to a hotel?

I reached down and grabbed one of Clay's talking dolls, shaking it and crowding out my angry thoughts until a gruff voice shook me from my playtime. "Help ya, bro?"

I looked up to see Dale, Gina's on-again, off-again boyfriend. Bald by choice and covered in tattoos, Dale's a failed rapper and a successful convict, one of those brothers always planning to get his act together. The best credit I could give Gina was that she hadn't fully committed to him. "He'll never be you," she'd said with a wink and a nod when I complained about him taking Clay to the movies once.

As the room shook with the low rumble of thunder, Dale walked into the middle of the room, bare-chested and flexing his pecs and biceps. "Gina ain't here," he said, scratching at the groin of his pajamas. "She gone to take lil' man to day care."

"I thought she usually took him earlier than this."

"Yeah well, she was a little tied up last night, so she's behind schedule." The self-satisfied grin on his face missed its mark.

"Look," I said, rising from the couch and crossing the scraggly brown carpet, "have her call me when she gets back." I hesitated, fiddling with my keys and staring back at Dale. At five foot ten or so, he was a little shorter than me, but I was guessing he was pure muscle. I couldn't help it, though, there was no sense being a punk where my son's welfare was involved. I stepped closer and looked him in the eyes. "We got some serious issues, me and Gina."

Dale's eyes grew wide. "Issues? Oh really?" He took another step toward me, flooding me with what smelled like morning breath mixed with Colt 45.

"Yeah," I said, coughing. "We have some things we need to straighten out. Matter of fact, I could use your help with her, you're the man after all."

"And how's that?"

"Well, she needs to level with you about your relationship with my son," I said, stiffening my back as Dale invaded my personal space. We were toe to toe now.

"What about Clay? You got a problem with me buying the boy nice things? You oughta be grateful, dog. You know how some of these brothers treat their girl's kids? You need to be thankin' God for me." When he suddenly shoved me, I wasn't quite sure he'd actually done it. Maybe I'd lost my footing?

"Watch it," I said, steadying myself. "Just tell Gina she and I need to deal. This is for Clay's benefit—"

I ducked when Dale threw a right at my head, then lowered my shoulder and charged him like the pit bull he was. We smashed into the opposite wall, knocking down the family portraits and some sort of African sculpture Djuana had probably bought at the local swap meet. I landed a couple of good punches before catching one from Dale on the chin, which sent me hurtling back against the couch.

I don't know how he was so quick, but somehow he lifted me into the air and hurled me straight at the front window. I curled into the fetal position as I hit the pane, so I wasn't sliced up too bad, but when I slammed into the wet asphalt outside, landing on my butt, the pain increased. As I lay there on the pavement, my head spinning and blood dripping onto my dress shirt, I heard Djuana scream bloody murder. I sat up on both knees and looked through the window, where I could see her pummeling Dale with her fists. She wasn't hurting him, but she was keeping him from finishing me off, probably because she was sick of him hanging around her house and forcing her to play grandma every night he was with Gina.

I took the chance to escape, letting them handle the mess and calculating Djuana would cover for us, more for her own sake than anything else. Her place had strict rules, and she'd probably get written up for having overnight guests if she didn't quickly and quietly fix things.

I went back home, knowing Nikki would be long gone, and cleaned myself up with another shower and some antiseptic. I was sore all over, but the bleeding had stopped enough for me to be presentable. Too pissed to bother with another oxford and tie, I threw on a short-sleeved rayon shirt and a pair of microfiber slacks. No monkey suit today. My bosses at the radio station should be happy I was even coming in at this point.

Around ten-thirty I sped back into town and pulled into the station's parking garage, near Clark and Chicago streets. I limped to the nearest elevator and rode it up to the seventh floor where

WHOT's offices were located. I picked up my mail from the receptionist and walked through the two large rooms where most of the employees sat. The feel of WHOT reminds me of the dot-com offices some of my friends worked at a few years ago—large, roomy spaces with spare but modern furnishings. All the desks and chairs are made of black Formica, except in the handful of executive offices, and everyone's computers are the little multicolored Apple iMacs. I walked through the "floor," as we call it, waving at people but hustling so no one could slow me down for a real conversation.

When I reached my office doorway, I got just the greeting I didn't need: My bosses were waiting for me. O.J. Peters, WHOT's star personality, and Tony Gooden, the station's co-owner and my old friend, were cooling their heels inside. Tony sat at my desk and O.J. lounged in the leather chair opposite him. O.J. had just gone off the air and was still in his studio gear—white T-shirt and navy Adidas cotton sweatpants with a loud pair of Nike cross-trainers. Tony as usual was dressed like a stockbroker, with a power tie, suspenders, and shiny leather shoes. When I saw the red toothpick dangling between his lips, I knew there was trouble. Tony didn't chew toothpicks on "good" days.

After I apologized for being late, blaming it on a doctor's appointment for Clay, Tony spoke first. "What's up, man? Have a seat," he said, rising from my desk chair and parking his short, trim frame on the ledge of my window.

I walked past O.J., who sat nursing a large mug of what smelled like hazelnut coffee. He stared ahead, grinding his teeth.

Pretending not to notice O.J.'s attitude, I sauntered past him to my desk and traded irritated glances with Tony as I took a seat. "What's the problem?"

O.J. leaned forward in his chair, meeting my gaze intently. "I hear you're too good for this job. Something you want to tell us?"

Before I let my reflexes get the best of me, I locked in on my desk photos of Nikki and Clay. Before I became a married father, I would ridicule coworkers at Empire Records who stuffed their cubicles with pictures of the wife, kids, and family dog. Always seemed inappropriate to me somehow, like they were bragging or needed some validation. Then I got a two-hundred-thousand-dollar mortgage, parental responsibilities, and a life partner. When you're a step away from telling the boss to "take this job and shove it," you need to be reminded of those commitments.

I cleared my throat and leaned back in my seat, looking between O.J. and Tony. "Why don't you guys tell me what we're talking about?" *Please tell me Shae didn't tattle. Please.*

Tony stopped jostling the toothpick between his teeth and met my stare, his expression grim. As station manager he was the man in charge, but the burdens he carried had his shoulders stiff with stress. "Shae's come forward with some accusations, man."

"Damn," I said under my breath. At this point there was no one to blame but me. If anything, I felt worse for Tony. As an owner of a new radio station with the fastest-growing audience in town, he had saved my ass by hiring me as business manager for O.J.'s professional exploits just a few weeks after my severance pay from Empire Records ran out. I coordinate O.J.'s personal dealings with attorneys, CPAs, and agents, and schedule all his speaking engagements. The station covers my salary, so in effect I'm just a nice perk Tony offered O.J. to get him away from his station in Atlanta. As a result, Tony feels responsible for me. It was one more humiliating aspect of a job that reminded me I was missing my calling, whatever that might be.

"How's about this," O.J. said calmly. "Why don't you tell me your side of what happened between you and Shae?"

I decided to go with honesty. "I asked her to handle some station business, and she told me where I could go."

O.J.'s eyes glazed over with skepticism. "And what station business was that?"

"Well," I said before coughing a couple of times, "I told her to make another call about a past-due invoice."

O.J. held up a hand, silencing Tony before he could jump in. "An invoice to someone who owed the station money?"

"The invoice was to the Hampton University Distinguished Speaker Series. It was for your speaking fee and expenses when you spoke at the campus back in January. They're months past due."

"Cool, except for one thing. That's *my* money on the table, Mitchell, not his," O.J. said, jabbing a finger in Tony's direction. "You need me to refresh your memory with a copy of the invoice? That Hampton appearance was an O.J. Peters Enterprises production. You are the business manager for O.J. Peters Enterprises, or have you forgotten? You can't be fawning off my money matters to some office clerk."

I looked at this brother, who's a couple years younger than me and several inches shorter, and glanced again at my photos of Nik and Clay. I could take him, and absolve myself of the shame of Dale's beating while I was at it, but it wouldn't be worth the cost. I had a wife, a kid, and a mortgage. "It was a misunderstanding, O.J., okay? I wasn't asking her to do anything sophisticated. She's a collection clerk for the station, she dials for dollars all day. I just wanted her to add one more customer to her list. It wouldn't have killed her."

"She was upset because she already had a full plate of *station* business. That's why she complained to me."

"Yeah, she would come to you, given that she was the first sister to properly welcome you to the station." I inhaled quickly, unfortunately not fast enough to draw the words back. O.J.'s reputation as a lover had been solidified quickly upon his arrival in town, and Shae had been all too eager to feed the office grapevine with tales of their night together. O.J., on the other hand, was not one to joke openly about his conquests. I wasn't helping myself, Nikki, or Clay with that jab.

Tony stood from his perch at the window and walked over to my desk, copping a squat on a corner. "Let's take personal issues out of this, all right? Matter of fact, let's take Shae out of it. You two have worked well together these last three months. We can fix this."

"Can I ask something?" O.J. looked up at me, wry amusement lighting his wide eyes. "Is your problem with me, or with the job itself? Or maybe you're too blinded by the belief you'll be the next E. Lynn Harris?"

I sighed. I was due for a retaliatory attack, so I let it go. Yeah, I'd self-published a novel a few months before. *Out of His Shadow* was the product of my plans for years to write a novel. My sister Deniece, who had divorced Willie, her abusive husband, around the time Clay was born, had been my inspiration. Niecy wanted to tell her story, but didn't want to do it directly. Next thing I knew, I was adding some embellishments, shaving a fact here and there, and we had her story in print. We hadn't sold a lot of copies, but we were getting good buzz on the Net and had even been favorably reviewed in *Today's Black Woman,* the *Sun-Times,* and *The Cleveland Plain Dealer.* O.J. thought he was being funny, but there was a part of me that looked forward to a day I could shove some literary success in his face.

That would have to wait. As it was, Nikki's salary was already higher than mine was: one hundred thousand versus seventy thousand, a difference that would grate on any real man's ego. Between our house note and school loans we needed every drop of income, meaning I had no luxury of chasing some "dream." Besides, at least with this job I wasn't working directly for "the Man."

Still smarting from O.J.'s barbs, I tried to explain myself. "I'm here to manage, guys. It hurt my heart when Empire sold my record label to Arista and laid me off, don't get me wrong, but I tried to find a silver lining."

O.J. crossed his arms, curled his lower lip. "A silver lining in getting laid off? What would that be?"

"I was sick of bean counting. I couldn't keep doing accounting and finance work when my heart wasn't in it. I took this position to get the hell away from all that."

I was getting nothing but silence, so I kept talking. "There's some cool aspects of this job, don't get me wrong. It's just there's no one to delegate to, you know? I have an MBA and eight years of work experience. Why should I play cash collector when there's a clerk down the hall who specializes in it?"

I realized suddenly that Tony was shaking his head. "I'll handle this," he said, getting to his feet and looking only at O.J. "Don't worry about it anymore."

Gripping his coffee mug, O.J. got up and looked past me to Tony. "Whatever. I expect some good news about all these past-due invoices real soon. If my current business manager won't handle business, I expect this station's gonna find me someone who will."

As O.J. slammed my door behind him, Tony walked toward it before turning back to me. He squinted, looking like he was trying to read my mind as he yanked the toothpick from his mouth. "What the hell's happened to you?"

"Don't know what you're talking about, man."

"You used to be a rock, Mitchell. The stable guy, the brother there in the clutch. Even with the baby-mama drama around you and Gina, you won Nikki back and you have a good marriage. You the man, man, except you're tripping professionally now. If you don't want to work here, go sign up for unemployment. Damn."

Before I could respond, my friend was slamming the door. No man could feel anything less than humiliated at that moment, and I didn't disappoint. *Be a man,* I prayed as I booted up my e-mail. I had half a mind to run over to Oprah's studios on the other side of town and see if she needed an extra guest, maybe get in a good cry while I was at it. I could have at least rung Nikki up for some affirmation after the start of a tough day, but in truth, that's not what we men do.

3

O.J.

Life can sure trip you out sometimes. I know mine still has me off balance. In six years I've gone from saving souls to spinning sounds, and I never really saw the change coming. I should say I never saw the disc-jockey thing coming. I knew I had to get out of the ministry when my pregnant girlfriend stuck a knife in my ribs. But that's another story for another day.

I've got a dream job that crept up on me. My pop says I've got a big mouth that never fails to get me noticed, and he's been proven right in this case. Now that I'm on a growing station in the country's third-largest media market, it's on. Every morning, after we sign off, my program manager briefs me on my latest guest choices for "The O.J. Peters Way." On last week's wait list: my man Johnnie Cochran, Vin Diesel, Martin Lawrence, Destiny's Child, and P. Diddy. It don't get no better.

I'm in this business to entertain, most definitely, but if I may humbly say so myself, "The O.J. Peters Way" is taking off because it hits folk where they live with timely talk, the latest jams, and a snatch of news. With the help of the lovely Liz Rivera, the more cautious co-host who keeps me in line, I deal with real issues but have fun at the same time. For instance, every Friday Liz and I ring up the homes of three deadbeat dads and offer them a choice: Pay that child support or receive another call the following week, while urban Chicago takes notes. Then there's the safe-sex seminars we work into the program during the last week of every month. Informative, but also full of humor nuggets. We get ya with laughter, we leave you thinking. I aim to be my generation's cross between Tom Joyner and Don Imus, and based on the latest Arbitron ratings, I'll get there.

Of course, nothing worth getting comes easy. After a peaceful few months getting settled into the Windy City, the drama kicked into gear today.

When my alarm buzzed me out of bed this morning, the shower was already running. It freaked me out. I've been in Chicago almost six months now, and besides my daughter, Cherrelle, who visits the first weekend of every month, this was my first time hosting an overnight guest. Since hitting town I'd put my "mojo," as my boy Austin Powers would say, on the shelf. Two reasons: One, romance can be very distracting, and two, I keep all but the most promising dates out of Cherrelle's sight. This morning, though, that was sure enough my shower running. I knew it had to be Saturday 'cause I'd never have a sleepover during the week, given my workdays start at three A.M.

Whoever was in the shower had tinkered with the damn thermostat too. As I snorted my way into consciousness and threw back my black silk sheets, I fought the shiver dancing along my spine and plopped my feet onto the cool maple of my floorboards. It wasn't even June yet, how could homegirl be hot, especially when my condo sits a couple of blocks from Lake Michigan? I stepped to my bedroom window, sweeping a blurry gaze over the landscape of Lake Shore Drive and the traffic already clogging the Loop. It was times like these I missed Atlanta, which may have the most convoluted highway network in Western civilization, but at least things feel spread out there. Downtown Chicago is always so *thick* with people, things, events. It may not match New York as the city that never sleeps, but it's way too busy for my country ass.

As I swayed back and forth in front of the window, the rush of water coming from the bathroom stopped. I looked back over to my king-size bed and noticed the bottles of Chianti lying at the foot. All but one were empty, and there was about a shot's worth of that left. I didn't feel hung over, surprising given how long it had been since I'd tied one on, but I was still trying to decide who was about to come out of that bathroom. I had it down to two candidates. Either I'd grown weak and brought Shae—the six-foot, long-legged accounting clerk from WHOT—home, or it had to be Alison Chavis.

Alison emerged from the bathroom, her long curly black hair pulled up into a bun. She was chilling in one of my towels, which was working overtime to cover breasts the size of healthy coconuts, a lean torso, and shapely legs honed on a Stairmaster. That was all it took: Instantly, I began to replay the night before, starting with our dinner at the P. F. Chang's near O'Hare Airport. She'd rented her own car, one of the new BMW coupes, and was planning to spend the weekend visiting old college friends. The friends were a side dish, though; I knew I was the main course.

"Oh, now you're up," she taunted, dropping the towel and pointing past me toward the bed. "You mind opening up my suitcase?"

I glanced past my belly button to my checkered silk boxers. No denying I was a bit sprung; the boxers had turned into a tent in the space of five seconds. A couple of months of abstinence will do that to you, I guess, especially when you're a healthy twenty-something brother. "What say," I said, taking a step forward, "we hold up a minute on that?"

She ran back into the bathroom in mock protest, where I followed after grabbing an extra-large Lifestyles condom and prepared to christen my wide oval sink and countertop. I was out of my boxers and T-shirt in moments, and as I'd provided plenty of kissing, petting, and stroking the night before, Alison impatiently pulled me inside her for a quickie. As I gripped the smooth skin of her taut hips and slid in and out at varied speeds, I tried to push aside the images coming at me.

We hadn't talked for weeks before she'd called out of the blue last Monday, announcing she was gonna be in town and wanted to hang out. The whole thing was awkward, because when it comes down to it I owe Alison for my career.

As I sped up for the final round of body blows, everything flooded over me: meeting her at Club Peachtree in Atlanta the year after I graduated from college, the strings she pulled to get me booked on shows on her father's radio stations as a social commentator, even the money she paid to help me get my FCC license. After that things kind of took on a life of their own, largely due to my stunning charm, of course, but in truth it wouldn't have happened without her. Alison alone looked at me—an unemployed, burned-out preacher with a baby daughter a world away in Washington, D.C.—and saw a star in the making.

We did cuddle afterward, even if the porcelain sink and counter were a little chilly. I stayed inside her warmth for a few minutes and stared back at her peaceful gaze. Finally, I couldn't help myself and went with an honest question. "Why are you here again?"

"Such a charmer. I don't want anything from you, O.J." She slid back enough to let me pop free. "I just like seeing you succeed. I'm here to see you in your element, baby." She slapped my chest and then held her hand there. "How much more weight have you lost? You trying to look like D'Angelo or something?"

I stepped to her side and eyed my ebony birthday suit in the mirror, flexing my biceps and rippling my abs a bit. "All praise be to the Atkins diet and to Gold's Gym," I said, patting my short, relaxed Afro back into place. "I work out Monday through Friday, soon as I leave the studio."

Alison grinned and ran a hand through my hair. "I guess Chicago women motivate you more than us country girls in Atlanta."

I smiled knowingly. "You know it's not like that. A brother's just not getting any younger."

"Well, don't forget where you came from," she said, hopping

down from the counter and smacking me square on the ass. "Let's wash up and then you can treat me to breakfast. By the way," she said as she opened the glass door of the shower, "I decided to stay in town until Tuesday, so I can visit the studio with you. Is that okay?"

Her immediate frown told me I'd failed to hide my real response. Had I rolled my eyes? "You wanna come by the station Monday, that's okay, but—" My grasp for an excuse was interrupted by the sudden bling-bling of my doorbell. "Be right back," I muttered after tossing on some sweats and a clean T-shirt.

Walking out into the hallway, I was less concerned with who was at the door than with my next move on Alison. I wanted to be grateful and all, but I'd just as soon see her on the first flight back to Hotlanta. She was a blinding reminder, a testament to my unrelenting shallow side. Truth was, I'd failed to become the man I'd sworn to be eight years ago, when Cherrelle was born.

I was twenty-one then, and had just thrown away my manufactured calling to the ministry. With no clear future and no convictions about what to do next, it was perfect justice that I, a notorious player who'd spent his college years hopping from one girl to another at clubs, classrooms, revivals, and gospel concerts, became the father of an innocent baby girl. I stood at her mother's bedside two weeks after she was born and held this little angel in my arms, swearing I'd live up to the challenge. It's a commitment I reflect on every day, and many days I think I live up to it. Alison, though, was a reminder that every now and then, I still fall short.

As I leaned forward and peered through the peephole of my front door, those concerns got a rude shove into the back of my brain. Standing in the hallway, with arms crossed and mouth in a predictable frown, was Keesa Bishop.

I yanked the door open instinctively, eager to look past Keesa and see my daughter. Cherrelle was in fact standing to Keesa's right, looking at the floor and twirling one of her dark curls of hair. Ignoring me as I stood in the doorway, Keesa looked down at Cherrelle and pinched her on the shoulder. "Stop slumping, girl, I'm not telling you again." She flicked a glance my way. "You letting us in or what?"

Still a bit startled, I stood back and let them pass me, steering them to the right, toward Cherrelle's bedroom. If Alison showed up buck naked right about now, the world wouldn't end, but I wasn't going around asking for extra drama.

Keesa walked to the threshold of Cherrelle's room and stopped abruptly, letting my daughter smack into the back of her splashy, tie-dyed sundress. As she turned to confront me, I caught myself admiring the sleek look of my ex's sculpted knot hairstyle and the snug fit of the sundress. Motherhood had left her with a few extra pounds, but they'd attached to all the right places. "You got company, don't you," she said, sighing.

Before I could lie, the rushing sound of water emanated from the master bathroom. I ignored the question and held my arms out to Cherrelle. "Come give Daddy a hug. Let me know what's up with you, girl."

My daughter, who has Keesa's delicate facial features, my mother's big eyes, and the baby fat it took me twenty-five years to shed, stiffened as I swept her up. "You stink, Daddy," she said, twisting her nose and looking past me.

"Can't argue with that one." I chuckled, though I didn't feel the least bit of humor in my gut. Here I was, dripping with sweat and Alison's bodily fluids, smothering my little girl in a pool of perversion. What were they doing here anyway? Maybe I had my weekends mixed up.

"I *do* need to shower," I said. "Let me get some money, and you guys can go get some juice, eggs, whatever you want me to fix for breakfast. We'll do it up when you get back."

Keesa took Cherrelle by the hand and extended her other palm to me. "The freak of the week better be gone when we come back, O.J. Don't think I'm not telling Sanders about this."

"Keesa." I held her gaze insistently, knowing I couldn't open up with both barrels until later. "Your lawyer has no place in this. This is not my designated weekend, what I do on my own time is none of your business." I softened my tone. "I'll get my wallet and be right back."

After they were gone, I leveled with Alison and, like a trouper, she was dressed, pressed, and out in half an hour. We agreed to hook back up Sunday, as long as I was out from under Keesa's surveillance by then.

Keesa and Cherrelle returned from the store ten minutes after Alison left. I had cleaned myself up and was in the kitchen, warming up my mega-griddle and stirring my Bisquick pancake mix. Holding my breath, I labored away on my Southern-style menu of grits, scrambled eggs with cheddar cheese, and fat slices of pure pork bacon. Cherrelle quickly hopped in front of my wide-screen TV, leaving Keesa to sit at the marble kitchen counter and stare me down as I made like my Granny Anna on a Sunday morning.

"I hear some D.C. stations are looking at your show," she said skeptically.

I sliced a slab of butter and tossed it onto the griddle, sucking in the lovely smell. "D.C.'s not the only one," I said nonchalantly. I didn't want to let on any more than necessary about my financial situation to Keesa, but the woman's raising my daughter. I can only afford to piss her off so much. "My station thinks they can get me syndicated on at least two stations by year-end. There's about six cities showing interest, so in the end we should at least snag a couple."

"Hmm. You'll really be all that then, won't you?"

I poured six pancakes onto the griddle and considered changing the subject. As of this moment, I'll give my girl Keesa credit, she's no gold digger. When her pregnancy interrupted her studies at the University of the District of Columbia, she admittedly had some issues at first. For starters, she lost her mind and damn near stabbed me to death outside my house, when I denied being the father. By the time Cherrelle was born, though, I'd recognized my role in all the madness and was relieved to learn I was the daddy. The girl hadn't gone postal for nothin'.

Anyway, after languishing for a couple of years at Mickey D's and getting used to motherhood, Keesa got an associate degree in nursing and moved up the ranks at a couple D.C. hospitals. Today she's a licensed RN, has a decent row house in northeast D.C., and covers her own car note. I've always provided for most of Cherrelle's financial needs, from medical insurance to clothing to school expenses, but I've never doubted that my checks go one hundred percent to support my baby. Keesa's come a long way, for sure, but there's a certain glint I've noticed in her eyes since my radio career's taken off.

"I'm in a building phase right now, you know," I said casually. "I doubt I'll see any real money for a couple more years at least, until I've proven I can stay on in the new markets that select me." This was only a small fib. Yes, my income had jumped fifty percent with the move to WHOT, and with just one syndication pickup I'd be well into six figures. That was play money in the eyes of my radio idols like Tom Joyner, Doug Banks, and Don Imus.

Leaning forward in her seat, Keesa smiled faintly, frightening me a bit. I was afraid she might be hiding a knife behind her back. "Well, I just want you to know a lot of people are proud of you, O.J., whether we show it or not."

"Hey look, you don't have to—"

"I mean it. I've been thinking about this a while now, the way I come at you hard all the time." She glanced over at Cherrelle, who for the first time since she'd walked in seemed happy, camped out in front of an episode of the new *Saved by the Bell*.

Keesa lowered her voice to a whisper. "I know she can be bitchy with you, but that's my fault."

You don't say.

"We're going to make it up to you. That's why we're here." There was that scary smile again. I held my spatula and turned away from the griddle, fully facing her.

"Keesa, you don't owe me anything. We just need to keep being civil, keep the peace, and–"

"We're moving to Chicago."

"Come again?"

"I said we're moving to Chicago."

This was a conversation we'd had before about Atlanta. I'd dodged that bullet; it was time to make Chicago falsely unappealing now. "Keesa, you've been in D.C. too long to up and leave. That's Cherrelle's home, for God's sake."

"Cherrelle was born there, but we don't have any family left to speak of. Mama's strung out again, as usual, my grandmother's got a new husband and doesn't have time to be bothered, and most of the girls I grew up with are still on welfare, or what's left of it." She yelled over to Cherrelle. "We ready for a new start, ain't we, baby?"

When Cherrelle's only response was a dismissive wave, Keesa pressed ahead. "I flew out here so I can spend the week interviewing with area hospitals."

I stepped back to the stove, flipping the pancakes first, then stirring the eggs. "There's a lot of nurses looking for work in this Bush recession, you know."

"True, but I got contacts. The chief of staff at Walter Reed is hooking me up with physicians at three different places here. He says I'm a lock to get something in cardiac care, his exact words. By the way, he says hi. Dr. Dickens?"

"Oh yeah, I remember him." *Thank you, Dr. Dickens.* I wouldn't soon forget the good doctor. He'd been the head trustee at my church in D.C., when I was a college student and star preacher. He'd never liked me, and he'd known exactly what he was doing by helping Keesa try to move here.

"I still think you should weigh this with care," I said, straining to sound cool. "I mean, I got no problem with it in theory, but I can't promise I'll be in Chicago forever."

"I want Cherrelle to be near her father, and Chicago's as good a place as any for me to build my own life from scratch. I've thought this through, run it past my girls at work, even wrote to Iyanla Vanzant about it." She reached into her purse and pulled out a folded sheet of paper. "This is a copy of Iyanla's *Essence* column last month, when my letter was one of the ones she answered. I'm famous!"

"Oh my." *Thank you, Iyanla.*

It was official, I knew it before the skillet had cooled and we sat down to eat. Like it or not, I was about to get me a complete family unit. It'd be hilarious if it were a bit on my show. Unfortunately, this is live and in living color.

4

Nikki

I had just forked up my first slice of smothered chicken when Mrs. Hanson interrupted my lunch with Mitchell. She kind of bum-rushed us, popping over to our table at Jonie's from out of nowhere. I actually dropped my fork, she startled me so much.

"How you kids doing? Lydia will be thrilled to know I've seen you!" A tall, heavyset lady of sixty or so, Mrs. Hanson was still sharp in her gold-trimmed navy-blue suit. She'd been fly as far back as I could remember, especially during my high-school years, when I spent every weekend in the streets with her daughter. Lydia has since gone off to Los Angeles to make a decent living as a model in direct-mail catalogs, but every time I see Mrs. Hanson she swears the girl's a week away from that magic movie role.

As Mitchell and I stood to give her hugs and salutations, I forced a smile onto my face and calculated how quickly I could get rid of Mrs. Hanson. She was cool people and all, but I'd asked Mitchell to meet me here for lunch because Jonie's, a buppie soul-food joint, usually has a slow crowd during weekday afternoons. A couple of weeks had passed since Gina's Mother's Day performance, and today was the day I was asking for a baby. We'd had a nice time since arriving, catching up on each other's day and holding hands, but Mrs. Hanson had interrupted me just as I was ready to go in for the kill.

We traded the obligatory news updates, summarizing our current careers and letting Mrs. Hanson update us on Lydia. She was convinced Lydia was about to land a supporting role in a Wesley Snipes film. I still talk to Lydia every couple of months, so I know she really spends most of her time chasing sugar daddies, but I didn't bother sharing that, of course.

"You all are just such a beautiful couple!" Mrs. Hanson said as she stepped over to her table, which was behind us, and grabbed her purse. Then, almost as an afterthought, "Lydia told me you're ready to start a family. You enjoy these last few months of freedom!"

I felt a nervous laugh squeak from between my lips. "We'll just have to let nature take its course, won't we?" I waved good-bye to Mrs. Hanson as she walked toward the front door and prayed the chill creeping into the air wasn't coming from Mitchell. I searched his face for signs of a reaction, only to find him focusing on his plate of Cornish hen, which he was slicing and dicing into cubes.

"Where'd she get that business from?" he asked, frowning and tucking his silk tie inside his shirt for protection. His eyes were still on his plate. "Lydia's full of it, but I thought she only exaggerated facts about *her* life. Now she's making up stuff about you and me wanting kids already?"

"Who knows," I said, swooping in but keeping my tone light. I kicked off my right heel and slid my foot over to one of his. "Lydia probably misunderstood me, but I do want us to start on a baby soon . . . baby."

Mitchell set down his knife and his fork, though he didn't move his feet. "Have you forgotten I already have one of those? Or don't you remember complaining when I downgraded our weekend in Hilton Head to one in Wisconsin, after those unexpected doctor bills for Clay last month?"

"I did *not* complain about those bills," I protested after chewing a tender bite of my collard greens. "Maybe I suggested you could have planned for them better, so that–"

"You're proving my point, right this minute," Mitchell said, leaning over his plate. "Kids cause stress, Nikki. Hopefully they cause a whole lot of love and fun, too, but the stress is guaranteed. I love Clay more than my own life, but I don't need another child yet. I'm up for it eventually, you know that. Right now we've got a marriage to build."

As Mitchell spoke, the restaurant, in its bright hues of red, orange, and white, swirled around me. Why was he dismissing me so quickly, without asking why I'd have told Lydia that in the first place?

The next thing I knew, I swear our table started to elongate, stretching from a small square into a lengthy rectangle. In my mind's eye, Mitchell was sliding further and further away from me, his entire focus now on his plate of hen.

I licked my lips and resisted the urge to scream that he pay attention to me. I had never had to go that far with the man I'd married a few months ago. No, he used to be Johnny-on-the-spot, eager to know my feelings and exceptionally thoughtful in responding to them. Who *was* this ogre sitting fifty yards from me?

I had two options that would reach him, and as my steaming plate of chicken, candied yams, and greens cooled I calculated which one to lead with. One felt too sentimental, the other was a double-edged sword. I took a deep breath, willed the room to stop spinning and reached over the table to grab Mitchell's left hand. "Baby, at Gene's funeral, didn't you promise we'd have kids as quickly as possible?"

A few months before our wedding, my father's abused heart finally gave out on him. The mention of his funeral, which was emotionally draining despite our distant relationship, drew Mitchell's eyes to me. He trained a determined gaze at me as his fork and knife clanged against the plate. "That was a tough time," he said, clearing his throat and looking me in the eye. "You'd just lost your dad and were worried about whether our children would get to know their grandparents, especially your mom."

"It was more than that. You do remember the conversation we had on the way home?"

Mitchell sighed. "You know men never remember complete conversations." He leaned back in his seat for a minute and took a swig of ice water. "I know we agreed not to waste time having kids, since our parents aren't getting any younger and we want them involved in their lives. I don't recall saying we'd have kids right away, though. We talked about this again, you know, a few weeks before the wedding."

"I know," I said, shoving my plate to the side so I could reach for his hand again, "but I guess I was in a different place then. Mitchell, you never committed to a time frame after Gene's funeral, but you did support me when I said I wanted to have all our kids before thirty-five. Do you remember why I was worried about that?"

"Look, I know we're not exactly spring chickens—"

I lowered my voice again, fought the tears pooling at the edge of my right eye. "Do you remember why I was *specifically* worried?"

Mitchell glanced away, just long enough to break my heart. "Yeah, I remember."

Now we were into option number two, the justification I had least wanted to use. When Mitchell proposed to me, I insisted we sit down and bare our entire sexual histories. Even though our partner count was comparable because of some "catching up" he'd done in the year before we hooked up, my history was a little more complex. I had dodged the worst bullets of unintended pregnancy and AIDS, but at least one hastily selected brother had given me a gift that kept on giving until the right medications cleared things up. All the same, I'd asked enough probing questions of my gynecologists over the years to know it could affect my ability to have Mitchell Jr. or little Ebony some day. As Dr. Gupta, my gynecologist, told me during my last checkup, "You already thirty, girl? Everything may be fine now, but if I were you, I hurry hurry!"

Mitchell reached back across the table for my hands. "Nikki, look. I love you regardless of those issues. More important, I'll love you whether we have children or not. There are always other .options."

Count to ten, Nikki. What was he talking about? Other options? "You really wouldn't mind if we couldn't have children together? Are you *that* infatuated with your son, that you don't need any more children?"

Mitchell held up a hand as he finished chewing his black-eyed peas. "I—I didn't say I don't need more children, baby, I said that if we can't have them naturally, there are other options, whether it's adoption or whatever."

"Or whatever? If my equipment turns out to be broken, Mitchell, you'll have only two options. Adoption, or go out and fuck Gina again."

As soon as it slipped out, I knew I was wrong. Mitchell's face turned as white as a Black man's can, and his jaw went slack. Several beats passed, then he shoved back from the table. "That's what this is about!" Standing now, he lowered his voice. "You've never forgiven me for what happened with Gina and Clay." He leaned over the table, his wide, beautiful eyes glowing like cinders. "It's not Clay's fault that he's here. God allowed it, and he has a purpose for that boy. You're wrong if you walk around resenting me, Clay, or even Gina for it."

I grasped at Mitchell's hands, which by now were flailing in time with his words. "Sit down, please," I whispered, noticing the growing interest of the waiter at the nearest table. "I was wrong for going there. This isn't about Clay; it's about us. I just want you to look at reality. Haven't you seen the recent news reports about fertility? Women peak in their twenties. I'm already over the hill. We may not have any problems at all, but the longer we wait to try, the more we're asking for."

"We're going to have to take some things on faith," Mitchell said calmly, though he continued to stand. "Trust me, we're not ready to start trying. For one, your husband here could get fired any day. And it's not like my second job pays any money."

"You're a gifted writer, you know that." I felt myself slowing my words, choosing them with greater care. As much as I believed in Mitchell's budding talents, his new love for writing scared me. I had married a reliable BMW (Black Man Working) only to find his life goal was to be a starving artist. "Someday your work will pay off, baby. Until then you'll have to be like the rest of us, and find the best day job possible."

"Some people," Mitchell said, removing his wallet from his sport coat, "are more successful in their day jobs than others. You seem to forget you're now the top breadwinner in this family."

I shook my head, annoyed at his indulgence in playing the victim. I'd gotten another promotion around the time he was laid off from Empire Records. I knew he'd been catching flak from his parents and others about my out-earning him, but was that my damn fault? "Mitchell, please. You're paying all the major bills right now. Most of my money goes into our retirement funds, savings, and to help Mama. We can afford a baby as long as you keep some type of real job."

"Yeah," he sighed, slapping a couple of twenties onto the table, "that's the problem." He leaned down like he was going to kiss me on the cheek, then paused in midair. "So, are we agreed that the baby thing can wait?"

I narrowed my eyes despite myself. "Have you heard a word I've said? Would it kill you to just let me come off the pill for a few weeks, see what happens? You said yourself Clay was meant to be, maybe the same goes for our first child."

Grimacing, Mitchell reared back from me and rubbed at his forehead. "Sure, you come off the pill," he said as he turned toward the door. "I'll be waiting in bed with a body condom."

5

Mitchell

The walk back to my office was about a dozen blocks, but it felt like a marathon. The pavement had turned into the jagged peaks of Everest, cutting into the soles of my loafers and turning every block into a mile. The weather was a partial distraction, now that late spring had brought us a sunny day, but with the sharp, insistent breezes blowing off the lake I still longed for an overcoat.

What the hell had I gotten myself into? I loved Nikki, but I was starting to question my timing. Should I have waited until Clay was older before I proposed, when I was ready to open the floodgates of my family jewels again?

She'd been dropping hints for weeks, I recalled as I plowed through a sea of college kids and worker bees massed on State Street. Fact is, I'd known even before Gina's latest antics that Nikki had ideas about getting the family thing going, but she'd never been this direct before. I had hated storming out of there, but her crack about Gina and Clay had just driven the sword of my guilt deeper into my chest. She was just going to have to get over it. I had made the mess; it was my responsibility to clean it up by being a good father, not hers to fix by giving birth to another baby.

When I stepped off the elevator into WHOT's lobby, Tony stood there waiting, his arms crossed and a green toothpick dancing between his lips. "What up," he said, smoothing the lapels of his suit. "At least you're on time. O.J. better move his ass. He was still stuck on the Dan Ryan when he called a few minutes ago."

"I told him we shouldn't schedule that remote on the same day he had to meet the good old boys." That was our euphemism for the Old White Men who really owned WHOT. Skip McClellan and Danny Waters had built a network of stations across the West from California to Colorado, before training their sights on Chicago. Tony had "networked" with them in his previous job as a top mayoral aide, and the access he'd granted them to City Hall had led the good old boys to make him a minority owner of their first midwestern station. My boy was a minority owner in the true sense of the word, too: the only one in touch with our Generation X, multiracial target market and the holder of a whopping two per-cent of the partnership's shares.

Tony checked his gaudy Rolex and pursed his lips. "Skip and Danny will be here any minute. O.J. better show up first."

"Stop your bitching," came a lazy drawl from over my shoul-der. We turned to see O.J. stroll in from the other end of the lobby, a pair of narrow sunglasses over his eyes. He was rocking a black pinstriped three-piece suit, white silk shirt, and bright red tie flecked with black. "O ye of little faith, I been waiting on you fools in the conference room for the last five minutes."

"Are you backsliding into the church or something?" Tony said, grinning. "Actually, you look more like an undertaker in that getup. No wonder you do the sweats thing so much."

O.J. flipped Tony the finger. "Next you'll be saying this is a per-fect suit for radio. Kiss my ass, Gooden."

"All right, boys," I said, shepherding them toward the back hall, "I'll play the grown-up here. Let's get into the conference room and make sure we're ready." Still cracking wise, we walked into the station's main conference room, a long, narrow rectangle with mottled salt-and-pepper carpet, a wooden table lacquered in black that seated twelve, and a single bubble window. We took seats near the head of the table and prepared for battle.

The good old boys showed up a few minutes after two, right on schedule. Skip, whom I'd met before, was tall and paunchy with a full head of black hair, dressed in a beige blazer and white shirt with no collar. Danny cut an immediate contrast: small and spindly with a head of receding blond hair, he looked ready to hit the dude ranch in his checkered shirt and black cowboy boots. We quickly got the usual bull out of the way and settled into seats opposite Danny and Skip.

"Tony," Skip said, leading off in his salty New York accent and punching the air with gestures, "let me just say publicly as I've told you before, we couldn't be more proud of the job you're doing so far." He kicked back from the table a few inches and slung one long leg over the other. "You've picked a skilled program manager, hired a strong sales force, and of course we're here today to talk about this star on-air man!" He swept a hand in O.J.'s direction. O.J. stared back with a smart-ass gaze, looking like the cat who'd eaten Skip's canary.

"We love hearing all that, Skip, Danny," Tony said, nodding at each man. "I'm excited to have you and O.J. share ideas to build on his early successes. As I mentioned, we also have Mitchell here to add background, since he handles O.J.'s business affairs."

"Well, let's just get to it," said Danny, a loose Southern accent oiling his words. He leaned toward the middle of the table, grabbing a glass plate and a large chocolate-chip cookie from the metal snack tray. "O.J., I'm fifteen years older than your core demographic, a white old square to boot, but I love what you're doing!" He paused to trade glances with Skip. "We're agreed, though, that you need just two modifications. Less politics, more gossip."

O.J. sniffed and reclined in his seat. "I don't know what you mean by that."

Undaunted, Danny clapped his hands together and gave a wry smile. "A simple example. The monthly calls you do to local churches, where you ask these pastors how they're drivin' Jags and BMWs when they got members who are damn near homeless?

Priceless. That stuff makes tongues wag, O.J., it makes for juicy gossip."

Danny paused, taking time to break his jumbo cookie in two. "On the other hand, these occasional rants you've started lately, take for instance last Thursday—"

"You mean my weekly 'get out the vote' episode?"

"Yeah, that one." Danny took a bite of the cookie and glanced at both Skip and Tony before continuing. "You were getting pretty damn specific with some of your comments, son."

I wiped a trickle of sweat from my brow when I heard Danny say "son." The air in the room was getting thicker by the minute.

O.J. smiled and clapped his hands, mimicking Danny's earlier motion. "Danny, the most specific thing I said was something like 'President Bush is an arrogant, ignorant windbag, hell-bent on sending the poor and the minorities of this country into immoral wars.' Was that too specific, sir? Should I have been a little more vague in my opinion?"

"Now wait a minute," Tony said calmly, removing a fresh yellow toothpick from his jacket pocket, "I think I know what you're trying to say, Danny. O.J. and I can talk about the political content. Our audience appreciates hearing something substantive every now and then, but we can examine whether we've got the right balance."

"I believe the balance is fine," I said, before I could censor myself. O.J. sat up straight at the sound of my voice, a curious smile in his eyes.

"At every public appearance O.J. makes, he gets more questions about politics and community issues than about Ja Rule's next CD," I continued. "I think people are tuning into 'The O.J. Peters Way' because it is a unique mixture of unpredictable comedy, slamming jams, and forays into things that matter. Doesn't seem wise to tinker with a working formula."

"So," Skip sighed, tracing a circle into the wood paneling of the table, "you're saying we can kiss your ass." He reached over, tapping Danny on the shoulder playfully and trading glances with Tony, who was clearly grinding his teeth. "We're just the bank anyway, right, Tony?"

"O.J. and Mitchell are just advocating their opinions," Tony said, scooting closer to the table and clasping his hands together anxiously. "We're open to considering—"

"I don't think O.J.'s open to considering much of anything," Skip interrupted. He crossed his arms as he towered over us. "I'm the one talking you up for a syndication deal, Mr. Peters." His intense gaze had turned this into a personal conversation between him and O.J. "I have programmers in several cities interested already. But the political stuff worries them. You're attacking a popular wartime president, and that sort of controversy scares away the big corporate sponsors."

"And it's not just potential syndication deals we're talking about," Danny chimed in. "If we're going to take you to the next level and keep chasing the mainstream audience in Chicago, we need to keep the show *fun* and steer away from these political icebergs. You get my drift, son?"

O.J.

I sat back in my chair and weighed my emotions as Danny spoke. Wasn't this a bitch? It wasn't enough that Keesa and Cherrelle were already across town looking at apartments, hungry for the chance to move here and complicate my new life, but now the station was trying to make me choose between the almighty dollar and some semblance of a positive self-image.

I left the ministry when I realized I wasn't there for the right reasons. That's why I love lampooning every wife-beating, money-stealing, choir-member-seducing man of God I can find. When I came into my own with my Atlanta show, though, I figured I'd found the real calling God had reserved for me. I may be a bit of a clown, but when I want to I can actually do some good too, and I know this is only the beginning.

Some day I'll be too old to spin the latest hits. When that day comes, O.J. Peters will step onto a larger stage, one where I can scoot aside the Rush Limbaughs and Sean Hannitys of the world. "The O.J. Peters Way" is a means to an end, to a day when I can run a national radio show that adds some true diversity to the mix—something that enlightens, informs, and entertains a multi-cultural audience. Something to offset the propaganda passing for programming today. I know I can make that dream a reality, but with every word Skip and Danny spoke, I could feel that dream being strangled.

"I've had six months to show you results, gentlemen," I said, standing and buttoning my suit jacket. "Your drive-time ratings are thirty-five percent higher today than when I first joined up here. I think that ends this discussion."

Skip stepped toward me, his damn hands chopping the air like it was wheat again. "You don't care about syndication then? I'm sure we could find a proven personality who does."

"Do what you gotta do," I said, feeling my cell phone buzz against my belt. I knew who that was. Keesa was getting a little too comfortable consulting me about every little decision behind her relocation.

I started toward the door, brushing Tony's firm hand off my shoulder and ignoring Skip and Danny's cold glares, their hushed profanities. When I reached the door, only Mitchell was at my side. I took a few more steps into the hallway before playfully punching him on the shoulder. "Partner." I looked him in the eye. "You sure you wanna be on this plank with me?"

"Like it or not, I'm with you, man." Mitchell smiled wearily.

"You're a success because you attack your show with passion, O.J. Water it down and your ratings will be watered down too. No sense selling out, least of all when you're holding the cards."

I gave a tight smile and slunk back to my office, praying he was right.

6

Nikki

It had been a couple of days since my blowup with Mitchell, and this morning we had to act as if the whole thing was over. It was one of those perilous moments where work and home collided.

I arrived at the WHOT studio with LaRae Summers around 7:15 A.M. LaRae, a tall, statuesque, thirty-something sister with manila-brown skin, plump lips, and a beautiful head of micro-braids shaped into a pixie, is a nationally renowned novelist. Girl's got eight books under her belt, total of four million copies in print. That's not even going into the three feature films and one Showtime series based on her work. Though some haters would say her biggest books have been Harlequin romances dusted with ethnic spice, LaRae's a literary powerhouse. On top of that I'm a fan, so I'd been honored to help her approach Empire Records about a marketing collaboration with her new publisher, Black on Black Books.

Our meetings the past couple of weeks had focused on LaRae's idea that Empire help increase reading among young Blacks by cross-promoting new authors in Empire's CD packaging. I'd immediately wondered why no one else had thought of it: Wouldn't the average Toni Braxton or Maxwell fan enjoy chilling with an Eric Jerome Dickey or Terry McMillan novel? Common sense.

I had helped LaRae pitch the idea to my boss, Chase Wells, last week. As the corporate vice president of promotions, Chase had been skeptical but I was confident we'd wear him down.

LaRae had been so grateful, she'd opened up to me about changes taking place in her life, including her recent relocation to Chicago from New York and the end of her three-year engagement to a former professor from her years at NYU. She had pretty much come to the Windy City for a fresh start, and was kicking it off by devoting the next year to projects that would increase opportunities for new writers. She was so cool, I'd invited her to meet some of my friends and suggested she appear on WHOT with O.J. to publicize her community-service plans and events. Not to mention, I figured it would give O.J.'s show a ratings boost and improve Mitchell's standing in his eyes. A sister's gotta look out for her man.

After being buzzed back by the receptionist, LaRae and I chilled in Mitchell's office, since we knew O.J. wasn't having her on until after the seven-thirty news break. I was proud of Mitchell; he dutifully made small talk without making one mention of *Out of His Shadow*. I had promised him I'd nudge LaRae into giving him some help when the time was right, but I didn't want to be blatant; I figured her "user" radar was razor-sharp.

Just after the half-hour Tony squeezed the office door open, grinning like a kid on Christmas morning. I surveyed his sculpted fade haircut, tailored suit, and puppy dog–cute facial features and tittered to myself. I had a love-hate relationship with Mr. Tony Gooden. An old high-school friend of Mitchell's, he had been the role model for the "player" persona Mitchell created when he first pursued me. In that way, I suppose I owe him for the happiness I have with Mitchell. By the same token, I also owe him for the pleasure of Gina's presence in my life. I like to think Mitchell would never have fooled around with her if he had stayed true to his real "nice guy" nature. That's water under the bridge, I suppose: It's not like Tony personally placed Mitchell's sperm inside Gina.

"Ms. Summers, it's an honor to meet you in the flesh," Tony said, crossing the floor and taking LaRae's hand reverently. "I hope you know you're welcome to come see us anytime. O.J.'s show, the afternoon mix, during the Quiet Storm even. Our door's always open."

"Thank you," LaRae said, looking skeptically at Tony's lips as he touched them to her right hand. "Are you here to tell me it's time to go on?"

Before Tony could answer, Mitchell's door swung open again. We all looked at the doorway to see Trey Benton, another old chum of Tony and Mitchell, swagger into the office. Six foot two, with curly blond hair à la Justin Timberlake, a well-groomed matching goatee, and a hard-body build, Trey was a prototypical "wigger." Early in the year, Tony had brought Trey in to interview for a role on O.J.'s show. O.J. had loved the idea and hired Trey as a sort of novelty act, the show's resident clown. In the tradition of Howard Stern's sidekick, Stuttering John, Trey had been known to rove the streets of Chicago far and wide on behalf of the show, embarrassing celebrities and upstaging public officials. The only difference now was that he knew how to turn the wigger act on and off. This morning he was on the respectable side, chilling in a pair of khakis and a striped rugby shirt.

"Ms. Summers," he said, stepping into the office and gently shoving Tony out of his way, "it is an honor." He got down on one knee and took the same hand Tony had kissed. We all rolled our eyes as he slowly raised it to his lips.

LaRae's eyes danced with amusement. "You're brave. You don't know where I've been."

Trey completed his smooch, just above her knuckles, before looking up at her. "Oh my fine sister," he said, his pearly-white teeth flashing, "you don't want to know where I've been."

LaRae shot me a smile before looking back at Trey. "Aren't you something. I may have to put a white love interest in my next book."

Trey straightened up, popped onto his heels. "Well, wouldn't be the first time I inspired a sister to new heights, if ya know what I mean."

I turned and flicked Tony on the head, ready for him to restore some order to the situation. You never knew if Trey might try to jump LaRae before she made it to the studio. The boy didn't just think he was Black; with six babies by five mamas, he was a player on par with Shaft.

After a few minutes of bullshitting with the boys, LaRae took Tony's hand and they stood, following Trey into the hallway. I smiled at LaRae as she turned back toward me. "Knock 'em dead," I said, giving her a thumbs-up.

She glanced between Tony and Trey playfully before winking my way. "Child's play."

Mitchell shut the door behind them and returned to his seat, moving past me without pause. He waited until he was planted in his seat, fingers clicking away at his PC keyboard, to address me. "You hanging out until she's done?"

"I did talk her into doing this," I replied, frowning. "I'd like to make sure everything goes okay. If we pull this cross-promotional project off, it will impact Empire."

"Mmm-hmm." Mitchell's curt response, his lack of eye contact, was palpable. We let the sound of the WHOT broadcast fill the dead space between us. Sitting across from Mitchell, looking out his office window at a view of the river and Wacker Drive, I tried to imagine LaRae and O.J. sitting down the hall in the studio. I pictured them fiddling with their headphones and making small talk as the sound of D'Angelo's version of "Feel Like Making Love" filled the airwaves.

O.J.'s scratchy voice rolled over the last few seconds of D'Angelo. "Seven thirty-nine, seven thirty-nine A.M. on WHOT, 93.9. Good morning, Chicago! We have an extra-special treat for you this fine morning. Trey, Liz, and everyone out there, please welcome a superstar presence we all know and love. I don't care how illiterate you may be, if you've seen the movies *The Sound of My Heart* with Nia Long, *The Longing* with Morris Chesnutt and Angela Bassett, or if you've caught a few episodes of *Sunday Dinner* on Showtime, you're familiar with this woman's work. Ladies and gentlemen, the talented, the beautiful LaRae Summers!" The air filled with a shot of canned applause.

"O.J., what's up, it's nice to be in studio with you."

"You been hearing about the show?" There were times O.J.'s ego leapt through the radio.

"Hearing some nice things, yes. They say anyone who's anybody needs to meet your listeners." LaRae was good.

"And you know that, huh? Well, LaRae, I know you're here to fill us in on your recent move to Chi-town. I'm very curious to hear your impressions as one who's recently relocated here myself."

"Where from?"

"Atlanta. What you know about the Mecca?"

"Oh, I've only based four of my books there, baby."

"Cool, we'll trade notes shortly. Before we get into anything else, though, can you tell us why you became an author? I meet famous folk all the time nowadays, and I know most of 'em got into show business because they need the validation, know what I mean? I always figured authors were different, though. Am I right?"

LaRae paused for the first time before answering. "Well, for me personally, I wrote my first novel while working on my master's degree in literature at NYU. I'd graduated with a degree in English from Fisk University—"

"Fisk Bulldogs are in the house. HBCU alert!" O.J. sounded his HBCU—historically Black college and university—siren.

"Oh yeah," LaRae continued, chuckling, "I loved me some Fisk. But at NYU, I was struck with a story about love and redemption, and knew I had to share it. I'd suffered some crises in my personal life, and even though my character faced some different problems, in a different era, telling her story helped me cope with my own stuff. My hope was it would do the same for others."

"That's all right," O.J. replied. "That first book wasn't published, though, right?"

"No. The story was set in Virginia during the first few years of Reconstruction and showed the coming of age of a girl whose father was a former slave-owner who'd fallen on hard times. The manuscript was represented by a famous literary agent, but she couldn't sell it to a publisher. They all said it didn't sound like something a twenty-three-year-old Black girl would write."

"So you flipped the script."

"Well, I wrote something closer to home, about a girl raised by a single mother who finds herself homeless when her mother is sent to a sanitarium. It wasn't my experience, but I'd seen enough drama in my Memphis childhood to relate to the character's challenges."

"And everyone loved it, huh?"

"Well, it was published to nice reviews and great word of mouth. I think the key was that so many young women related to the alienation and damaged self-esteem of my heroine."

"Would you say that's still the case, that your books connect with women because they reflect real-life struggles?"

"I'd probably agree."

O.J. cleared his throat suddenly. Then, "Just how much affirmation do the sisters need, LaRae?"

"How much?"

"Yeah. I mean, let's be real, you go into any college or corporation today, you'll find three, six, sometimes a dozen Black women for every brother in the place. Black men still lead the pack in homicide rates, illness, and incarceration. Meanwhile, the sisters are improving in just about every statistic that matters. Why do so many books cater to women only?"

Still sitting in Mitchell's office, I shifted in my seat, waiting anxiously on LaRae's answer. Mitchell even stopped his typing, pausing to trade glances with me.

"Black women don't exactly have it easy now," we heard LaRae respond, a slight chuckle layered over the new edge in her tone. "We may show more of a work ethic and earn more educational and financial progress, but a lot of us return to empty homes every night."

"Empty homes? Please," O.J. replied. "You all come home to find a kid or two you had with some bozo, or bozos, a Bible you don't follow, and a coffee table full of LaRae Summers books. Shallow, male-bashing screeds that blame dogs, players, and every other type of Black man for your problems."

It sounded like LaRae gulped. I know Mitchell did. "I'm not sure where you're heading with this," she said, her tone thick with menace.

"Don't get mad, stay calm, girl. All I'm saying is someone of your stature, your power, can help turn things around. You 'sister girl' authors have got to stop—"

"Excuse me, I am not a 'sister girl' author. I am a professionally trained writer and scholar of—"

"Do your books focus on female heroines whose main problems are caused by men?"

"That's only one way of interpreting—"

"I rest my case. Now hear me out. You women authors have got to stop telling these sisters that all their problems are the result of brothers' shamming. It's not doing our people or society in general any good. Let's just keep it real, okay?" The air filled with the thumping beat of O.J.'s theme song. "Seven forty-five, seven forty-five on 'The O.J. Peters Way'! We're coming back in a minute to continue this vein, along with your phone calls. Stay right there!"

As a stream of commercials began, Mitchell and I hurried from his office down the hall, where we ran into Tony, who was also headed for the studio. We let him shove the door open.

He stood in the doorway, hands on hips, staring straight into O.J.'s flippant gaze. "What the hell?"

"You don't like this, Tony?" A crooked smile on his lips, O.J. straightened in his seat. "You don't want any more politics, right?" He took a quick swig from his bottle of diet Vanilla Coke. "You take away one hook, gotta add another. Less politics, more sex and gossip, right? How else we gonna keep folk talking?"

Tony looked at LaRae, who sat with her crossed legs pumping like oil derricks. "Ms. Summers, my apologies. This feels like an ambush, I am so sorry. Are you all right?"

LaRae waved a hand at Tony and stared across the studio at O.J. "I can handle this little twerp."

"Oh God," Tony whispered, running a hand over his head and yanking his tie further from his neck. "Clean it up," he said sternly, pointing a finger at O.J. "And at this point, just keep Trey and Liz out of it. Just get out—"

"Ten seconds before we're on air," O.J. said, turning away from Tony and adjusting his headphones. "While you're in your office, boss, check the call volume before you decide whether you like this."

Tony shut the studio door behind us just as the lovely couple went back on the air. Mitchell and I exchanged anxious grins as the dance resumed, blasting through the hallways on overhead speakers.

"You know," LaRae was saying, "after seeing you in person, O.J., I understand why you chose radio."

"Give me a few minutes off air and you'd change your tune."

"Please. Only an impotent, insecure half-man would be threatened by books that empower women."

"Trey, help me out," O.J. replied. He was breaking another rule already, inviting Trey's silly ass to wade into the water with him.

"It's like this." Trey jumped on the invitation. "As a white guy who's probably had more 'sisters' than the average 'brother,' I think LaRae's type of books trap the sisters in a pattern of victimization. Sorry, Ms. Summers, you're foxy, but y'all can do better."

From down the hall, a yell from Tony: "Dammit! That's it, they're both dead!"

Walking toward Tony's voice, I followed Mitchell back into his own office. As the air filled with another round of charges, insults, lies, and replies, Mitchell and I faced each other across his desk. His weary, weak smile told me we were mercifully on the same page: grimly amused, tired, and guilty. This on-air "battle of the sexes" was a reminder we were miles from getting our own shit together.

7

O.J.

I'd had a pretty good morning so far. We were down to the last hour of the day's broadcast, and I was interviewing our spotlight child for the week, Jayvon.

"Jayvon, tell us your age, money," I said, smiling at the little guy seated across from me.

"I'm ten and three-fourths," Jayvon said, adjusting his headphones clumsily. He was small for his age, so we'd piled a couple of phone books on his chair. He leaned forward gingerly, trying to stay upright. "I'll be in sixth grade next year."

"What you wanna be when you grow up, player?"

"I'm not sure," he replied, flashing a gap-toothed smile at Liz and me. "Maybe a doctor. I want to help heal people."

Liz, a trim little lady who packs six feet worth of intelligence and energy into her five-foot frame, leaned into her studio mike. "Why do you want someone to adopt you, Jayvon?"

"So I can figure out what I can do with my life. You know, get some regular help with schoolwork and stuff like that."

"Yeah," I said, "the right parents could help you figure out how to become a doctor someday. I feel you, Jayvon. You'd probably be happy to have just one parent, wouldn't you, man?"

"I'll take anything."

I shook off the pain behind the boy's words. Had to keep the pace moving. "Brothers and sisters, ladies and gentlemen, again I present for your thoughtful consideration little Jayvon Edwards. Almost eleven years old, starter on his school's basketball team, solid B student, and a lovely head of nappy hair. Plus, the boy knows how to mind, if the last few minutes are any evidence. Give

us a call now to apply to adopt Jayvon. Remember, you ain't got
to be a banker, you ain't got to be married with two-point-five
kids. If you're an upstanding citizen, the Department of Children's Services is here today as they are every Thursday morning,
and *they'll work with ya*. Do the right thing, y'all, call now. In the
meantime, here's the four millionth rotation of Nelly and Kelly!"

I signed off, punched in the well-worn single, "Dilemma," and
gave Jayvon a high-five and some station paraphernalia. As the little dude climbed out of his stool and walked to the door, I eyed
Liz. To be honest, her looks—clear, smooth skin the color of a ripe
banana, head of shoulder-length jet-black hair, and pouty lips
most women can only get with implants—had played an initial
role in my choice to hire her. I'd long since learned my lesson.
Yeah, the little lady was fine, but it wasn't her looks that kept the
show running smoothly. I'd come to realize I needed Liz: She was
the leavening in the show's bread, the playful but studious presence that balanced my spontaneity.

I rubbed my jaw and stared at her as she sat at her studio desk,
shifting papers around. "What you got next?" I asked. "It's been a
slow news day."

She smoothed her feathery hairdo and barely glanced my way.
"I got it."

"I'm just saying, don't be having me call you out on the air because there's nothing worth making fun of. The last hour's segment was weak, babe."

Liz looked at me and smiled. "Kiss it, O.J."

"So it's like that?"

I was interrupted from my verbal play by a rap on the glass. The
simple rhythm of the tapping reminded me that today was it, my
day of reckoning. Standing there on the other side of the glass
wall, a cautiously eager smile on her face, was Keesa.

The time had come to help select a happy Chicago abode for
her and Cherrelle. I think I'd blocked it out of my mind until I saw

her standing there, flanked by Mitchell and his fine wife, Nikki, who looked like she'd nearly been poured into her aqua-blue business suit. There wasn't an observable flaw in that girl's figure. Combine that with Mitchell, whom I'd probably compare to singer Brian McKnight looks-wise (not that I judge guys, of course), and those Stones make a right handsome couple. Mitchell may get on my nerves with his uppity self, thinking he's too good to deal with bookkeeping and other stuff he was *hired to do,* but he scored points when he convinced Nikki to help Keesa find a good deal on a place.

I was surprised when Nikki stepped up, given how pissed I know she was about my "ambush" of LaRae Summers a few weeks back, but I think she knows what I did was as good for LaRae as it was for me. Our little on-air battle still had people calling to weigh in, and I understand that her Chicago-area book sales spiked in the first couple weeks after the interview. It's just a matter of time before she comes crawling back for another go-round.

Nikki's girl Leslie Forbes was some sort of heiress whose father's estate owned property north of the Loop, not far from the Northwestern Law School campus. Leslie worked some magic and it was looking like she could get us something at a ridiculous price. All we had to do was go see whether it was suitable.

Keesa was so eager to get everything done that she'd insisted on meeting me at the station so we could take off immediately. She wasn't playing, showing up while there was still thirty minutes of the show left. She was looking nice too, to her credit: still working that long sculpted knot hairstyle, skin glowing like roasted chestnuts, outfitted in a sharp red-and-black blouse with red slacks. She looked good, but to be brutally honest, in my eyes she was still just Keesa.

Shortly after ten A.M. I emerged from my cave, where I nearly ran over both her and Nikki. "You ladies eager to go or something?"

Before they could answer, Mitchell strode toward us from the other end of the hall, his suit jacket over his shoulder. "I can drive," he said, twirling his car keys.

"Thanks, hoss," I said, slapping him on the shoulder as I nodded toward Nikki and Keesa. Although it was awkward to have Mitchell and Nikki sandwiched into the tense air surrounding me and my ex, I appreciated having them along for the ride. Hopefully we could keep the day focused on business that way.

When we pulled out of the parking garage, we drove into a light drizzle. "You'll like this location," Nikki said to Keesa as we rode north on Clark, the pitter-patter against the roof serving as a soundtrack. The girls were in the back seat, with me and Mitchell holding court up front. "You're getting a ridiculous deal considering how close this is to O.J.'s place, the station, and Cherrelle's school." With help from Tony, whose political background made him an expert on the desirable neighborhoods and schools, I had already enrolled Cherrelle at Saint Andrew Elementary, a Catholic institution a few miles south of my crib in Lincoln Park.

"Well," Keesa said, looking at me in the rear-view mirror and smiling faintly, "it definitely makes sense for me to be close to O.J. We may have fought like cats and dogs over the years, but when you share a child with someone, you're going to be close whether you want to or not."

Just then, a banged-up Chevy Cavalier hurtled through our next intersection, despite the fact our light had just turned green. Mitchell slammed his brakes to bring the car to a sudden stop but said nothing. Nikki was quiet too. It took a couple of silent, tense moments for me to remember that Mitchell has a baby mama of his own. I clenched my stomach and jaw, fighting valiantly against the chuckle lodged just beneath my Adam's apple. I didn't mean to take pleasure at anyone's pain, but damn if it wasn't nice to remember I wasn't alone.

There was no complex decision to make when we stepped into

the apartment. The place had it going on: two-story townhouse, hardwood floors in the foyer and kitchen, thick carpet everywhere else, plus recently renovated appliances. CTA train stations were a block's walk, and good shopping and dining were another two blocks away.

Mandy, Leslie's professional, perky property manager, was ready to give us the whole show. She dutifully ran the dishwasher, washer, and dryer for us, pointed out the recessed lighting in the family room, and walked us over every inch. By the time we sat down to talk the specifics of rent, my clenched stomach told me the time had come to bite the bullet. We weren't going to find a better deal than this; Keesa had been looking for almost a month now, and nothing else in this area came close. Her only other options were further west in Oak Park and as far south as Calumet City.

"Why don't you all go on back," I suggested to Mitchell as Keesa and I pulled our chairs up to the kitchen table with Mandy. "We'll get the unpleasantness of money out of the way and then catch a cab back to the station."

"You sure?" Mitchell took Nikki by the hand, looking a little too eager to escape. "We can wait, or go get some lunch and meet you back here."

"No," I said, waving him off. "Get a sandwich with your lovely wife, drop her back at work, and get ready to spend the afternoon making those cold calls for me. I need to scare up some speaking engagements, man! Brother needs some dollars before he gets fired, know what I mean?" I was smiling, but my heart was laced with anxiety. Our argument with Skip and Danny about the show's content wasn't over by any means. It was starting to look like I'd have to back off on the politics or head back to Atlanta.

"You're not going anywhere." Mitchell looked me in the eye and shook my hand briskly before looking at Nikki, who in turn winked at Keesa.

"Everything okay, girl? I know this must be overwhelming."

"It's good," Keesa sighed. "I'm really excited about this opportunity, Nikki. Thanks."

"We're out then," Mitchell said. "See you at the office."

"I'll call you, Keesa," Nikki said quickly as Mitchell stepped
past us and yanked her from view.

"All right, Mandy," I said, turning to her and chuckling, "let's
get this show on the road."

Once Keesa had signed the necessary papers and I'd put down
the first month's rent and security deposit, we walked a couple
blocks south to Pearson Street and hailed a cab. Though the skies
were still overcast, the rain had stopped, making our search for an
available taxi less annoying. When a white-and-brown station
wagon screeched to a halt at the corner, we slid into the raggedy
back seat and stared at the back of our driver's head. A big man
with an unruly Afro, he turned and grunted at us in a heavy West
Indian accent. "Where you want t'go?"

I yelled out the address for him real slow and settled back
against the punctured leather seat, keeping my eyes on Keesa the
whole time. She sat there with a forced smile on her face, rubbing
her fingers over the seat's greasy texture. "There's days, O.J., when
you make a sister feel she's in the way."

You don't say? I rolled my eyes before meeting her gaze. "Everything's cool, girl, don't trip. We got your place squared away now,
Cherrelle's ready to start school in a couple months, and your job
at St. Joseph is a done deal."

"I know all that. Everything else is in place except for *you*, O.J."

I felt my nostrils flare defensively. "What the hell's that supposed to mean?"

As the cab slowed amid a snarl of traffic, Keesa hiked a knee up
onto the cab seat and scooted toward me. "Are you happy with
your radio career? I mean," she continued, tilting over just enough

to give me a glimpse of the cleavage beneath the neck of her blouse, "do you see yourself doing this five or ten years from now?"

I reared back, leaning against my door. "You don't think of radio as a serious career? You do realize this career is what's allowing you to move into someplace livable, instead of the hovel you could afford on your own?"

Now Keesa's eyes flashed defensively. "You want me to go back now and rip up the lease? I took this deal 'cause I thought you'd matured enough to want to help your child and her mother, O.J. If I was wrong, then I don't need your damn help!"

I looked out the window. *Are we there yet?* "I was out of line, okay? If you're going to live here, I want you and Cherrelle to be safe and comfortable. What was the point of your question?"

"I meant," she whispered, sliding away but keeping her eyes on mine, "how much longer do you want to have episodes like we had with your little trick Alison a few weeks ago? When are you going to settle down, professionally or personally?"

"You have got to be kidding." I was laughing, but I didn't feel it. I turned to face Keesa head on. "You been single just as long as I have."

"I'm not single by choice, I'm just very picky about who I let into my life, out of respect for Cherrelle. She doesn't need to get her hopes up about a new stepdaddy until I know there's a good chance."

My lungs inflated with indignation. "Sh-she *wants* a stepdaddy?"

"She wants to see someone make me happy, if that's what you're asking. She's already outgrown that 'why won't you marry Daddy' stage, O.J. You pretty much shot that one dead after she met your fourth or fifth girlfriend."

I tried not to pout. "I never let them stay over when she's with me. I told her they were just friends."

"Well, guess what? Your daughter's no fool. She's already onto you."

I rubbed at my forehead, glad to feel the cab speed up underneath me. "Again, what's the point of all this?"

"I'm just laying it out there. When you want to grow up and simplify your life, I'm here. At least until Prince Charming sweeps me off my feet."

I looked at the floor of the cab. "Keesa, come on—"

"We're not kids anymore, O.J. If you could never love me and you know that for sure, let this go in one ear and out the other. Otherwise, I'm just saying the door is open, when you're ready to do this right."

As if on cue, our cabbie screeched to a halt as Keesa finished. "Twelve-fitty, please."

"All right," I yelled slowly, "I'll pay you for this leg, then you'll take her on to St. Joseph Hospital." I couldn't stay silent as I fished the money out of my wallet. "Keesa, why on earth would I be interested in you just 'cause you've moved here? We've come a long way, girl, you know it, and I'm ready to go another ten years for Cherrelle's benefit. But you're tripping now, plain and simple."

"Never mind then, Peter Pan," Keesa said, shoving her door open, "keep playing your little games."

I took my change from homeboy and climbed out on Keesa's side, where I stood facing her on the curb in front of the office. "Like you *really* want to get back into my life? You just insulted my profession and my character." I paused, gathering myself as she climbed back into the cab. "If you weren't Cherrelle's mother I'd have some choice words for you right about now." I raised my voice over the blast of traffic. "Welcome to Chicago."

Keesa grabbed the door, her eyes growing cold. "I'm going to keep praying for you. I don't need you, but unfortunately Cherrelle does." A last glare, and she slammed it shut.

I watched the cab speed back into the stream of traffic, feeling myself shrink with each passing second.

8

O.J.

When I left the gym that afternoon, my temples were still pulsing from memories of Keesa's scolding. She was wrong. I was not some irredeemable whore; I ought to know, I used to be the genuine article. I'd slept with two, count 'em, two women since coming to Chicago six months ago. For most single men, that was a monk's existence. Keesa was just tripping because I wasn't with *her*.

As I walked toward my building, cooling in a new nylon sweat suit and Nike cross-trainers, I flipped my cell phone open and stared into it. Who could help me sort through this mess? Somehow the life of radio, plus the move to Chi-town, had made life increasingly solitary for me. If I wasn't at the station or out playing "O.J. Peters," it seemed I was wrapped up with Cherrelle, Keesa, or Tony and one of his many women. I'd lost touch with most of my boys from college, with the exception of my former housemates Larry, Brandon, and Terence. Larry is executive vice president of his father's retail holding company in Cincinnati, Brandon's a medical resident at Emory University, and Terence is a partner in an engineering consulting firm in Silver Spring, Maryland. All of them are married, and Larry and Brandon have kids, both born within wedlock, a small fact I try not to envy.

I couldn't talk to them brothers, not right now. They weren't out there anymore, swimming with the sister sharks. I started to dial my pop's number. I nearly broke his heart the year Cherrelle was born, when he first learned I'd made a mockery of God's pastoral call on my life, and to be perfectly honest, he's not overly thrilled with my current vocation. Nevertheless, Pastor Oscar Peters is always ready with a word from above, and as one who knows most of my dirt, he can pierce my macho façade to the quick.

I paused at the doorway to my building, sucking my teeth when I heard Pop's voice mail click on. I shut the phone just before his greeting reached the "may God bless you mightily" part, and stood amid the cool breeze of evening, dreading the thought of going into an empty apartment loaded with nothing but anxiety. Why did Cherrelle want a stepdaddy?

She's already onto you.

I started to zip my sweat jacket and considered calling it a night. That's when my neighbor Asha walked up. "What's up, O.J.?" Short, full-figured without an ounce of excess fat, Asha reminded me of a shorter, stockier India.Arie. She had that earthy quality I always admired in sisters, a self-empowered air. Her hair was a short natural, a cut that framed her oval face, narrow brown eyes, and plump little nose perfectly.

I stepped to the side so she could stand under the front awning with me. "Hey, Asha, just ending my workday. Trying to decide how early to hit the sack."

"Hmm," she said, sliding her leather shoulder bag around to a hip and looking up at me with a wide smile. "You don't look like you want to hit the sack."

I smiled instinctively at the raspberry scent of her perfume and privately gave her dap for the minty-fresh breath. "I'm feeling a little restless tonight, I guess."

"Well, I know WHOT wants their star to get his rest, so I better stay out of this." Asha smiled wickedly, sharing an inside joke given that she was the sales director for V103, the lead station WHOT was trying to take down. We naturally traveled in some of the same circles, but as a rule Asha and I kept things to "hi, bye" to avoid conflicts of interest. Right now, however, "conflict of interest" sounded like some irrelevant legalese. This girl had me sprung.

"You got some ideas?" I stepped a few inches closer to her, leaning over just enough to keep our eyes level. "You name the bar, I'll buy."

"I don't have no time to run all over the city on a worknight, boy," she said, cutting her eyes and slapping my chest.

"Oh, excuse me then." I reached down for my workbag. I'd shot my one bullet for the night.

"What I *can* offer," Asha continued, looking into my eyes as I straightened up with my bag, "is a bottle of wine and some kick-ass leftovers. My sister and I made veal parmigiana last night. Got some broccoli and carrots to go with it. Wanna stop up, say in half an hour?"

"Oh, sure. A family meal's always nice—"

"My sister doesn't stay with me, I live alone," Asha said, cutting me off and tapping my chin. "And as far as I can tell from the grapevine, so do you. Are we on the same page, O.J.?"

I had been on the sidelines so long, I nearly gulped at Asha's boldness. I'd forgotten that self-empowered often coincides with sexually liberated. She stood there, looking as devious as she looked tempting, and over her shoulder I swore I saw Keesa standing with arms crossed, mouthing *She's already onto you.* Those petty words were now a self-fulfilling prophecy.

I reached over, slid Asha's bag off her shoulder, and steered her toward the main entrance. "Girl, we're on the same paragraph."

9

Nikki

Gina was thoughtful enough to give us a wake-up call this morning.

The phone's purring jarred me from sleep first. I blinked a few times, stared at the blinking phone light, and noticed the time on the clock: Four-thirty. I wanted so bad to pick up the receiver and slam it back down, but on the off chance it was an urgent matter, I groped to my left and pulled the phone to my ear. "Hello?"

The tone, the cadence, the arrogance in the voice required no introduction. "Put Mitchell on the phone, please."

"He's asleep, Gina. Try calling back after six, please." If she hadn't blurted out anything about Clay being sick or hurt by now, I figured the little booger must be okay. That was all that mattered, far as I was concerned.

"Nikki, this is important. Wake his ass up."

"Is something wrong with Clay?"

"That's between me and his father, ain't it?"

This bitch. "Good-bye, Gina." I set the phone back into its cradle, nice and slow. As I pulled my hand back, my pulse picked up its pace.

Mitchell stirred next to me. "What was that?"

"You mean who?" I turned toward him, searching for his eyes in the dark bedroom. "Who do you think?"

His only response was to turn his back to me, a common occurrence the past several weeks. Since our blowup at Jonie's, we'd made love exactly three times, if you could call it that. The tension about our baby argument hung in the air like a foul stench, and infected what for three years had been rapturous sex. He'd even had the nerve to pull out before we finished last week.

The phone purred again.

Curled up into a near-fetal position, I bit my lower lip and kept my eyes closed. On the third ring, I felt Mitchell rise, reach over me, and clumsily pull the phone to his ear.

"Yeah?" He paused to cough as I heard Gina's whine kick into gear. "Is something wrong with Clay?" Another pause as he waited out Gina's fusillade of a response. "Gina, why is it my problem if you and Dale broke up again? Least of all, why's it my problem at four-thirty in the morning? 'Cause it impacts Clay? Don't even go there." I heard Mitchell's voice strengthen, felt him sit up. "These roller coasters are exactly why I should challenge for full custody. Are you even home with him now?"

Mitchell rustled the sheets and climbed out of bed, stomping into the bathroom and shutting the door behind him. I sat up on my elbows and tried to act like I didn't want to hear the snatches of conversation coming from behind the door.

"Don't threaten me with this silliness again. . . ." "You best believe I keep records of every dollar of child support I've paid. . . ." "Dale's giving you advice about what to expect from me? Are you kidding?"

I fell asleep before Mitchell came back out.

With a full Friday ahead of me, I was up and showered before he was out of bed, and I didn't bother sticking my head into the shower to interrogate him before I left the house. Wasn't my problem.

10

Nikki

That night after work, I had a much-needed girls' night out. Leslie and Angie met me at Empire's offices, and we went to dinner at Morton's before driving over to LaRae Summers' condo, which was on the near South Side, a few blocks from Twenty-fourth and Wabash. We were heading to an "Eighties Revue" concert at United Center: the Gap Band, Kool and the Gang, New Edition, DeBarge, and Teena Marie. We were all hyped to hear our respective favorite artists, but I knew LaRae would have fans of her own tonight.

As we idled on the street in front of her condo, a recently renovated red-brick high-rise, I called LaRae on my cell to let her know we were out front. As I punched my phone off, I turned to beg mercy from my girlfriends.

"Please don't fawn," I said, rolling my eyes. Both Angie and Leslie had spent many a night cuddled up on a bed, couch, or loveseat living vicariously through LaRae's characters. So had I, but as an entertainment executive, meeting celebs didn't really faze me. I was much more worried about Leslie, whose family fortune was built in workaday industries like real estate and hair care, and Angie, a former journalist whose life was now consumed with screaming babies, *Blue's Clues,* and *SpongeBob SquarePants.*

"We's professional women, girl, shutty," said Leslie, waving at me from the back seat and using her expression for *shut up.* "We know how to act up in here."

"Ain't that the truth," Angie chuckled, rubbing her growing belly. "We do have a little home training, you know."

"I'll believe it," I sighed, tapping my steering wheel, "when I see it."

We sat there for another ten minutes or so, waiting on LaRae and reminding ourselves she was a busy woman. As I continued watching for her, I noticed that each time I glanced toward the bright green canopy over the main entrance, the same guy was always there, standing near the gold-trimmed revolving door, and he didn't look like anybody's doorman. Lean, close to six feet tall and dressed in black denim jeans with a long-sleeved T-shirt, his hair in the "twisty" phase of pre-dreadlocks, the brother was cute but menacing. At a condo like LaRae's, where I'd heard the units started at four hundred grand, he didn't quite fit.

When LaRae emerged from the front entrance of her building, dressed in a white silk blouse, sharp wine-colored blazer and navy denim jeans, things got stranger. The brother didn't bother her, didn't speak, but rather turned his back to LaRae as she stepped onto the cement walkway. Oblivious, she threw her black Coach bag over her shoulder and waved frantically in our direction.

I looked over her shoulder as she climbed into my passenger seat. "You know that guy near the front door?"

"Hmm?" LaRae settled in, fastening her seat belt before looking back. "Can't say I've seen that one before, though that scar in the middle of his forehead caught my eye." She shrugged. "He was acting funny or something?"

"Maybe it was my imagination, but he seemed like he was waiting on someone to come out, then he ducked out of your way like he didn't want to be seen." I looked back again. "Now he's walking away. Who else was he waiting on?"

LaRae shook her head as I pulled away from the curb. "I usually come and go through the parking garage anyway. This place is pretty stalker-proof. I have bigger worries than that."

Seeing she wasn't worried, I let it go and pulled out into traffic. The mood lightened quickly and I made introductions. LaRae fit right in. She got us arguing about why a city as major as Chicago had no WNBA franchise.

"Folk are just not supporting the sister ballers the same way they show their love for the average baby-making NBA whore," Leslie said. "But don't sleep, the revolution's coming."

We arrived at the United Center a few minutes later and hopped out of my Infiniti. Leslie had rented a luxury box for the night, so we were lucky enough to have the rectangular room with a large glass window all to ourselves, with the exception of Leslie's cousin O'Dell and his wife and four kids. We introduced them to LaRae and played with O'Dell's youngest boy, the only sociable child, before congregating in the back row of the box seats.

During the intermission, after Charlie Wilson, Kool, and Teena Marie had taken care of business, we shifted into real girl talk. Angie started it all, whining about her sore nipples (baby Milton's fault, not husband Marvin's), swelling feet, and fidgety fetus.

"Girl, stop your crying," I said, laughing like a hyena as I poured myself another glass of Zinfandel. "You knew what you were in for when you let Marvin poke you without protection."

"Excuse us for building our family," she snapped back. She twisted around in her seat, looking most directly at LaRae. "My girls here are still childless by choice, LaRae. I forget, do you have any—"

LaRae crossed one leg over the other. "Just a couple miscarriages."

Angie put a hand to her mouth. "Oh Lord. I am so sorry."

"Hey," LaRae said, grabbing Angie's hand and removing it from her lips, "no harm. I almost carried one of the babies to term, so I can relate to some of what you're going through. Don't let these haters get you down!" She shot a playful grin at Leslie and me.

"I'm happy as I am," Leslie said, smiling ruefully. Leslie's partner, Sarah, was a sweet middle-aged white woman who had us over for dinner every couple of months but wasn't into hanging with us. "I'm happy to play godmother the rest of my life," she continued, "the one who's hating is Nikki."

LaRae cocked her head, meeting my eyes. "You ready for a baby, Nikki?"

I looked down at my wine. "Well . . . I guess I wouldn't mind."

"You just got married, right? Some say it's best if couples wait two or three years, to let the relationship solidify."

I set my glass down and clasped my hands. "Those *some* people aren't thirty with potential health issues."

"I heard that," Angie said under her breath.

LaRae leaned around Leslie, scooting a little closer to me. "What's hubby say about getting down to baby business?"

"He's just, well, he's got some other things he wants to handle first. Like keeping me from killing his son's mother."

Leslie flicked a glance my way. "You mean keeping your girls from forming a posse and taking that freak out."

Angie put a hand on my shoulder. "Have you all cleared the air yet, after your talk a couple weeks back?"

I quickly summarized the encounter for LaRae's benefit. "Well, he hasn't said he'd leave me if we get pregnant right now. He did say he'd start using condoms if I come off the pill."

"Then keep your ass on that pill," LaRae said, looking stonecold serious. "That doesn't mean you can't keep working on him in the meantime, though."

Angie nodded. "Not to mention, it doesn't mean you can't prepare the way now, so that you two are as potent as possible when you're ready."

I ran down the things I was already doing to increase the odds: zinc supplements slipped into Mitchell's morning coffee, monitoring our caffeine intake, and replacing all of my man's tight brief underwear with roomy boxers. Angie, the baby factory, was unimpressed.

"You've barely scratched the surface, girl. Are you still hitting those high-impact aerobics classes at Bally's? That stuff will over-heat your ovaries and fry your insides."

"What?"

"You heard me! Look into yoga, much easier on the reproductive organs. What about taking a daily dose of folic acid?"

"Covered."

"And calcium, your twelve hundred milligrams a day?" She shook her head at my dazed expression. "Look into a supplement like calcium carbonate or something. And make sure you get regular helpings of dark-colored vegetables, like kale, sweet potatoes, fresh spinach."

LaRae piled on. "What about lovemaking techniques? You all know what to do to increase the odds?" She paused at what I know was my irritated expression. "Look, girl, I've been pregnant a couple of times, okay?"

Leslie excused herself, chuckling as she headed for the buffet table in the corner. "I'll come back when I can be of help, girls. Anyone else want a slice of that Black Forest cake?"

Angie raised an eager hand before smiling at LaRae. "Let's help Nikki out with this conception thang. You go first."

LaRae pointed a finger at me. "Throw away all them lubricants, even the non-spermicide stuff is gooey enough to take Mitchell's little soldiers out."

Next up, Angie. "Focus on the missionary position! All the acrobatics are cute, but nothing gets those little guys closer to the eggs."

I decided not to jab Angie with the obvious; missionary was probably the only position Marvin, who'd been a virgin until twenty-five, was any good at.

"Make him get the job done every other day at a minimum," LaRae chimed in, "whenever you're ovulating."

"Finally," Angie said, "make sure to put a pillow underneath—"

I felt a slight headache coming on. Wasn't this supposed to be a fun night out? I waved a stop sign at the girls. "I've heard the pillow tip, I got it." I looked over at Leslie, ready to join her at the buffet table. "I'll get started on everything I can, at least until Mitchell agrees to let me off this pill." I was sounding far more at peace than I really was.

The rest of the evening flew by with Ralph Tresvant's crooning, Johnny Gill's belting, and El DeBarge's shrieking. In between, we girls played at small talk, jokes, and LaRae's stories about the celebrities she'd sexed over the years. Girl had spoiled some of our most precious images by the end of the evening. It was a great time.

When I pulled into our driveway a little after midnight, my face streaked with tear tracks from hysterical laughter, my heart froze. Parked in the middle of the drive was Gina's Saturn.

I screeched to a halt, popped my seat-belt buckle, kicked open the car door, and let myself into the front door. As I stepped into the foyer, Gina's honey-smooth voice wafted in from the kitchen. Steeling my nerves, I balled both fists and strode straight ahead.

Mitchell was sitting at the kitchen table with a sleeping Clay in his lap, Gina standing over his shoulder. She was holding a copy of *Out of His Shadow.* The smell of pizza, one of the miniature Chef Boyardees we keep on hand for Clay, hung in the air.

"Hey, hey," Mitchell said, shifting Clay in his arms as I walked up to them. He stood, threw Clay over his arm, and leaned down to give me a full kiss. "How was the concert?"

"Fine." I looked at him just long enough to thank him for the kiss before turning toward Gina. "What's up?"

I could swear Gina rolled her eyes before answering me. "I had Mitchell keep Clay this evening. I went to a recruiting reception at Roosevelt. I forgot about it until this morning, but Mitchell said he was free while you were at the concert."

How convenient. I looked at his novel in her hand. "You hadn't seen the book before?"

"I'd seen it, but I just started reading it when I stopped over a few minutes ago. Mitchell, you have real skills." She placed a hand on his shoulder. "You go for it, make your son proud."

"Clay's a little young to really know the difference." I was annoyed at the sound of my voice, dismayed that I was even bothering to get in the way of her little come-on. When was the last time I had encouraged Mitchell's writing? It was hard to know anymore.

Clay's little eyes suddenly opened. He wriggled anxiously in Mitchell's arms, prompting my husband to play with him. "What's up, boy, where you trying to go?" He tickled Clay's tummy and began to swing him back and forth.

"Now stop it, you're gonna get him all excited, and he'll keep me up all night!" Laughing, Gina eased Mitchell back into the kitchen-table chair and reached over his head to rub some crust out of Clay's eyes. "That's my baby."

From his cradle in Mitchell's lap, Clay wiped a hand over his nose and pointed at the book in Gina's hand. "Mommy, wha's that?"

"This is Daddy's book, he wrote it himself." Gina's eyes sparkled as she traced a finger over Clay's face. "Daddy's going to be a big success someday." She tapped Mitchell's shoulder. "When are you going to focus on this full-time? Your talent's obvious."

That's between me and Mitchell. The sentence was the absolute truth, but it wasn't my place to speak it right now. I stood there watching Gina's act and wondered whether Mitchell had already forgotten about today's wake-up call.

"I'll write full-time when writing pays me full-time," Mitchell sighed, glancing at Gina before returning his attention to Clay. "Nikki's been a great support—"

"I hungry," Clay yelled suddenly. "Daddy, I hungry," he announced, tapping Mitchell's chest.

"Okay, okay." Mitchell stood, let Clay stand on his own two feet, and walked to the refrigerator.

"I have one thing to cover before we go," Gina said, looking at Mitchell's back but glancing at me with a dead expression that turned my stomach. "We have to decide on his preschool for next year. I brought all the brochures and information with me."

"It's late. Why don't we review it tomorrow," Mitchell said, walking back over to the table with a can of soy milk and a couple of cookies on a napkin. "I'll come by in the morning, on my way to the gym."

Still standing a few feet from the kitchen table, I shook my head. Here she was, in our home after midnight, and in the morning she'd have my professionally frustrated, recently sex-deprived man in her spider's lair of a home. It was getting real old.

"Whatever," Gina sighed. She looked down at Clay, who stood between her and Mitchell, slurping his milk and holding a crumbling cookie in his fist. "I have some news I should share with you, though."

I felt my eyebrows arch. Mitchell's back tensed as he slid his hands into the pockets of his sweatpants. "What would that be?"

"Well, it may be nothing." Gina blushed, looked back down and patted Clay's head. "Dale proposed to me today, at lunch."

You could have heard a pin drop.

Mitchell relaxed his shoulders, kept his hands in his pockets. "You guys just broke up last night. You're kidding, right?"

Gina's lips split in a crooked smile. "You know I can't stay mad at him. We made up this morning, after I dropped Clay at day care."

Mitchell and I exchanged a look, no words.

"Anyway, he wants to set a date around the holidays," Gina continued. "The other thing I don't get? He wants to adopt Clay when we get married. Crazy, huh?"

Mitchell crossed his arms, furrowed his brow. "Is that a threat? If so, it's laughable."

"I'm not saying I think Dale's right," Gina replied, her eyes growing wide. "I just thought you should know."

Mitchell's arms were crossed, but the emotions he was suppressing bubbled up through his throat. "I'm not giving you marital counseling, Gina, not my job. But if you think his interest in Clay is anything other than another shot at me, you're missing a few cards from your deck."

Gina gave a low chuckle and rubbed Clay's head again. "Come on, sweetie. Time to go home. Daddy's getting upset."

I couldn't take any more. My heart pounding with a rhythm loud enough to dance to, I turned and walked upstairs without another word, breezing through our master suite until I reached the bathroom. Exhaling loudly, I yanked open the medicine cabinet and retrieved my last pack of birth-control pills. The image of Gina, Mitchell, and Clay danced in my head as I walked to the toilet and, one by one, dropped each pill into the still waters.

Nikki

Keesa and I were standing in line at Carson Pirie Scott when I saw the tears form in her eyes.

She stepped to the sales register and carefully placed two dresses and one cotton pantsuit onto the counter. As the lady at the register searched for the tag on the first dress, Keesa looked into her shoulder bag and rummaged for her wallet. A stray tear plopped onto the store's marble tile.

I stepped forward, placing a hand on her shoulder. "You okay?" We'd had quite a range of conversations all afternoon, in between shopping our way up and down Michigan Avenue and State Street, but most of it had been filler. After all, this was really like a first date for Keesa and me. Sure, I'd helped her find her apartment a couple weeks ago, but we were still no more than acquaintances, folk who'd never have met if her baby's daddy wasn't my man's boss.

Keesa stared longingly at my hand on her shoulder, as if it was a life preserver she'd been waiting for in vain. "I'm all right, really. Sometimes you just have to let a little something out, know what I mean?"

"I feel you."

After Keesa had paid for her clothing and complimented me on my shopping tastes, we stepped back onto State Street, where a faint breeze from the lake tickled my spine. It was nine in the evening now and most of the stores were closing. In truth I'd done my duty for the day: showed Keesa where Chicago's finest afford-able shopping could be found while giving her an insider's tour of the city along the way. That was all she'd asked for when she called me earlier this week. I'd had my hands full with family events during the July-fourth festivities, but I'd cleared today's schedule for Keesa. The shopping was done now, but I didn't feel like it was time to go home yet.

I tapped my watch and leaned closer to her, shouting over the roar of a passing waste truck. "My man won't be home for a couple more hours." Mitchell and Clay were at Marvin and Angie's, helping paint the latest baby room. "What time do you need to be home for Cherrelle?"

Keesa crossed her arms playfully. "I ain't *got* to do nothing but stay Black and die." We both chuckled. "You wanna do something else? I'll call O.J. and tell him he's keeping his daughter overnight. It's simple as that."

"I just thought you might want to go somewhere, chill, talk, you know." I held out an arm. "Let me take a couple of those bags, homegirl. Just follow me!"

We made our cell phone calls home as we walked south to Adams Street and headed over to the Bennigan's on Michigan. The joint was jam-packed, with a proclaimed waiting time of forty-five minutes. Fortunately the host in charge was a twenty-something brother, a rail-thin little thing with a goatee and an eager spirit that perked up when we approached his station. We were both wearing jeans and silk blouses, and given the fact neither of us looked her age, it's not surprising we had him sprung. Keesa followed my lead, and with a little flirting and shaking we were seated in a back booth in minutes.

I ordered water with lemon and she took a vodka with orange juice. By the time the drinks arrived, we were getting to each other's good part. "I'm just wondering whether I should have kept my ass in D.C.," Keesa said between her initial swallows of vodka. "O.J. and I are on the warpath already."

"Why, is it something he did?"

"Naw, it's about what he won't do. I just want him to settle down, Nikki, you know, build a stable home setting for Cherrelle."

I sucked on a couple of ice shards before responding. "You want him to build that stable environment with you?"

"I'm not gonna lie, I do love him. In a perfect world, girl, I could help O.J. be all that he can be, and then some. I've seen his gifts clear as day from the first time we met ten years ago.

"But it'll never happen." Keesa signaled our waitress for a refill. "He respects me now, much more than he did back when I first had Cherrelle, and he is a responsible father. But he'll never view me as wife material. I screwed everything up back in the day, letting him play me and disrespect me too much."

Seeing the gleam of fresh tears in her eyes, I reached forward and grabbed Keesa's quivering hands. "That's his fault, not yours. You've obviously grown since then, maybe more than he has."

"Yeah, I know," she said, sniffling. "I'm over it, really. I just want to see him shut me up by getting a good woman in his life, so Cherrelle will respect him. That girl can hold a grudge."

I smiled lazily as I started to peruse the menu. At this hour salad was the only thing my figure could withstand. "You know, you could make the stable home for Cherrelle yourself, find a Mr. Right of your own. We may not quite be Atlanta or Chocolate City, but Chicago has its share of eligible brothers."

Keesa's eyes flashed so bright they warmed my heart. "You better tell me about it! Why you think I want O.J. to spend more quality time with my baby? While baby's away, Momma can play!" She offered me a high-five, which I quickly slapped. "I have to be honest, Nikki, I love spending time with you, even if you and Mitchell make me jealous as hell."

"Hmm. All that glitters is not gold." I smiled through closed lips, remembering I'd barely slept last night, afraid that Mitchell would surprise me with an early morning lay. Not that there was anything to worry about for a few more days, while my previous pills were in my system, but after that all bets were off. Assuming everything was actually okay with our plumbing, four pokes from

Mitchell's pecker and I could be with child, whether he was ready for it or not. Despite Gina, despite our disagreements about his career, I still didn't know if I had the nerve to stake my claim that way.

Our waitress showed up to take our orders. When she walked off, Keesa and I compared notes about our history with men, our fathers (both were absent during our childhoods), and our mothers (mine a saint, hers a little less so). As the night went on, our differences became more obvious, but our similarities won out by miles. Here I was, a buppie executive and DINK—double income, no kids—with a University of Chicago education, hanging tight with a former welfare mom. It felt snobby even thinking about it, but Keesa was a rarity amongst my current circle of friends. The girl had survived more than her share of hard knocks and was just a few years removed from life on the streets. I could learn plenty from her resilience and tenacity. I was looking forward to it.

Once I'd picked over my blackened chicken salad and Keesa had knocked off her Monte Cristo sandwich, we paid our bills and strolled out to the front lobby, where we patiently milled through the throng. Imagine my joy when I heard my name called out.

"Hello, hello, hello! Ms. Nikki Coleman!"

I knew the voice before I saw the face. Chuck "Lowball" Spencer, my first boyfriend and my first, period, lounged against the wall of the lobby, surrounded by two guys who looked a little younger than us, probably in their early twenties. Like Lowball, they were dressed in leather sweat suits and wore their hair in tight cornrows.

"What's up, girl," Lowball crowed, rising from his seat and stepping into my personal space. Around Mitchell's height, he was still wiry but had the workings of a double chin and noticeable bags under his eyes. The smell of his cologne, a sharp, spicy mix I'd never sniffed, shot into my nostrils way too fast.

"Hey, Chuck." I assumed he'd outgrown the nickname by now, but who really knew with these types?

He grinned wide, flashing a couple of gold-capped teeth. "It's like time stopped for you, like you just stepped out of MLK's halls and updated your wardrobe."

"You're way too kind. By the way, the name's Nikki Stone now." I stared back, hoping my curtness would back him off before I had to introduce him to Keesa or make phony small talk. The few slices of chicken from my salad started souring in my stomach.

When I realized Lowball had gently grabbed my arm, Keesa was at my side, staring a hole through him. "Hey, no harm," he said, smiling at Keesa but maintaining his grip. "Just want to say congrats on your nuptials. I heard 'bout you and Mitchell a few months back. Never figured you to roll with such a straight arrow, but I'm sure y'all make a nice couple."

"We're happy."

"Any kids?"

My brow grew warm but I smiled. "No."

"Hmm." Lowball let his eyes take a trip down my neck, over my breasts, and alongside my hips. "I been married five years myself, two kids and a set of twins on the way."

Oh, spare me. "How about the other three you had by Latrina, Trichelle, and Vanessa when we were in high school? I mean, before you dropped out?"

Lowball's grin twisted into a frown. "You think you funny now, huh? You wasn't too good for me all them afternoons in my mom's basement, now was ya?"

"Excuse me, we're going." Keesa calmly, forcefully addressed Lowball while shoving a hand in his face. "You have a good night."

I followed her out into the street, pushing through the rest of the crowd and ignoring the chuckles of Lowball and his crew.

For summer, it was cold as a witch's tit outside. Wind swept through the air, chilling the night's last touches of warmth. Rubbing my arms briskly, I checked my watch. "It's almost eleven, girl," I sighed. I had not meant to keep us out this late. At this hour hopping the El train back to Keesa's, where I'd left my car, was feeling questionable. I paused at the end of the block. "You want to hail a cab?"

"Girl, we may as well save a few dollars." Keesa brushed a curl out of her eye and put a hand on my arm. "That nigga in there was getting to you, wasn't he?"

"It's just the irony of seeing him at this moment in my marriage, is all. Like I said, me and Mitchell aren't perfect. Maybe the problem is I expected we would be."

Keesa chuckled to herself as we came to the Adams/Wabash train station. "You mean you figured life would be easier if you chose a brother with something on the ball like Mitchell, rather than that scrub?"

"I guess." I glanced toward Keesa as we climbed the steel-covered steps leading to the wooden platform. "I thought I was getting a package deal when I chose Mitchell over roughnecks like Lowball. I mean, Lowball gave me plenty of pleasure once upon a time, probably still could. But I always knew, even in my teens, that pleasure would come with a price of other women, other children, etcetera. What I didn't count on was having the same mess with a so-called good man."

"You're my nightmare," Keesa whispered as we crossed the pitted, gummy platform and stood at two automated ticket machines.

I let it slide until we'd crossed through the gates for the northbound tracks. We were all alone. "I like you and all, Keesa, but what's up with the nightmare comment?"

"I mean it in the way I'm *your* nightmare, Nikki." Keesa's urgent words met the cool air, leaving behind faint puffs of steam. "Whenever O.J. does find the right woman, by definition she'll have problems with me, especially if she envies the bond I have with him through Cherrelle."

I tapped her wrist as we took a seat on a bench. "Keesa, you're nothing like Mitchell's ex Gina. I know you wouldn't–"

"No, you really don't know what I'd do. I mean, I've had some good girlfriends who were some of the most mature people I knew, until their babies' fathers married other women. Almost every one showed her ass." She looked off into the distance, where a group of loud teens clambered up onto the platform. "It's tough. Sometimes I think with blended families, there's no one who's wrong or right. Just people trying to survive."

I started to respond when I looked over Keesa's shoulder to see that the teen gang–roughly eight Negro and Hispanic knuckle-heads–were headed our way. I checked my watch, ready to see an orange or green train roll up any minute.

"What up, mamas." A squat, heavyset boy with olive skin and fat cheeks strode up, loomed over our bench. "You got anything for us tonight?"

I sighed and looked at the boards of the platform, shaking my head. "No. Shouldn't you boys be home in bed about now?"

"Ain't nobody laughin' here." The boy took a closer step toward us, his face coming within inches of ours as he leaned in and pulled a knife from his right pocket. "Give up the bags and whatever cash you got, and we good."

I have to admit, Chicago native or not, the knife left me in a state of shock. Eight years out of college, traveling in the finer cir-cles of Chicago, a girl had gone soft. As I inhaled sharply and stiff-ened my spine, it was Keesa who took the lead.

"Get that shit out of my face." With a liquid motion, she stood and grabbed the teen's knife hand, twisted it, and sent the knife flying down into the train tracks. As he gaped at his precious weapon, Keesa shoved the surprised boy off to the side, where he stumbled to his knees. She put her hands on her hips and looked down at him. "Don't play with grown women, boy, it don't pay."

Not quite believing what had just happened, I shifted nervously on the bench, warming my hands and shaking with laughter at Keesa's heroics. I wasn't the only one amused. The rest of the gang, which had slowly approached us from the start, now stood ringing the bench and laughing their heads off.

For a few seconds, it felt like we were all on the same page, ridiculing the so-called leader and his incompetence in the face of a determined sister. It didn't take long until I realized the tide was turning. As Keesa stood laughing a few feet in front of me, just inches from the train tracks, the boys' taunting of their leader grew increasingly nasty.

"Punk-ass bitch! Marquise can't even get the job done with a little woman!"

"Thought ya knew, Jay! You 'member he couldn't get it up with that trick over on West Jackson either." A fresh wave of giggles and roars, some of the boys walking over to Marquise and jabbing fingers in his face, mouthing "faggot."

We were still the only folks on the northbound platform. An arty-looking white couple on the other platform huddled together and looked away.

The failed leader, the one I was assumed was Marquise, slowly gathered himself. Moving back amongst the rest of his boys, he traded four-letter curses with them before stepping back out from the group, eyeing me first and then Keesa. The look in his eyes did not escape her.

"Can I help you?" She faced him, her fists balled at her sides. "I know you don't want more of this." From behind her, the platform trembled with the approach of an orange train. Thank God.

Marquise lumbered back across the platform, pushed past me before I could get out of my seat, stood in front of Keesa. "You think you funny, bitch? You think you gonna show me up in front of my boys?"

"Nobody told you to fuck with me, son."

Flecks of spit flew from the boy's mouth. "I can't show my goddamn face on my street now."

"Not my problem. Now get out of my way—"

That's when Marquise did it. Raised his closed fist, reared back like he was Roy Jones Jr. Keesa ducked, kicked the boy square in the family jewels, and shoved him out of her way.

Only then did she realize what she'd done. Marquise, fat sloppy bastard he was, had lost his balance and was catapulting off the platform, straight into the tracks.

"Oh God!" Keesa turned back lightning-quick, reached for his hand.

I jumped to my feet. "Keesa, don't!"

From there, gravity had the final say. Keesa followed Marquise's pull, tumbling into the tracks behind him. By then the train was yards away.

I screamed and everything went into slow motion. The piercing screech of the train's brakes ringing in my ears, I turned from the carnage and raced across the platform, cursing every last boy on that platform and reaching for my cell phone with rubbery, shaky hands. No way was I looking back onto the tracks. I couldn't remember Keesa that way.

12

O.J.

Mitchell and Tony greeted me my first day back on the job, a week and a half after Keesa's funeral. The both of them looked like they'd been beaten with bags of ice: eyes bloodshot, rings under the eyes, heads hanging but just high enough to meet my gaze.

I sat in my office chair, staring back at them through my darkest pair of square-framed sunglasses. I felt no duty to remove the shades.

The two of them stood there in their respective suits—Tony wearing a double-breasted Armani, Mitchell sporting a more casual navy-blue number with chalky stripes—and shuffled in place.

"You can say what's up, boys, if you want an honest answer." I stuck my tongue back into a cheek and continued to review the day's outline.

Mitchell touched a hand to his lower lip. "O.J., if there's anything we can do at all, man . . ."

"You know we have your back," Tony continued, nervously twirling a blue toothpick stuck in his teeth. "You weren't returning my calls, but your father said you received all the—"

"Yeah, yeah. The cards, the food platters, it was great, man. Can we get on with life now?"

"Whatever makes you comfortable." Tony's lips were pursed and I could feel him suppress further words. At least he realized he wasn't some trained grief counselor.

Mitchell glanced at his watch. "You go on the air in a minute, so I guess we should leave you be. Again, you need anything—"

"I got it, guys." I inhaled deeply. "Thank you. Cherrelle and I love you for it, but we have to adjust in our own way, on our own time."

Tony pulled the door up behind him and Mitchell, sticking his head in the doorway before shutting it. "We'll be right down the hall."

I didn't respond, just let him click the door closed.

When I breezed into the studio a couple minutes later, I was greeted by Liz and by Bobby, my studio engineer. We'd already had our initial talk an hour earlier, so we were ready to get down to business without any excess drama. I'd sat up on the phone with Liz several nights while I was away, and in addition to sharing a corner of my emotional shock, I'd prepared her for today's major segments.

We spent the first half-hour talking small, kicking around the latest dramas from the mayor's office, the Sox, and the police blotter. The question of the day was *How many is too many? How many partners makes a woman "loose"?*

We were on a six-thirty newsbreak when Bobby tapped his side of the glass window. I frowned, fearing what was coming. "Yeah?"

"O.J.? Uh, the mayor's office is on the line, wants to offer condolences to your family and promise help in prosecuting—"

I grabbed my overhead mike, yanking it to my lips. "What did I tell you?" The studio shook with the blast of my response. I took a deep breath. "No on-air references to Keesa or Cherrelle. Period." I wasn't turning this into some *Real World/Big Brother/Survivor* spectacle, with me carrying on about my problems and the fact my little girl was now motherless. As if I hadn't disappointed Keesa enough when she was right here. No way was I going out on her like that.

The rest of the show passed with few incidents. We did a segment over the second and third hours, browbeating the people at Sprite's corporate headquarters. They'd been running ads featuring this little racist rocker, Deadpan Jan, for months, and with some prodding I'd convinced my audience we were tired of it. Even while I was out, the staff had collected another thousand electronic petitions, threatening a Chicago-area boycott if Dead-pan Jan wasn't dropped as a spokesperson. Don't you know by the end of the morning I had Sprite's VP of corporate communications promising they'd pull the ads? I punched the air around me like a boxer at the bag.

As soon as we signed off, ten sharp, I stalked past Liz, tapping her on the shoulder without stopping. My shades still firmly affixed, I continued down the hallway to my office, wordlessly passing the stares of numerous folk. I felt their questions, their concerns as viscerally as I felt this black hole of guilt in my heart, but there was really nothing to say.

I hurried through my office, quickly closing the window shades and grabbing my notes for tomorrow's program. On the right corner of my desk, another somber reminder: a clean stack of insurance and health-benefit forms to complete, all to update my new status as Cherrelle's only source of support.

I was standing in the middle of the office, my bag over my shoulder, the forms in my right hand, the station's music buzzing like static in my ears, when Mitchell walked in.

We stood staring one another down, filling the room with our tension. After a minute, maybe two, I shrugged at him and waited. Again, not much to say.

"I couldn't say this at the funeral." He cleared his throat and crossed his arms, looked me in the eye. "Nikki's a basket case. She feels—really, *I* feel—responsible."

"It's not a good time, man," I whispered, looking past him and stepping toward the door.

"You're right," Mitchell said, stepping aside but smacking one fist against the other palm. "Whenever you're up for it, though, let me know. There's nothing we won't do to help, O.J."

"Let me tell you this much." I looked up at my business manager, realizing his need was not something to trifle with. "Keesa was grown. I know she handled the situation the way she'd have handled it with or without Nikki there. My beef is with the misguided waste of breath who died with her, and the culture that produced that whole gang of bastards. What can you tell me about that?"

Mitchell straightened his back, looked me in the eye. "Nikki's given her statement and reviewed it with the police several times. Sounds like they're closing in on some suspects, likely associates of that Marquise punk."

"Associates, huh? I think you mean fellow bastards." I sucked my teeth, but couldn't stop myself. "I'm gonna have to be there when Nikki fingers whatever kids were involved. I don't care if they did just egg the kid on, they gotta be held accountable."

Mitchell didn't flinch. "Nik feels the same way."

"That's all I need to know. Tell Nikki to come down off the cross. Leave that to me and Cherrelle."

Mitchell clapped my shoulder, dipped his head. No words needed.

When I arrived home, my dad and Sister Lucy, my stepmom, were cleaning up the place. Sister Lucy was up front in the kitchen washing dishes, while Pop was vacuuming in the family room and had set out a broom and pan for the floors.

I went to Sister Lucy, kissed her gently on the cheek, and waved my arms for Pop to cease and desist with the vacuum.

He shot me a gap-toothed smile as the buzzing of the vacuum petered out. "So, how'd it go?"

I filled them in on the morning's happenings, then nodded toward Cherrelle's room. "She napping again?"

"Oh no," Sister Lucy piped up. Sister Lucy's a short, plump, beautiful Sunday-school teacher at Pop's church. At forty-five, she's ten years his junior but has the warm, boisterous spirit I first saw in my own mother. "Cherrelle went back to day camp today. She was in a much better mood."

I felt my brow furrow. "She was up last night crying, saying she didn't want to go back this week." She'd been fine Monday, but on Tuesday it seems the subject of Keesa came up several times. Lucky me, the majority of her classmates' parents are at least part-time fans, so there was no way Cherrelle could hide from reality, even among her peers.

"She was just caught up in the moment last night," Sister Lucy said, smiling and patting me on the back. "You can't always believe the first thing a child says, O.J. Have to watch their actions more than anything, mmm-hmm."

I felt a slow burn creep up my spine. "With due respect, I think I know my child, Sister Lucy."

My father scratched at his short silvery Afro, which was frayed through the middle. "O.J., come on over here and have a seat. You've been working all morning—"

"Pop, this is not nerves, okay? I appreciate you all's help, God knows I do. But I think it's about time I got used to rearing Cherrelle without human training wheels."

Pop placed his hands on my shoulders, smiling weakly as Sister Lucy disappeared back into the kitchen. "O.J., you have nothing to prove, son. Do you remember how callous you were when Cherrelle was still a baby in Keesa's womb? Look how far you've come. You're going to be a great father, just give it time."

"There is no time," I said, feeling my breath grow short. "The moment has arrived." I'd spent nearly a week in D.C. burying Keesa, then spent the past week cleaning out her apartment and moving in all of Cherrelle's things. "From now on, I'll be responsible for how she turns out."

Pop removed one hand from my shoulder but continued staring into my eyes. "Yes, you will, but that doesn't mean you can't do with some help."

"I'll take the help, Dad." I tried to soften my tone. "I'd prefer to take it over the phone for a while."

We continued our dance the rest of the afternoon, them cleaning up around me while I begged them to hit the road the next morning. We would have kept it up interminably, if Cherrelle's camp counselor hadn't called. Apparently Cherrelle had flattened a kid's nose for cracking wise about her mother. I walked over to Grant Park to pick her up, leaving my parents to complete the maid service.

The camp counselor, a thin freckled white girl named Jenny, was completely cool about things. She explained the incident to me then said, "I'm not sending Cherrelle home as punishment, I can just sense that she needs to be with family still. I'll take her back tomorrow if you want, though."

I told Jenny we'd keep her home for the rest of the week, meaning I'd have to allow my parents to stay that long at least. *Oh joy.*

We took the long way back, winding around the shore of Lake Michigan, heading toward Navy Pier. Given our emotional state, the weather almost felt like a cruel joke. The sun was out in high beam, the few clouds overhead were bright and puffy, and the sky's color was richer than I'd ever seen. It was the type of day that lets some people forget all their problems.

After a few minutes of silence, I gently took the book Cherrelle was reading from her hand. I came to an abrupt stop when I saw the name on the book jacket: *LaRae Summers.* What was my baby doing reading romance stories? Then I realized this was *April's Secret,* LaRae's children's book from last year.

The irony of my daughter's reading a book by a woman who hated me was almost mind-boggling. "You like this?"

"It's good so far. Can I have it back now?"

I reached out for her hand and started up our leisurely pace again. "You can have it back in a minute. What did those kids say to you?" I wanted her version for the record.

"Some of the boys said Mommy got killed 'cause she jumped bad, thought she was Jackie Brown. They all laughed." Cherrelle looked up at me, her face still streaked with angry tears. "Who's Jackie Brown anyway?"

"It's not important," I said, clasping her hand tighter. "What they did was wrong, Cherrelle, but you can't react to every wrong person, you hear me? You do that, you'll spend your life picking fights and getting sent home from school." I sucked in some air and realized we'd need that child psychologist Liz had recommended. I felt like a traitor. How could I tell my baby she was wrong to defend her mother's memory? As much as it sickened me, I was in need of professional help to guide her through this.

I looked down at my daughter as we walked on in silence. My child was motherless at the tender age of eight. I lost mine at thirteen, and I've never been the same. Nothing else has shaped me more decisively. My mother's absence left me without a female role model, left me with no one to compare the girls crossing my path with. As an only child reared by a single father, the concept of treating a girl "like a sister" held no meaning for me. When my talent for the preached word turned me into a mini-celebrity, nothing was there to counteract the normal tendencies of a horny teen.

The streets of Atlanta and D.C. were littered with the broken hearts of women who'd paid for my sense of abandonment. I could only imagine what such emotions might do to my bright, moody, determined little girl. Any emotional demons, or nasty little boys for that matter, gunning for her would have to go through me.

I tightened my grip on her little hand, grazed my fingers over her precious locks of hair. I'd failed her mother, but Cherrelle would get everything Keesa had longed for.

13

Mitchell

I walked in the door at six-eighteen this evening and made love to my wife.

Things had been pretty frigid for weeks. We'd never fully resolved her desire to come off the pill, nor her unease over Gina's interference in our marriage. I was doing everything I could to keep Gina on the fringes of our life; by paying full court-ordered child support, I had left her with no official leverage over me. The problem, of course, was that whenever a woman is the primary caretaker of your child, she has an unofficial power that needs no name and no court enforcement.

Keesa's death had plunged us into a new level of crisis. On the one hand, it brought us closer. When Nikki had first called me from the train station, she'd sounded pretty strong. Shaken, yes, but clear-minded and solidified by outrage. Once we'd come home, though, after consoling O.J. and explaining everything to Tony, my baby started fraying around the edges.

She blamed herself, felt she could have somehow defused the situation before Keesa and the hotheaded kid took it to a hostile level. Even if there was a grain of truth to that, I couldn't let her think that way. I knew Nikki well enough to know that she'd handled the situation as wisely as she could. Most likely she had tried to defuse things, but Keesa's more streetwise defense ratcheted things beyond her control. With the exception of this fool Marquise, it hadn't been any one person's fault, just a jacked-up situation.

O.J.'s first day back on the air, I came home from work and marched right upstairs, where I found Nikki lying in bed just as I'd expected. She'd only missed two days of work after Keesa's death, most of which she had spent recounting the experience to the police and aiding their search for the kids. However, though she was back to work, her energies were limited to Empire Records. Every night she would come home and cry herself to sleep.

"Wake up, sleepyhead." I flicked on the recessed lights in our master bedroom, stood over her still body. It had been almost a month since we'd been intimate, and I wasn't proud of the last few times. I had spent the last week and a half cooking dinner every night, stroking her hair while she slept, even placing some after-hours business calls on her behalf so she could conserve her energy. Now I was ready to fill her up with every ounce of love I'd withheld these past few weeks. I walked to the dresser, grabbed a match from a drawer and lit both of the apple-scented candles that sat on top.

Nikki's eyes opened slowly, her cocoa-brown irises focusing on me as she shifted onto her elbows. "Hi."

I turned back from the dresser, looked into her eyes. "O.J. came back today."

"I heard him. Had him on my office stereo. He sounded too normal."

"He's got a shield up as thick as a glacier, but you can look in his eyes and see the pain. He just knows how to perform."

She turned back the sheet and comforter covering her, revealing the soft slope of her neck and her silk camisole top. "Did you speak to him?"

"He wasn't very talkative," I said, stepping slowly toward the bed, "but he said he appreciates everyone's thoughtfulness." I sat down and scooted over behind Nikki after throwing off my shoes.

"Did you tell him about me, about—"

Sitting behind her, propped up by her four satin-covered pillows, I touched her chin, turning her to face me. "He confirmed what I already knew. It's not your fault." I pulled Nikki's face to mine, kissed her deep and long. "I know it's easier said than absorbed, but that's from the horse's mouth."

"Mama wants me to see one of her friends at the center."

"Makes sense to me." I pulled the covers back from the rest of my wife's busty, athletic frame, admired her curves and her rich maple-brown complexion.

"I have to think about it," she said, yawning and turning onto her side before looking at me suspiciously. "What are you looking at?"

"I'm looking at the best thing to ever happen to me, is what I'm looking at. Someone without whom I can't imagine this life. God Nikki, if that had been you—"

"It wasn't, though. We're blessed, why I don't know."

"Yeah, we are blessed," I said, the crotch of my slacks ready to burst from sexual pressure. "Let's try to act like it." I flipped over on my side, laid Nikki flat against the mattress, and let my right hand travel beneath her outfit to her thighs. With smooth, swift motions I began to trace familiar circles on those thighs. As I felt her back arch and savored the smile teasing her lips, I used my free hand to peel her top off. Getting onto my knees, I poised myself over her and continued past her thighs to the increasingly wet space between her legs, as I simultaneously licked her quivering breasts. When she'd had her first orgasm, a loud, thrashing experience I attributed to our self-imposed strike, she grabbed at my erect penis and guided me deep inside her. Our new mattress squeaked and squirmed beneath us as I spread her legs wide, wrapped them around my waist, and plunged in and out with a soft, slow rhythm.

As good as Nikki felt, as well tuned as we were, the time away caught up with me. I boiled over a little faster than usual, but we were still spent and covered with sweat. We lay naked in each other's arms and let everything—Clay, Gina, Keesa—sit outside the bedroom door for a few minutes.

Nikki

I was in good shape until I realized we'd just made love for the first time since I had come off the pill, a withdrawal I'd failed to share with Mitchell. The romance and warm fuzziness rolled off me like a fog. God, what had I done? I'd never made up my mind about whether to get back on the pill before Mitchell and I made love again, then everything with Keesa had put the whole thing on the back burner. As Mitchell's eyes fluttered closed and he began to snore faintly, I kept a hand on his chest but started to bite the nails on my other hand. I knew from reading that even the most fertile couple takes at least four times to conceive, on average. Maybe there was nothing to worry about. Bottom line, though, I owed it to Mitchell to warn him that a baby might be on the way now, or would be if we kept this up before I got back on the pill. I patted his chest and vowed to handle it later in the evening.

The phone woke us, around eight-thirty. The lights were still on, so we both jumped quickly at the ring. Mitchell grabbed the cordless phone from his side of the bed.

"Hello?" He inhaled deeply, gave the familiar "Gina" pause. "Yeah, of course I know I need to get him from day care tomorrow." Another pause as he sat up, a gathering of civility. "How'd your interviews go?"

I shook my head, reached over to lovingly palm my man's head, and climbed out of bed. Mitchell looked over at me as Gina talked and smiled wide, sticking his tongue out at me like we were on the playground. I walked up to him, loosely grabbed his dangling johnson, and mouthed, "All mine." I gave him a quick squeeze and headed into the bathroom.

A few minutes later I had washed my face, brushed my teeth, and tightened my cornrows. Turning from the sink, I nearly ran into Mitchell, who stood wordlessly before me, the phone hanging loose in his hand. I grabbed on to his wide shoulders and narrowed my eyes, gazing up. "What's wrong?"

"Gina's, uh, weighing a job offer from CNN."

"Cool, something with their Chicago bureau, huh?"

He looked away, exhaled a breath full of emotion. "No, *the* CNN. Atlanta."

I chuckled, stifling the surge of fear welling up in my chest. "She's just talking, baby. Gina of all people wouldn't move to a new city and lose all the support she has here in Chicago."

"She can cash my checks in Atlanta as easily as she cashes 'em here."

"But she wouldn't—"

Mitchell put his hands on his hips, a motion that caused my arms to slide off his shoulders. "Unless I can prove she's unfit, there's nothing she can't do, Nikki. She could take my boy as far away as she wants." He smacked his fists and his eyes boiled with anger. "It's so damn wrong!"

"You can't think that way," I whispered, pulling him back to me. "You can't, okay? She's just talking, trying to get in your head again. Trust me, baby, trust me."

Mitchell, still looking limp as a string bean, dropped his forehead to mine but tightened his grip around my waist. It seemed my pep talk had worked; either that was a hammer in his Jockeys or he was happy to feel me. It was time for another round, either in the bed or here on the countertop, and Gina had just convinced me to keep my mouth shut. It was time we had some leverage to balance her misuse of Clay.

I touched my lips to his, opened my mouth, and prayed for a new addition.

14

Mitchell

I was stuck in traffic on Cermak, sweating buckets thanks to an ailing air conditioner, when Tony rang my cell phone. Stifling a cough at the exhaust of the belching eighteen-wheeler next door, I punched the SEND button. "What now?"

"Hey, man, you ran out of here pretty quick. I went looking for you a little after five, you'd already cleared out."

I sighed, then inhaled. "I told you I had that reading at Chicago State tonight."

A pause on Tony's end. I could just see him rubbing his forehead. "I'd forgotten." He chuckled grimly, probably pausing to pity my hopeless dreams. "When you getting home?"

"The program ends at eight." I reached overhead with my free hand, grabbing my sunglasses from my sun visor. "Can't this wait until tomorrow?"

"Uh, no. Did you forget I'll be gone the rest of the week?" Tony, who worked twelve- to sixteen-hour days, was taking a well-deserved vacation to Montreal.

"And?" I was so far behind keeping up with his women, I didn't try to figure out which one was going along for the ride.

"Well, I had a special project for you, one I meant to cover before you left tonight. You're gonna have to come back through here or let me swing by your crib, say around nine?"

Inching my car forward, I slid my sunglasses on and shook my head. "Knock yourself out, we'll leave the light on. You wanna tell me the nature of the project?"

"Let's just say you'll get to use your MBA."

"Dammit, Tony–"

"Look now. I just learned that Holly's taking family leave time." Holly was the accounting manager, and had just had twins with no time off. "Everything finally caught up to her."

"And hiring a temp's out of the question."

"It is when we have an able-minded accountant—excuse me, financial analyst—on board. I'm under pressure to minimize expenses right now, you know the damn drill." Aside from O.J., WHOT was struggling to get credible ratings in its major time slots.

"Fine," I said, rapping my steering wheel. "I'll get out my green eyeshades and pencils. See you later." I punched the phone off and tossed it onto my passenger seat.

There was nobody to blame but myself. My business-manager gig was so ill defined, I was becoming more and more susceptible to extra odd jobs like the one Tony had planned. I was beginning to feel like Michael Corleone—just when I thought I was out of accounting, this job was finding ways to pull me back in.

I continued down Cermak in fits and starts, finally turned onto Calumet, and eventually reached Dr. King Drive in one piece.

As I pulled into the parking lot on CSU's campus, I tried to mentally change hats from corporate worker bee to *artiste*. I'd read numerous accounts of how the most successful Black novelists—from E. Lynn Harris to Parry Brown to Kimberla Lawson Roby—had broken onto the scene while holding down corporate jobs. For me, such a balancing act was proving disorienting.

It had been a couple months since I'd had time to promote *Out of His Shadow*. Between the increased demands at WHOT, spending time with Clay as well as with my mentee, Terry, the new tensions with Nikki, and Keesa's death, my plate had been too full. Now, as I walked toward the auditorium filled with authors and demanding readers, I wondered whether I was ready to re-enter the arena.

Still wiping my damp forehead, I stepped through the doorway and was dismayed to find the lights already turned low, the auditorium full, and the stage packed with authors. A row of them, mostly female with a smattering of brothers, were seated at a long wooden table. In front of them a heavyset, middle-aged sister with beige skin stood at a lectern, reading emphatically from her book.

"I picked that child up and ran down the street as if I'd been set aflame. . . ."

Frozen in the doorway, I checked my watch frantically. It was six-fifteen; the program was supposed to start at six-thirty.

An usher, a college-age girl with a well-groomed Afro, stepped over and handed me a program. Plastered underneath the logo was the start time: Five-thirty. Somehow I had misunderstood. Small wonder given everything on my plate.

As new beads of sweat swamped my forehead, I shuffled down the right aisle and took a seat in the second row. A few seconds later, I felt an insistent tap on my shoulder and turned.

"One more seat up there for you." Carolyn McKneese, the program coordinator I'd met in passing earlier this year, pointed over my shoulder. "Go ahead, you'll be the last one on, but you're up next."

Confused, frustrated, I stewed in my chair, not wanting to step on the toes of the sister at the lectern. Walk in and read, no warm-ups, no foreplay, no lubrication. Could I just go home maybe?

In seconds the sister was finished and the emcee, a tall beefy brother with the fresh face of an undergrad, butchered my introduction. First he pronounced my name "Michael," then proceeded to selectively read from my bio, skipping important stuff and mixing in factoids that must have come from someone else's. Then, "Please welcome Michael to the stage."

I walked up the steps, back arched, shoulders high, butterflies in my chest. *You the man*, I thought, trying some ethnic self-affirmation. *You the man*. It was true, really. I had the love of a beautiful, bright wife, was a responsible father to a handsome son, had a loving family, and had found time on the side to write and publish a novel worth reading. I was the man, but there in the moment, as I looked at the sea of amused, somewhat skeptical faces, I didn't feel it.

My head was empty, so I dispatched with attempts at opening humor or small talk. "*Out of His Shadow* is a story about the strength of the human spirit. Dominique is a successful physician whose husband, Andre, has abused her for years, keeping her at his side with a mixture of deception, mind games, and threats. Her challenge is to defy him and rebuild her life. I'll read from Chapter Nine, which is a key turning point in her story. She's made her first attempt to move out of town, and is holed up in a hotel a few hours outside of New York, where the story is set."

I fidgeted with the book, realizing I had lost my bookmark. I heard faint chuckles in the distance but kept flipping pages, for what felt like an eternity. Finally I reached the appropriate page, which I clutched between my right thumb and index finger. As I got rolling, I tried to effect my best vocal impression of James Earl Jones—low, smooth, mellifluous—the type of authoritative vibe a reader probably imagines when reading in the privacy of her home.

Sad fact is, I was shooting that fantasy voice to hell. I'd been away from the material too long. I started and stopped numerous times, losing my place. Paused to make eye contact with the audience, build rapport, and lost my place again. Felt my whole body stiffen like Al Gore in front of a camera. I was butchering my own handiwork, rendering it dull, lifeless, probably even painful.

When I slapped the book shut, silence rang throughout the hall, until Carolyn's tepid claps reminded everyone to applaud out of pity, if nothing else. I wiped my sweaty forehead, shook the moderator's hand, and walked off the stage. Coming to the bottom of the steps, I looked straight ahead and hurtled down the aisle and across the back row of the auditorium, until I was back out in the parking lot.

Shaking my head, I stuffed my book into my leather satchel

and grappled with what might just be the truth. Life was complex enough without these delusions of literary grandeur. Maybe it was just time to—

There was a hand on my shoulder.

I pivoted, dropping my satchel as I stopped a few feet from my car.

The hand belonged to Dale, my rival for my own son's affections. Dressed surprisingly well in leather loafers, gray slacks, and a two-tone dress shirt with power tie, he was cheesing from ear to ear. "Righteous job up there, dude. Don't hang that head!"

I had forgotten Dale was an on-again, off-again CSU student. He'd probably only enrolled this last time to please Gina. I brushed his hand away and bent back down, retrieved my satchel.

I could hear, and smell, Dale still standing over me. "I give you a pep talk, and you give me the silent treatment, huh?"

I unlocked my car door, opened it, and looked at this fool over my shoulder. "No offense, Dale, I just have nothing to say."

"Aw, come on. So you can't have everything, Mitchell. You'll never cut it as a creative type, you ain't got the personality, the cool. We both know it. I'd still trade places with you, partner. You got degrees, you talk the King's English well and all that shit. You'll always have a place in the corporate world."

I turned all the way around, stood toe to toe with the brother once again. "There's something you don't understand about human communication, Dale. You don't give a person your opinion about shit that's none of your business, unless they ask you for it."

Dale rubbed his hands together, a smirk twisting his lips. "Oh, it is my business, son, 'cause it impacts your dealings with Gina and Clay. And Gina and Clay are definitely my business."

I didn't bother fighting the smile that spread across my face. "You're right," I chuckled, scratching my neck anxiously, "Gina and Clay are your business, because I really believe she's going to marry you."

"That, and then we'll see about me adopting Clay."

"I've got an ironclad record with the courts, asshole." I caught my breath. "Unless you've got pictures of some judge in a compromising situation, you're dreaming. Why don't you figure out how to make Gina take you seriously?"

"The fuck you mean by that?"

Fists formed at my side, but my smile spread even wider. "Can't you see you're just something to do?"

Dale raised a hand, balled it up. "You better watch your tone, mutha–"

"Mitchell!" The shout, from over Dale's shoulder, stopped us both where we stood. LaRae Summers ran toward us, flanked by a dozen or more pursuing fans.

"Hold up one minute, okay?" Sporting a sleek gold-colored pantsuit, her braids pulled back into a neat bun, LaRae scribbled off autographs for the women surrounding her, then excused herself. Though Dale still stood in front of me, boiling like a teakettle, LaRae walked right past him and gently took my arm.

"Save me," she whispered through clenched teeth as we edged away from Dale and the adoring crowd. "There's more where they came from. If they think we're together, maybe they'll let me get out of here."

I let her tug at my arm and smiled. "How about I walk you to your car and we call it a day?"

LaRae looked over at Dale, who stood a few feet away staring us down. I hoped he wasn't offended I hadn't made introductions. "Why don't you drive me to my car?" LaRae whispered. "I'm on the other side of the auditorium." She raised her voice and turned toward Dale. "I hope you don't mind me stealing him away. I'm friends with his wife."

Dale shrugged and glanced at me. "Whatever. I'll deal with Mitchell later."

LaRae chuckled as I made an obscene gesture behind Dale's

back and opened my passenger door for her. "Look, there's a serious reason I flagged you down," she said as we slid into the car. "I come out to events like these to scope talent, Mitchell, and I think you've got it."

Starting my engine and letting down the front windows, I rolled my eyes before looking at LaRae. "What convinced you of my talent? My inability to read my own material, or my striking white oxford shirt?"

LaRae giggled as I drove into the adjoining parking lot. "Hey, I'm not saying you can't improve as a performer, but as far as what's between the covers of your book, you've got it. *Out of His Shadow* was an excellent read!"

I hit my brakes suddenly, so suddenly LaRae and I both hopped in our seats. I gently hit the gas again. "Don't toy with me, ma'am. Nikki put you up to this as a practical joke, right?"

"Oh, Nikki slipped me a copy of the book all right, but she was very low-key, almost apologetic. I'm so happy she did, though, because it's very good. Here's my car." We stopped at a black Jaguar. "The book's not perfect yet, but if you'll agree to work with me on some light revisions, I'll submit it to some agents and publishers on your behalf. Never know what might happen."

I fought the goofy smile spreading across my face. "Let me know when you want to talk, I'll make the time."

"No problem." LaRae touched a hand to my chest, smiling peacefully. "It's a blessing to help good people with real talent. Just make me one promise." She winked playfully.

I tried to ignore the tingling down south that her touch had caused. "Uh, what's that?"

"When you get rich and famous," she said, opening my car door, "promise me you'll go on every radio show but O.J.'s. It would serve his ass right!"

We had a good laugh until her face turned serious. "How is he? I mean, really?"

"The picture of strength and responsibility. I know he keeps a lot of it inside, though."

LaRae looked down at her hands, which still rested in her lap. "I guess I keep thinking about his little girl. I lost my mother at a very young age."

I nodded. "That's a tragedy no one should have to suffer. Keesa was an impressive lady, on top of that. The type that made lemonade out of lemons."

"Well," LaRae sighed, "hopefully O.J. and I can patch things up someday. I'm sure he needs space right now."

We talked a little more, then LaRae zoomed off. My head filling with visions of good things, I insisted on sober thoughts as I turned the ignition again. I dialed Nikki up as I shifted gears.

"Hey." Her tone was sullen, disappointed.

"Everything okay?"

"I guess. I'm just sitting here strapping on a pad, the old period arrived this afternoon."

"You almost sound surprised."

"No, no, not at all. Just—well, never mind. When will you be home?"

"I'm headed there now. I have encouraging news, though you probably won't be all that surprised. I'll tell you when I get home. Nikki?"

"Yeah?"

It had occurred to me that though we'd been pretty hot and heavy the past three weeks, we'd never officially settled on how soon to try to get pregnant. "You *are* still on the pill, right?"

A momentary pause. "Why wouldn't I be?"

"No reason. Look, I love you."

"I love you too."

I hung up and pulled out into the street, my spirits lifted but my heart oddly wary.

15

O.J.

"I'm gonna send Marcy next door to Landon's." Dr. McIntosh, or should I say the Reverend Doctor McIntosh, peered at me over the rims of his bifocals. "What you want? I recommend the fried fish platter or the chops."

I shifted in my seat, a few feet away from the good pastor's desk. I had come to meet him in his wood-paneled study this evening, after avoiding him for most of my time in Chicago. Dr. McIntosh had been my pop's mentor in ministry, reaching back to their days as seminary students in Kentucky. Now that Cherrelle's well-being was on the line, I had sacrificed my pride and come calling for his wisdom.

"What you want?" he asked again, dangling a tattered take-out menu in front of me. "You don't like fish or chops? Have a looky there, they got other selections. Chicken-fried steak's nice."

I was starving like a mug, but I'd have to be hog-tied before I'd eat anything McIntosh had named. In the month since Keesa had been gone, I'd already gained about ten pounds. It was time to get back on track. I patted my stomach. "I'm not hungry, just ate." I didn't have time to argue.

"All right. Marcy!" McIntosh shouted so loud, I wondered if Marcy was up the block. "Bring me a fish platter, extra fries. An apple cobbler on the side."

I heard Marcy rise from her chair, just outside the office doorway. "Yes, Reverend," came the low, reverent reply.

"All right, looky here," McIntosh said, eyeing me as he flipped through a deck of cards on his desk. "Your daddy told me to leave you alone about this, but if you're gonna come in here asking me to counsel you through your bereavement—"

"It's not counseling, Reverend." I knew I was stepping on toes, but in my years away from the church I'd lost patience with its obsession with classifying everything. "I'm asking to come and just talk every now and again."

McIntosh leaned back in his chair. "Aside from your bereavement, what else you need to talk about?"

I wiped a thin film of sweat from my brow, wishing McIntosh wasn't so thrifty with his air-conditioning. "Full-time parenting is a new challenge, for one. Plus, there's the matter of my job." Despite my bereavement, Skip and Danny were working overtime to intimidate me into dropping every ounce of substance from the show. According to Tony, they were trying to initiate talks with John Ray, an emerging star out of Philly. Anything to remind me I was expendable.

"Well," McIntosh said, nodding at my list of concerns, "I'm sure the Lord will provide us with answers on these challenges and more."

"I respect your feedback, but I'm not looking for answers or specific counsel."

"Call it what you will, son." He clasped his hands and leaned forward, staring me down again through the bifocals. "If you want my help, I want something in return."

I waited.

"Your butt in my pew on Sunday morning, right next to that precious little girl's."

"Reverend, please—"

"No, that's my condition and I'm sticking with it. You Negroes always think you can get something for nothing. You of all people should know better, Junior."

"Sir—it's O.J. You called me Junior when I was twelve, sir."

"You'll be O.J. when you start bringing little Cherrelle into my sanctuary. You'll be blessed here, son, trust me."

I slapped the back of my head, let the hand slide down to my neck. I guess it beat going to see some sexually deviant, manipulative, price-gouging shrink. "Jesus would be proud, Reverend. You win."

"Praise the Lord. Let's say Thursdays at six P.M., okay? Some weeks I may have other commitments, if so we'll talk via phone." He reached across the desk, waved both hands at me. "Link up, let's pray."

As I pulled out of the parking lot in my Jeep, leaving Stony Island AME in my rear-view mirror, I tried to convince myself I hadn't sold out. Maybe I'd be all right as long as I drew the line at my "counseling" and attending Sunday mornings. I didn't trust myself with anything more; Stony Island, like any church, would be too full of opportunities for abuse if I got in too deep.

My cell phone purred against my belt. I flipped it open, saw the number, and blew air through pressed lips. I let it ring a couple times, considered letting it go. Then I bit the bullet.

"What's up, Asha?"

"Hey." She was trying to sound playful and easy, but an underlying resentment drowned those efforts. "Did you get my message last week?"

"You were on my list to call."

"Look, O.J., I'm not trying to cause drama, least of all now. I've been cutting you slack."

I screeched to a stop at Seventy-first Street. My right thumb itched, eager to mash the END button. I'd spent two nights with Asha before Keesa's death and one since. Problem was, I had no idea what that meant.

She finally took a cue from my silence. "I always said I wasn't looking for anything, and I was serious. But, I'm just wondering now, I mean, it's clear there's a lot on your mind."

"Mmm-hmm."

"I'm wondering if you feel it's right for us to carry on, with everything you've got bottled up right now, with Cherrelle living with you."

My words exploded, unedited. "If I was you, Asha, I'd write me off."

"Don't say that."

"I'm not gaming you, girl. You're beautiful, ambitious, and great fun. But if you're looking for more than compliments, I'm not ready for you."

"You don't know that."

Lord Jesus. What does it take to get rid of some women? I didn't know any better, I'd think she was getting turned on.

"Look, there's someone else," I said, hoping this would actually help. "You've heard of the Chavis family?"

"The ones who own Chavis Communications, out of Atlanta?"

"Yeah. You know I mentioned that Alison Chavis helped start my career down there?"

"Uh-huh."

"Well, let's just say I started her up first, if you know what I'm saying."

"She live in Chicago now?"

"No, but she's coming into town next weekend. She's talking about moving in to help me and Cherrelle. You may as well know, it'll save some awkward moments."

Asha coughed a few times, started to laugh. "Okay, fine. You take it easy, O.J." The line went dead.

I probably wasn't done fending her off, but I shut my phone and prayed for peace. Truth was, Alison was heading into town next weekend, and I was already at work on how to back *her* up off me. As much as I'd enjoy venting my burdens via some acrobatic sex, I couldn't afford to wave any more bedmates in Cherrelle's face. I'd creeped with Asha that one afternoon while she was at day camp a couple weeks back, but if I let Alison through my apartment door she'd try to play house and win Cherrelle over. The day would come when I'd let a courageous woman take a shot, but it would have to be someone I loved.

16

O.J.

I picked Cherrelle up from her day camp and we went out for pizza at Gino's East, which she prefers to my favorite place for Chicago-style, Giordano's. In the name of doing something different, we drove out to the Gino's near Midway Airport. Even after wading through the saturated blocks of Ninety-fifth Street, it was barely six o'clock, still sunny out but cooling nicely. On the way into Gino's I grabbed a copy of the *Sun-Times*, looking to delve deeper into the sports and politics sections.

Cherrelle and I sat at our wooden, graffiti-covered table and kicked each other's legs playfully. I read up on the Cubs and she flipped through the paper's sections like a madwoman.

I looked across our booth, tried to sound stern. "Cherrelle, stop playing with the paper. If you're not going to read anything, just fold it up."

"Oh, whatever." She gave me a characteristically nasty look but slid the Arts section aside and neatly folded the rest.

I fought tears of joyful surprise at her sudden cooperation. Cherrelle and I still hadn't had "the talk" her grief counselor thought we needed: the one where she'd come out and tell me how much she resented me for never marrying Keesa, where she admitted that she hated having to come live with me now. The one where she talked about the hole that losing her mother had left in her heart.

That said, chips of the ice between us were melting day by day, and this chip hit home more than others. I reached over, tapped her little hand. "What makes you want to read the Arts section?"

"Movies," she said evenly but with a hint of a smile. "I like the ads and stuff."

"All right, have at it." I went back to my Sports section and ignored the latest rumble of my stomach as a waitress walked by with a deluxe pan pizza.

I'd gotten through the second page of sports when Cherrelle's voice startled me. "Ooh! Look, Daddy!"

I lowered my paper to see my daughter pointing an eager finger at a half-page ad with a photo of LaRae Summers. Her braids framed those familiar lively eyes, the high cheekbones, and beautiful, bronzed skin. From the paper, it seemed she was staring me down, her smiling mouth saying *I'm still the queen.*

I stared back at the image, looked between it and Cherrelle's beaming face. "What you know about her?"

"I have her book, remember?"

"Oh yeah, that's right."

"See what it says?"

I leaned over to take a closer look at the ad. "Looks like she's doing a book signing tomorrow, baby. Afrocentric Books, noon to two. That's during your day camp."

"Can I go, please? I want her to sign my book." Cherrelle had always been an introspective child, an avid reader since first grade. Now she was already turning into an author groupie. How sad.

"Baby, I just told you you'll be in camp—"

"Will you go for me? You're not working at noon."

I chuckled. The child has no idea; I "work" from four until ten every day, then for a good piece of the afternoon doing informal research and networking. "Well, I could go during my lunch break, but tomorrow's really not a good day."

She crossed her arms and smiled smugly. "Then you have to let *me* go."

*   *   *

The next day at twelve-thirty I took reluctant steps out of the office building and footed it over to State Street and Jackson, Afrocentric's location. This was love, all right, walking two dozen blocks round-trip. I'd even made myself more presentable than usual for a workday, wearing a pair of my favorite Perry Ellis slacks with a coordinated white rayon shirt.

Adding to my fun, the skies had opened up on Chicago for the afternoon, with warm droplets of rain pinging randomly against the sidewalk. I looked up into the relatively blue skies and willed the drops to cease. I didn't need a bunch of "bee-bees" popping up in my short 'fro.

I had Cherrelle's book in one hand and a prepared script in my head. Since my daughter had bullied me into coming, I figured I may as well apologize for the "battle of the sexes" I'd started with LaRae. Somehow my motivations and methods from that day didn't feel right anymore.

I stepped inside the Jackson Street entrance to Afrocentric's shopping center and ran smack-dab into a line of LaRae's admirers. The line stretched from the other end of the plaza, across the little food-court area, to the door I'd entered. Each person in line was clutching a sheet of paper. I huffed and puffed my way through the crowd and found the end of the line, after speaking curtly to a few fans who recognized me and suffering a cursing rant from another sister who thought I was cutting in line.

I took my place at the very end, behind a tall, wiry young brother in a short-sleeved denim shirt and a baggy pair of Levi's 501s. I chuckled despite myself and tapped him on the shoulder. He whipped around, faced me with his head of short dreadlocks and the dark scar in the middle of his forehead. Didn't see that every day.

The brother looked down at me, eyebrows raised. "What's up?"

"Hey man, just tripping off seeing a fellow brother in the house. You notice how many women are in this line?"

He looked at his shoes, then over my shoulder. "Yeah, seem like most of her fans are women."

"Well, I'm here for my daughter." I held up a copy of Cherrelle's book. "You actually read this romance stuff, or did your little woman send you over here too?"

He jammed his hands into his pockets and turned around. "No woman tells me what to do."

I was about to say "Excuse the hell out of me" when a smiling, brown-skinned sister around my age walked up. "Hi, please take this," she said, extending a small slip of paper to me. "Write down the name you want Ms. Summers to use when she signs your book."

"Okay, sure," I said. "You work here?"

"Yes," she said, shaking my hand, "I'm Tamatha."

"Nice to meet you. I'm O.J. Peters."

"Oh that's right!" She covered her mouth with a hand. "I thought you looked familiar. From WHOT?"

"In the flesh." I jotted Cherrelle's name onto the slip and slid it inside her book.

Tamatha gave me a cross look, though her lips were still curled with a playful smile. "I know you're not bringing an old book into the store for signing. The idea is you support the author *and* Afrocentric."

"It's for the kids, Tamatha, it's for the kids." I chuckled and waved the book in front of her.

"Hey, that's all you had to say," she said, chuckling back.

I winked at her. "I'll pick up a few copies here anyway, how's that?"

When Tamatha returned to the store, I decided to leave homeboy alone and endure the line in silence. Afrocentric was pretty efficient, because despite the crazy-ass line it took only half an hour for me to reach LaRae. She was seated in the middle of the store at a table, flanked by two greeters whose clear role was to shoo the fans away before the ink on her signature dried.

As the brother in front of me stepped inside the store, he moved aside suddenly. "Go on."

Confused, I screwed my eyes in his direction and tried to wave him ahead of me. "You go on, player, you've waited just like me."

"Nah, uh, it's okay. I've seen enough." The words weren't completely out of his mouth before he'd blown past me, back into the hallway. One strange dude.

I stepped up to the table. Dressed smartly in a long-sleeved pink silk blouse and matching white slacks with pink pinstripes, LaRae smiled, then did a double take. The greeters, cute college-age types, quickly recognized me, paid their respects, and stepped back as I laid Cherrelle's little book onto the table.

LaRae looked down skeptically and shook her head. "Are you returning this because you hated it?"

That caught me off guard. "This is my little girl's book. For some reason, she enjoyed it."

I saw a flicker of sober recognition in her eyes. "Oh, I'm honored that she wanted it signed. This *was* her idea, right?"

"Damn right. I mean, yes."

She took the book, flipped it open and began to attack it with her black felt-tip pen. "You can never start them too early. I applaud you."

I looked over my shoulder, glad to see no more than a dozen folks languishing back there. I placed a hand on top of the book as LaRae continued writing. "Look, while I'm here, I wanted to say I hope there's no hard feelings about our little radio battle."

My personal foray piqued the interest of the two greeters. Both sisters angled in. One touched LaRae's shoulder. "Get him with both barrels, girl. He know he was wrong for the way he played you."

I cocked an eyebrow at the rabble-rouser. "You gonna stand there and talk mess after kissing my drawers a minute ago? I bet you still listen to 'The O.J. Way' every morning, don't ya?"

She looked at her greeter girlfriend, batted her eyelashes sheepishly. "This ain't about whether I still listen, it's about you trying to ambush my favorite author." The girl was toying with me, probably thought LaRae and I were secretly friends or something.

I sighed, fixed my eyes on LaRae again. "Let me buy you some coffee when you're done," I whispered. "We don't have to do this now."

"I'm all right." LaRae suddenly drew herself up and looked past me. "Ladies and gentleman," she said, speaking to the rest of the folks in line, "can you excuse me one minute? I need to visit the little girls' room."

The crowd murmured its assent and Tamatha stepped forward. "I'll walk you to the closest one."

LaRae looked at me suddenly. I got the message. "I can show her the way, Tamatha, you stay here."

I felt the attention our little exit caused, heard the whispers announcing who I was and wondering whether this was a bathroom break or a booty call. We stepped into the nearly empty hallway and I headed toward the restrooms, the smell of the food court—tacos, sticky buns, and French fries—closing in on us. "Look," I said, holding up my hands, "all I was saying is, I've thought about how things went down and I hope I didn't offend you."

LaRae stopped and placed herself squarely in front of me. "I'm sorry, O.J., but unfortunately I can't stand in for your little girl's mom. My heart goes out to you, honestly, but I think I know enough about your type. You're projecting your guilt about whatever you did to her onto me."

I stood there with my mouth frozen, my breathing stopped.

"Whatever happened between you two, remains between the two of you. Just because she's gone doesn't mean you can't deal with it. Just don't put me in the middle."

I took a deep swallow, felt a salty brine build up in my throat. "What are you saying?"

"I'm saying you'll be pulling the same stunts on someone else in a few weeks, whether on the air or off. That's your right, I just don't want to play games with you in the meantime." She extended a hand, which I left untouched. "Don't lose any sleep over me."

I watched LaRae turn and go into the ladies' room, then high-stepped my way back out onto the street. I was so pissed I caught a cab in the shortest time ever. A driver with no passengers tried to pass a brother by, and I damn near flung myself in front of him, bringing his racist ass to a screeching halt.

I was in the cab, still steaming, when I realized I'd left Cherrelle's book behind.

17

O.J.

"Cherrelle!" I tapped on her bedroom door. "Come on out here. You forget we were supposed to go over your history flash cards after dinner?"

The door creaked open a sliver, just enough that I could see my little girl's four eyes stare me down. I'd treated her to a new pair of wire-rimmed glasses after she'd been named the best reading student in her day camp. "I'm not done with this book. Can I come out later?"

"No. Let's cover this now. You know bedtime's coming up for us soon." It's a little embarrassing, but in order to be up at three every day I hit the sack about the same time Cherrelle does, between nine and ten.

She trudged out into the family room and we sat in front of the wide-screen TV, which I had on mute so I could keep up with the latest scores on *SportsCenter*. With this nightly exercise, I was carrying on something Keesa had begun. Each flash card held important facts about someone in African-American history; Cherrelle's job was to match the facts to the person.

"Okay, this man invented the stoplight."

"Garrett Morgan."

"Okay, next. This doctor's discovery of blood plasma is still used in transfusions and surgeries today."

"Charles Drew."

"What else is important about him?"

"He died 'cause a hospital wouldn't give him the treatment he came up with."

"Right." We went on for another fifteen minutes, and were

winding down when my intercom buzzed. Still holding Cherrelle's cards, I walked to the front door and pressed the response lever. I sure wasn't expecting anyone. "Who's this?"

"Hello, is this the home of O.J. Peters?"

I felt blood drain from my face. "LaRae?"

"Yes. Do you mind if I come up?"

I let go of the lever, let her meet some silence head-on for a minute. Stewing in place, I looked over at Cherrelle, whose eyes were full of curiosity. She probably was wondering if she'd heard right. I considered going down to the lobby, limiting LaRae's influence to me only. Three days wasn't enough to erase the sting of her words to me at Afrocentric. I didn't really want her up in the midst of my apartment nor in my daughter's face.

The intercom buzzed again. I hit the lever. "Yeah?"

"I don't get the message with silent treatment, O.J. If I can't come up just say so."

I wasn't leaving Cherrelle upstairs by herself. "Freak it, come on up." I hit the entrance release and turned back to Cherrelle. "Sit tight, honey. I'm gonna go meet Ms. Summers at the elevator."

"Bring her back with you. Pleeease," my daughter pleaded, her eyes earnest and her hands clasped as if in prayer.

When LaRae stepped off the elevator, looking like she'd come from the gym in her black bodysuit and rayon sweat jacket, I inhaled sharply. Tall, curvy like a sister who'd had her share of sweet potato pie and fried chicken, but with the firm thighs and small waistline of one who practiced high-impact aerobics. I had to stifle my reaction to her beauty. Not that I'd never been aware of it, of course, but somehow there was a difference when a woman was on your home turf, just a few feet away from your bed.

She was holding Cherrelle's copy of her book, along with a hardcover version of *Take It All,* the one that was being made into a movie as we spoke. "These are for you," she said, handing them to me and flooding me with her fresh apple scent. "In recognition of your support for my work. I don't want our personal issues to cloud that."

"Very nice," I said, taking the books and barely making eye contact. "Look, uh, I've gotta get my daughter through her paces before bedtime and then get my beauty rest."

"Okay. I don't have to come in if it's a bad time."

I crossed my arms, looking up at this beauty towering two inches over me. "After your slam on me, I don't quite see there being a good time, LaRae."

"That's fair," she replied, her arms open as if being searched. "I did want to apologize, quickly, for not accepting your mea culpa about our 'battle.' Even though I stand by what I said about you and Cherrelle's mother, it really wasn't my place. I should have accepted your apology regardless."

I took her words in, feeling frightened by my reaction. Suddenly I needed her to understand what she'd done. "I'll accept *your* apology, okay? But just know that it's actions like yours that reinforce a brother's emotional walls. I mean, I was already full of guilt about everything with Keesa when I rolled up on you. You took that guilt and turned it into a knife, drove it straight through me."

"Again, I am sorry."

"I just want you to know," I said, feeling my voice tremble slightly, "that I'm not what you probably think I am. Be honest, you stiff-armed me 'cause you thought I was trying to get with you, right?"

"The thought crossed my mind."

"Well, there was a time when I was that simple, LaRae. A time when I'd have been so turned on by our angry chemistry, plus your fame, I would have made it my life's mission to bed you for the sake of it.

"I'd already outgrown that phase, okay, but Keesa's loss fast-forwarded me out of it all the more. I stepped to you that day with pure intentions and got jacked for it."

"I guess I shouldn't judge books by their covers."

"Absolutely right. I suppose I need to take the same advice."

LaRae chuckled. "We both got issues, huh? Maybe we'll do a group outing sometime, you know, just hang out with no strings."

"We can do that. You obviously know how to find me."

"You can blame Nikki and Mitchell Stone for that."

"Duly noted." I filed that little factoid away, wasn't sure if it improved Mitchell's standing with me or not. I extended a hand playfully. "Give up your digits, please, so we're on even ground."

She pulled a business card from her purse, wrote a couple of extra numbers on the back, and placed it into my hand, real slow like. The warmth that passed between us was undeniable. "You keep that confidential now," she said, smiling and tapping the elevator button.

"It won't go unused." We talked small as we waited for the elevator, and I couldn't help myself. I watched the sleekness of LaRae's figure and instinctively plotted what I could do with every inch of that body. It would be so easy.

Soft pecks on that long, graceful neck.

Light, wispy passes of my hands over the tips of those attention-getting nipples.

The whirring and clicking of my flexible, easily adjustable tongue as it wound its way up her thighs, headed home to—

A door creaked open behind me. "Daddy?"

I turned to see Cherrelle standing there, rubbing her knuckles over her eyes. "Where's Ms. LaRae?"

Lord Jesus. I gave myself a mental slap. My baby just a few steps away and I'm sitting here plotting the next place to stick my horny moneymaker.

"Hey girl," I said, smiling wide and holding up her signed book, "see what I got here?" I turned back to LaRae. "Elevator's still not here. Maybe that's a sign? Why don't you come on in, we can do coffee and Cherrelle can quiz you about her book."

LaRae rolled her tongue around her mouth and looked past me, to Cherrelle. "Hi, Cherrelle, aren't you something? You mind some company for a few minutes?"

Of course Cherrelle was okay with it, so in minutes LaRae was on my couch with Cherrelle at her side. They talked through every possible storyline in that kids' book while I made coffee and hot chocolate. We sat around and had a nice enough time, until I had to send Cherrelle to bed. As my daughter grabbed her book and began to mope her way down the hall, LaRae called after her.

"It's okay, Cherrelle, you get a good night's sleep, all right? Maybe we can go to the library some time, and I'll show you some of the books I read when I was your age?"

Cherrelle stopped in mid-trudge and looked at us over her shoulder. "I'd love that. Good night, Ms. LaRae." All I got was a mumbled, "See you, Daddy."

We laughed as her door closed behind her and stared uneasily at each other, she on the couch still and me reclined across my matching loveseat. I let my curiosity get me. "So, a fine celebrity author's been here for a few months. How many men are you fighting off these days? Or are you fighting at all?"

LaRae crossed her arms and legs, started pumping her legs again like in the studio. "How about none?"

"None? Whew, must be a story there."

"For starters, I moved to Chicago specifically to lose about one hundred and fifty pounds."

"Huh?"

"My fiancé. He's old, authoritative, and I owe him for most everything I've accomplished. It just got too tiresome. I felt so indebted, you know?"

I eyed her carefully. "You all must have been together quite a while."

"Total of eight years."

"Ouch. So the next brother who steps up has to be compared with the . . . old man."

LaRae took a sip of cold coffee. "Who knows whether I'll let another brother step up. Can I get a little more java?"

"I got ya." I took her mug and walked back into the kitchen. "I admire anyone who can last eight years in a relationship. I'm a pretty short-term guy, not that I always want to be."

LaRae chuckled as I started to fill her mug. "Aw, widdle O.J. is another player on the surface who's really a softy? Tell me anything."

I kept my back to her as I seasoned her coffee with another dollop of hazelnut cream. I guess she thought she was being funny, but the "softy" crack was getting a little close to home. "Well, pardon the hell out of me, but there was a short window of time, years ago when I was a chubby adolescent, when women failed to find me charming. Ya might say they failed to find me at all."

LaRae leaned forward in her seat, searching my eyes as I turned to face her. "I'm betting you made up for lost time."

I held her refilled mug but stayed by my counter. "Oh, I blazed enough trails to compensate, played plenty of games."

"The games got tired for me real quick, that's why I stayed with the old man for so long. Those games can get deadly serious. My mother learned that the hard way, killed in a bar fight when I was three. Two stupid niggers trying to prove they could win her over. She got caught in the crossfire."

"Well, yeah," I sighed as I returned her refilled mug, "I've seen my share of craziness out on the scene." Next thing I knew, LaRae and I were playing emotional show and tell, peeling back a little of our false fronts. It was natural, just conversation and comparing notes more than anything. When she finally made a move to go, it was after ten-thirty.

"It was cool of you to stop by," I said as I held the front door open. *Friends, O.J., friends,* I reminded myself. "A nice gesture."

"It was my pleasure," she replied, holding her purse at her hip. "You take care of that sweet girl, we'll talk again."

I stood in the hallway as she headed to the elevator, watched the rhythm of her hips. *You bet.*

18

Nikki

My assistant, Sylvia, pulled me out of a conference call with Milos, one of Empire's hottest acts, around one this afternoon.

I stepped into the hallway behind Sylvia, pulling the door shut behind me. "What is it?" Sylvia knew better than to personally grab me for anything less than an emergency.

"It's the police. A Detective Bruce?"

I sighed, ran a hand over my forehead. "Don't tell me. They're ready for me finally?" I had given my statement to them already and handled some follow-up questions over the phone, but since then I'd been waiting for them to find Marquise's friends.

Sylvia rubbed a hand up and down my right arm. "They've got several of the boys at the station house, Nikki. They need you to come in immediately, I guess they can only hold them so long."

I took Sylvia's hand, rubbing it in thanks. "I'd better get going. Will you call Mitchell for me?"

"Sure."

When I arrived at the precinct, nothing felt real to me. A desk sergeant near the entrance flagged me down. "Yo, where you headed?"

I licked my lips and asked for Detective Bruce. In a minute the short, bearded man was at my side. We'd met before but, just like the last time, I barely registered his appearance or his words. He led me up some short, fat concrete steps into a rectangular office space lined with glass partitions and a low ceiling.

"Mr. Peters is here already," I heard him say. "Would you like any coffee before we go into the observation room?"

"No," I heard myself say. "I'm ready to get this over with." As eager as I was to help ensure justice for Keesa, the thought of seeing familiar faces in that room frightened me.

Detective Bruce paused at an office near the back of the floor, up against the south wall. He clicked the door open and stepped aside, ushering me in. I crossed the cement floor and took a seat across from O.J. at the low metal table. The room was dark except for a couple of grimy light bulbs swinging overhead. I peered at O.J. cautiously.

"Hey doll," he said in a whisper. He slid a hand across the table, squeezing one of mine. "Be strong. I have faith in you."

I choked back tears as Detective Bruce explained the process to us. In a minute they would parade a lineup of various teenagers through the room on the other side of the large windowpane in front of our table. If I recognized any of them as kids who'd been present the night of Keesa's death, I would simply call out the number hung around his neck. Afterward, Bruce and his partner would interrogate the fingered kids about the night's events and prepare to bring the appropriate charges.

I felt like I was having a heart attack when the door of the other room opened. As the seven perps walked in, I could only make out profiles but I was already having flashbacks. They were all dressed like the kids that night: oversized jeans hanging off their asses, heads shaved bald or covered in cornrows, loud-colored T-shirts or sports jerseys. My heart pounded even louder as they finally came to a halt and pivoted to face the one-way glass.

With the first glance across the row, I had nothing. Faces went fuzzy on me, fear clotted my throat, and I could barely breathe. I heard O.J. whisper, "Nikki, are you okay?"

I took a deep breath, reminded myself this wasn't about my discomfort, my anxiety: It was about honoring Keesa's memory. Drawing up in my chair, I started back over the row of faces, from back to front this time. "Number two," I said, not recognizing my own shaky voice.

Detective Bruce stepped closer to me, kneeling down so we were eye to eye. "You're certain? Do you need to see them from another angle?"

"I know that one was there," I replied, my voice steadying. "He just had an Afro that night, that's why I didn't catch him the first time. He's bald now, but that's the same kid."

Bruce stood to his feet again. After he had mashed an intercom near the window and relayed my announcement to his lieutenant, he turned back to me. "Are you able to tell us where this kid fits into your overall account? Was he one of those egging Marquise on?"

I glanced at O.J. first, trying not to betray too much emotion. "He was the first one to start taunting Marquise, and everyone else jumped in afterward."

O.J. slammed a fist onto the table. "That's it, right, officer? If nobody else, he's got to be held accountable."

"That'll be for the D.A. to figure out," Bruce replied evenly. "That said, you best believe my partner and I won't be as kind in the opinion we offer this punk." He stood over us. "Thank you both for your time. I'll escort you out before they release the lineup from the other room."

O.J. helped me up from my seat but kept his eyes on the detective. "When will we know about next steps?"

"Probably in a couple of days. We have to grill this number two first, then bring in whatever kids he gives up to save himself."

When we arrived back downstairs, in the lobby, the detective shook both our hands vigorously and excused himself, leaving me and O.J. there to share our anxiety. "Mitchell should be here any minute," I said, barely making eye contact. "I want to wait on him, but I don't think I can stay here any longer."

"You shouldn't have to," O.J. said, gently pulling me off to the side of the front desk. "I'll hang out here for a minute, wait on him. I may want to question some of the kids that get released from that lineup anyway."

"That's not your job," I said softly. "I understand how you feel, but getting personally involved with prosecuting the case isn't your calling. Your place is with Cherrelle."

"Tell me this." O.J. shoved his hands into the pockets of his slacks. "Was Keesa's death a murder or an accident?"

I inhaled sharply, afraid to respond on instinct. "Marquise caused her death by trying to mug us."

"Did he? You said she defended herself, then tried to save him from toppling onto the tracks. I'm just trying to make sure I understand, Nikki."

"What you said is what happened. You could call it an accident, but it would have never happened if Marquise's friends hadn't humiliated him after Keesa knocked his knife away."

"Should they have seen that coming? Was his death, or hers, a foreseeable outcome?"

I tapped my right foot and crossed my arms. "I don't think that's relevant."

"I'm just asking so I can press the police to bring appropriate charges. If this kid you picked out started the taunting and had any clue Marquise was fool enough to attack you guys again, his ass should be grass. But for the others, who may have been mindlessly playing along and maybe thought Marquise was too wimpy to take another run at Keesa, well, maybe they deserve another chance." He clearly saw my look. "Maybe."

I waited for a second, then pulled O.J. into a quick hug. "You sure you're through preaching? Not many of us could even *try* to think that way." I patted his shoulder and turned toward the door. "Call me when you want to talk some more. Anything I can do, I'll do."

He smiled at me, his lips barely parting and his eyes growing tired again. "I know, thanks."

I stepped out into the street, unable to get Keesa's face out of my head. How many dreams had she missed out on? With the gift of precious life still flowing through me, I considered my dreams, and was reminded again where they started. More than ever, I was ready to build a family.

19

O.J.

The night after Nikki identified the infamous Number Two from Marquise's gang, Cherrelle had a bad dream. I was tossing and turning myself when a series of loud hiccups jolted me out of my half-sleep. I rolled out of bed, flicked on the halogen lamp near my window, and jogged through the family room over to Cherrelle's.

I cracked the door open and flicked on the overhead light. Cherrelle lay on her bed, her back turned to me, her shoulders shuddering. "Don't, Mommy," she screamed, "don't!" I recognized her wails as the hiccup sound, then ran to her. I didn't say anything, just held her as I fought back my own tears.

When she came to, I took a thumb and started to wipe the tears away. She was nearly limp in my arms, looking back at me and blinking every three seconds. "I'm here, Cherrelle," I whispered, "I'm here."

We sat there several minutes until she shared her nightmare with me in halting fragments. I was wondering if I'd done enough to shelter her from my conversations about everything, because her dream was nearly a reenactment of Nikki's testimony.

I was still trying to calm her when she asked, "Will they get the electric chair, Daddy?"

"The boys that were involved?"

"Yeah, them."

I swallowed my top lip and looked at the floor. "I don't think so, honey. They're all under eighteen, which means they'll be charged as juveniles. They'd have to be adults to get death."

She tugged at my silk pajama leg. "Do you think they should get the death penalty, if we could change the laws?"

She had me there. I'd prayed, for the first time in years, about that very issue. The theme that kept coming back to me was grace. The grace I'd had to show Keesa years earlier, when she'd attacked me after careful planning and scheming. I hadn't pressed charge one because I knew what had started the whole thing. Technically she hadn't deserved a break, but I'd granted her one. *Grace.*

"Cherrelle," I said, enclosing her little hands in mine, "the first thing we have to do is hear their side of the story. There's a possibility Mommy's death was a horrible accident. The other boy, the one that died too? If he'd lived, he'd definitely deserve the harshest punishment. But with these others, we don't know that they really caused what happened."

Cherrelle frowned. "Weren't they wrong, just being there with that boy?"

"In a way, yeah." I placed an arm around her. "This is a case where we'll both have to pray, baby, and let God guide our hearts."

"Like Grandpa always talks about?"

I nodded. "Like Grandpa always talks about. I probably don't say it enough, but he's right."

Her expression still stony, Cherrelle looked up at me then. She didn't smile, but her eyes brightened as she said in a small voice, "I'm glad I can live here, Daddy, I like being with you. I didn't think I would."

Embers of joy stirring in my heart, I fought back tears and played calm. "Cherrelle, please don't ever doubt that I love you. I know we've had hard times, but from now on, I'll always be here for you."

I held her close and felt Keesa's presence with us.

20

Nikki

The alarm clock startled me awake, filling the room with Jonathan Butler's "Do You Love Me?" I opened my eyes and looked to my right, happy to see Mitchell's side of the bed empty. From the bathroom, the hiss and rush of the shower said my man was out of sight for a few more minutes. Just the time I'd need to check my basal body temperature, see how magic a day this might be. Now that I had been studying my body's signals for nearly two months, I trusted my judgment more with each passing day.

Careful to stay under the sheets, I flicked a hand over to the nightstand and pulled my digital thermometer from the drawer underneath. I angled it between my lips, underneath my tongue, and lay back, shutting my eyes tight. I was anxious but confident; it had been nearly two weeks since my last period, and my daily check of the feminine equipment and fluids told me I was ovulating. Better yet, I was pretty confident that today would be my peak day, if my daily charts of mucus, secretions, temperature, and texture were any indication.

The thermometer beeped and I yanked it out, looking soberly at the numbers staring back at me. My temperature was low enough, that was for sure. I probably still had a few days left, but odds were my levels wouldn't be any more optimal than today. The timing was perfect, too, coming in the middle of the week: With Mitchell's increased concerns about Gina's threats to move or marry Dale, he was getting Clay more and more often. At this point, we had him every weekend, sometimes from Thursday until Monday. Nothing cools the romantic heat in a home like having a young child underfoot.

I climbed from bed and traipsed innocently into the bathroom, where Mitchell was still showering. I watched his muscular shoulders and back, sighed at the contours of his high, tight buttocks through the clear glass of the shower stall. Looked lovingly at his slight love handles, even inhaled and thanked God for a minute before tapping on the glass.

He turned around and faced me, his package dangling. "Hey."

"Good morning." I blew him a kiss and walked over to our marble sinks, where I washed my face, brushed my teeth, and ran my hands through my newly permed hair. I'd jettisoned the cornrows a few days before, anticipating that impending motherhood would require a lower-maintenance do. After readjusting my silk head wrap, I walked back to the shower door and clicked it open.

Mitchell smiled at me through the enveloping steam. "Coming in? I'll wash your back."

"I want more than that washed." I reached down for his magic wand, trying to figure out the best timing. It would really be best if we did the final deed on the bed, where the little soldiers had the best odds of getting the job done. But here was my chance to warm him up.

"Whoa, whoa, whoa." Mitchell's shoulders stiffened more than the body part most on my mind. "I have to get out of here by seven, babe. Skip and Danny are coming into the station for an all-day operations review today. Tony's got me serving as his right hand on the financial review as well as some issues around O.J.'s show. I can't be late."

I exhaled, letting my lower lip pout. "Come on, I'll let you be a two-minute man, just this once." I continued tugging on his chain.

"Nik, come on." He stepped back, slid my hands off of him. "We've only been going at it like rabbits lately."

"That's what newlyweds are supposed to do."

"You're right. Look," he said, opening the shower door and

slipping around me, "I'll make it up to you tonight." He squeezed my left hip, held it like a man who knew it was all his. "Promise."

"And when will you be home?"

"Well, we have to take the guys out for dinner, so probably by eight or nine."

I started to chew my lower lip. My peak fluids would probably be dehydrated as dry ice by then. I'd have to come up with a plan B. "What if I wanted to take you to lunch today?"

"The way these guys have the day scheduled, I'm gonna grab a sandwich in my office."

I smiled wickedly. "I'll come eat with you."

He turned back, looking at me through the shower door. "Knock yourself out. Are you bringing lunch with you?"

"I'll bring you plenty to eat, don't worry."

I watched Mitchell walk to the sink, where his shoulders shook with laughter. "What they say about women peaking sexually later than men is no lie, huh?"

"So you saying I'm old?"

"Okay, I'm shutting up now." With that he headed back into the bedroom.

After Mitchell had left and I'd dressed and eaten a quick bowl of oatmeal, I climbed into my car and pulled out of the garage. I plugged in my cell phone, threw on my headset, and dialed Trey's number.

"What up, Nikki?" I knew Trey would recognize my number; I'd been calling him weekly for the past six weeks.

"Hey Trey. Just making sure you're monitoring your boy's work-out, keeping him on the straight and narrow." Trey and Mitchell had been working out at the same Bally's for almost four years.

"I'm on it, babe. Mitchell and I've been focusing for three weeks on aerobics and Nautilus training only, no free weights. I told him it was my idea after reading about the dangers of free weights in

Men's Health. I convinced him we should take a month's break and see if we can get comparable results from Nautilus."

"Genius. You don't get your due, Trey."

"Hey, I'm all about making a happy home. When you first asked me to get him off the weights to protect you all's ability to have a little one, I had to do some research myself. Here's one thing I ain't figured out though."

"What's that?"

"I was pumping much iron when I made all six of my babies." Six babies, five mothers, the last actually a candidate to become Mrs. Benton. Small wonder Trey had been one of Mitchell's "ladies' man" instructors in the days we first started dating.

"Well, Trey, some people can get away with more than others. I don't want to take chances, you know?"

"I can't blame you, especially with us gettin' on in years."

"Now you've really got me depressed." I tapped my steering wheel, ready to wind the conversation down. "You haven't mentioned any of this baby business to Mitchell, have you?"

"I just told him he needs to be careful with the weight training, to make sure you all can have kids eventually. I know my boy, he definitely wants to be a father again." Trey had the long-term facts right, the short-term wrong. "Any little role I can play to help, it's a joy to me, ya know?" He paused, sounded like he was clearing his throat. "Let me ask you a quick favor, girl."

"What's up?"

"You good friends with that fine LaRae Summers, right?"

I smiled, suppressing a surge of pride. It felt funny to hear someone else state it that way, but despite the fact she could buy and sell me, LaRae and I were getting to be pretty close. I knew a lot of the Chicago "in" crowd, she had the money to go out every night of the week; you put that together, and we were pretty useful to each other. Besides that, she was cool people.

"LaRae and I are definitely cool. What, you want me to put in a good word?"

"Well, it's just, you know, that day at the station, it was clear baby girl was feeling me. But since everything happened with O.J.'s old lady and stuff, I don't think I should step on his toes."

"You think O.J.'s holding for LaRae?"

"Oh please, that day she was in the studio you could have filled a lab with their chemistry. I just wanna know if she's waiting on him to make a move. If not, then Trey's ready to step up to the plate."

I stifled a chuckle. "Trey, are you slipping? You really need my help?"

"Never mind, babe. I'm tripping anyway. I'm supposed to set a date with Sharonda soon."

"Well, don't walk that aisle if you're not sure, honey. Smooches." I punched the phone off and dialed up my boss, Chase Wells, ready to get my business day going.

Mitchell

The morning's meetings with Skip and Danny were a procession of brushes with professional death. By now the good old boys were on the warpath. O.J.'s ratings continued to be the only real bright spot, but at this point it hardly mattered. On a net-net basis, WHOT was losing more money than they'd projected in their business plan. O.J.'s impressive ad rates were being swallowed whole by the dismal performance of our midday and afternoon drive-time hosts, and we were getting our asses handed to us worse during evenings.

"There's no fuckin' cohesion," Skip said in his gravelly tenor, shaking his head as I walked them through the year-to-date income statement. "It's as simple as that, you know?"

Tony rapped the conference table, clearly struggling to keep his cool. He knew he was supposed to be providing the cohesion. "Skip, if your concern is whether we have a well-executed strategy, I'd have to frankly say the answer is yes. What we have on the air is a compatible mix—a controversial morning show that mixes hip-hop and R&B, afternoon programming that's less personality-focused but plays comparable jams, then evening programming that mixes talk aimed at teens and young adults with more jams."

"Yeah, the same 'jams' four other stations are playing." Danny rested his forehead on a palm. "Skip, you thinkin' same as me?"

Tony shifted in his seat, drew himself up taller. "Gentlemen—guys, please let Mitchell finish his presentation. We can get into strategic considerations during review of my exhibits, that's next."

Things pretty much went downhill from there. When I was done detailing all the red ink, Tony walked through a PowerPoint presentation on strategy that the boys shot full of holes. By the time O.J. stopped in for a debriefing around eleven A.M., everything was going to hell. O.J. stood his ground on playing with politics when he felt like it, and Danny and Skip raised the stakes one more time.

"You don't understand." Danny's voice thundered across the table, loud enough to make me wish I had a remote to turn him down. "At this point, we're ready to scrap the entire lineup of WHOT, maybe even bring in a more experienced station manager." He accentuated the snipe with a glare in Tony's direction. "Your ratings are nice, O.J., but they're not enough. You keep that in mind next time we make a suggestion."

O.J. sat back in his seat, arms crossed. He stared over at Tony, ignoring the silent but smoldering Danny. "You gonna let him talk to us like that, T? Fine. Here's the deal, gents. You either stop talking to me like this or fire me now. You don't think I can get hired back on with a good station in Atlanta, or anywhere else now that I've set records here? Please." Shaking his head, he bolted out the door.

I was never more relieved to see Nikki than I was that day, shortly before noon as we wrapped a review with Roman, the beleaguered afternoon deejay. She walked by the glass window of the conference room, pausing long enough to blow a kiss my way. With her new perm coifed into her familiar bob and a sleek tailored mauve business suit caressing her curves without broadcasting them, my baby was both professional and irresistible.

Skip's eyes widened, a grin coming to his thin lips. "Who is that?"

"My wife," I replied, trying to keep a straight face.

Rubbing his hands together, eyes glinting, Skip smiled wickedly. "Well done, Mr. Stone, well done."

I led the men out of the conference room and went straight to my office, knowing she'd be there. When I walked in, Nikki was seated at my desk, her suit jacket off and her high-cut skirt showcasing her crossed legs. Behind her, on my windowsill, sat a lone burning candle she'd brought from home, its French-vanilla scent permeating the room. Looking at her sitting there—shining, sparkling hairdo, rich complexion, hourglass figure—I marveled again that I'd ever won this woman's heart.

I played at being annoyed. "What are you doing here?" I really hadn't thought she'd bother coming over.

She sat in my seat, twirled a pen playfully. "How much time do we have?"

"I have to be in the next meeting at twelve-thirty. Let's run downstairs and—"

With the swiftness of a gazelle, Nikki leapt from the chair and stepped to me, pinning my shoulders against the wall. She'd already drawn the blinds and I'd shut the door when walking in, so when she reached over my shoulder and flicked off the overhead light, she plunged us into dusky dark.

I met her hungry kisses head-on, felt myself rise to the occasion. "I can't believe," I said, gasping, "we're doing this." I'd made love in quite a few places in recent years—on a blanket along Lake

Shore Drive with Gina, at a Miami-area rest stop with a girl whose name I've since forgotten, and in a cave with Nikki on Maui's Mt. Haleakala, during our honeymoon. The office, however, had remained a sanctum sanctorum.

I broke through this barrier with great ease, I'll admit. First Nikki slid to her knees, nearly broke my trousers open, and started me up like she was a porn star. It was almost scary to witness her vigor, but truth was it was a nice benefit of having a wife who knew how to throw down when it mattered. When I felt ready to burst, I eased her over to my desk. Trying not to be a movie cliché, I took a second to neatly remove my paperweights and financial documents, and began setting my keyboard on top of my PC.

"Come on, baby," Nikki whispered, her tone rich and husky. She stepped around me and shoved everything but the PC onto the floor. "I have to work today too."

Her spontaneity almost brought me to tears, but that didn't stop me from simmering for her. I reached around her waist, grabbed those toned hips, and slammed her onto the desk, simultaneously sliding her skirt and panties to her knees. Feeling her grab instinctively for me and guide me inside her, I caressed her breasts, using them for traction, and joined her in a romantic, rhythmic dance.

After my second orgasm, I collapsed on top of her. The extra weight made the desk jump just enough that the PC began to slide off the edge.

"Aaahh!" Still on top of Nikki, I shot out my left hand and grabbed the central processing unit, holding it as steady as possible. As I felt it settle into place, I looked into Nikki's eyes. Sweating, we both began to laugh. I bent down and kissed her full on the mouth. "You're going to get me fired."

As I stood with wobbly knees, Nikki stayed on her back, checking her watch. "By my count, Mr. Stone, you've got seven minutes to get back to your meeting."

"Yep, now you can help me straighten up in here."

Still on her back, Nikki looked away briefly before meeting my gaze again. "Can you go get me a drink of water? It'll help, really. You want me walking out of here like a hooker stumbling out of a whorehouse?"

"Okay," I said. "You can get up off the desk, though, can't you?"

Another glance away. "I'll be up by the time you're back with the water. Be a sweetie."

I got another of those knots in my stomach as I eased out, shut the door behind me, and headed for the water cooler. Things were crazy at work, yes, and Gina was still trying to get that job in Atlanta, never mind what Dale was up to. On top of that, I was already behind on LaRae's revisions for *Out of His Shadow*. There was plenty of madness in my life, but this new knot had something to do with my wife's surprise visit. Why was she still on her back?

21

Mitchell

"Bro'ham, I really think you're worried over nothing." My big brother Marvin shot me a concerned glance as he eased his beige Lincoln Navigator into a space in the Home Depot parking lot. We were near his family's new subdivision in suburban Homewood. They were still in that phase of going broke on extra trinkets for their new half-million-dollar digs, and having just come through that time myself, I was along for moral support.

As Marvin shifted into park, I jumped out of the passenger seat and opened the back door, reaching in to unleash my niece Sarah. Now that she's almost two, Marvin finally trusts me to handle her, never mind that I became a father before he did.

I looked at my brother as he opened the opposite door, where baby Milton was seated. "What makes you an authority on whether I should worry about Gina taking my boy to Atlanta? If I'm concerned, you as my brother should be concerned."

Little Milton, who'd been asleep, came to and started to whimper, probably wondering where his mommy was. Marvin rubbed the little guy's wispy head of hair and gently fed him a pacifier before reaching for the dual baby stroller.

"All I'm saying, Mitchell, is that Gina clearly enjoys being a boil on you and Nikki's life. She moves away, she sacrifices some of that power." He winked at me as he pulled Milton from his car seat and placed him on one side of the stroller. "This is just part of the game plan to make you pay for not marrying her. She's not going anywhere."

There were times I thought Marvin relished seeing my agony at

Gina's hands. Seeing as how he'd advised me against turning my-self into a player and pursuing women like Gina years ago, it was a virtual "I told you so" for him.

"You don't know her, man." I shut the door, held Sarah over my right shoulder, and walked around to place her in the stroller next to Milton. "You've never known her. I do. She's got the talent and the looks to get on board at a major outfit like CNN. I don't think she's bluffing."

"Well, I did some checking." Marvin took command of the stroller as we headed toward the store's main entrance. The same night Gina had first mentioned she was interviewing in Atlanta, I had asked him to update me on my legal rights should she actually jump town. He had just been made partner, so he was able to get candid analysis from a heavy hitter. "According to my man Aaron Decker, the firm's expert on family law, if Gina was to actually move, you'd have to completely change the game to keep Clay here with you. Given that you've already accepted your full paternal obligations and expressed satisfaction with the current custody arrangements—"

"Both of which you advised me to do."

"Uh, yeah, and both of which were the right thing to do. The thing is, given that things have gone peacefully for almost two years, you'd have a hard time arguing that the move would harm Clay. From what you say, Gina's a reasonably fit mother."

As we came to the entrance, I paused, letting the whiz of the automatic doors delay my response. "What say we pull out the dirty laundry, all the facts about her relationship with Dale? He is an ex-con, not to mention that some nights she stays out with him and makes her mom serve as Clay's caretaker."

Marvin frowned, stopping to survey the array of housewares and hardware surrounding us. "Are you saying her mom's unfit to watch over Clay every now and then? I've never heard you allege anything on her personal conduct. Remember this could go both ways if Gina contested your letting Nikki, Mom and Dad, or me and Angie watch Clay when you're busy."

"Well, none of us live in subsidized housing or have spent time in jail."

"You know I feel you, brother, but the courts will never let classism trump the rights of a reasonably fit mother."

"Stop with the 'reasonably fit' crap, will you?" I felt my brow grow hot, tried not to look enviously at my niece and nephew. As long as Marvin continued to treat Angie right, he'd never have to let a stranger in a robe determine the nature of his relationship with them. "You're saying I'm screwed if she takes this job, aren't you?"

"Your words, not mine." Marvin bent down and kissed Sarah, who had begun tugging at his calf. He looked back up at me. "You've come a long way, little brother. From a guy desperate enough to let Trey and Tony turn you into a player, to a responsible father and loyal husband. If you have to be a long-distance dad, you'll make the best of it. God will give you the strength."

God will give you the strength. I didn't bother to tell Marvin that was a hell of a burden. God would say if I'd kept my pants zipped a little bit more, I wouldn't be in this situation in the first place. "Tell me what you want me to pick up," I said, resting a hand on his shoulder. I was ready to get out of there, get home, and clear my mind some.

The next morning I stood in front of the bathroom mirror, smoothed my suit, tightened the knot of my tie, and told myself Gina wasn't taking Clay anywhere. Fully dressed for work, I was ready for battle and shifted my thoughts to that arena.

O.J. had set up a lunchtime meeting with KISS FM, a Washington, D.C., station that had expressed vague interest in picking him up for syndication. In the end they'd have to work through

Skip and Danny, of course, but O.J. was cagey enough to expect the good old boys to sabotage any deal, just to keep him in place while they decided how to "re-engineer" WHOT and put all of us on the unemployment line. If we could work out the parameters of a deal with the station first, get them committed, they would probably come to Skip and Danny with a deal they couldn't refuse, thus securing O.J.'s future and perhaps WHOT's in general.

I walked downstairs, my back straight and head high, determined to think positive about life. There was much to be thankful for. Nikki and I had found peace again, our romantic life at a high hum and no pressure about having babies right away. Not to mention, I had just finished my revisions to *Out of His Shadow,* and LaRae had been impressed enough to submit manuscript excerpts to a handful of her "people." It was a nice stamp of approval, even if it didn't lead anywhere.

Finishing my morning scripture, PowerBar, and coffee, I yelled out good-byes to Nikki and stepped out into the garage.

As I backed out of the driveway, tapping the garage remote, my eyes narrowed at the car sitting in my rear-view mirror. The hoopty, a black Chevy, was plenty familiar to me by now: I'd seen Dale's car parked outside Gina's place more times than I cared to count.

The damn Chevy, belching a steady stream of smoke, was parked in the street, blocking the driveway. I screeched to a halt, told myself to count to ten even as I kicked my door open.

Dale emerged from his ride just as I did. He yanked his sunglasses off and crossed his bulky arms over his white T-shirt. "What's up, Mitchell."

Rays of sunlight temporarily blinding me, I pumped my arms and rolled toward Dale like an out-of-control skier. I had no idea what I was about to do. I stormed down the driveway until I was a couple of inches away from him. "What?"

"Bee-yootiful place you got here, dude. No wonder Gina's jealous of your woman. I had a crib like this, I could pull Janet fuckin' Jackson."

I shifted my weight, my balled fists at my side. "What!"

"Yeah," Dale said, stroking his chin and continuing as if he had me on mute, "it'll be good for G when she, Clay, and I move to Atlanta." He raised a pleased eyebrow at me, probably reveling in the ashen look of shock spreading across my face. "You heard, right? She got that CNN offer late last night, was going to call you this evening 'bout it. I thought I'd save her the trouble."

I bit my lower lip, feeling like Bill Clinton the day he admitted to that "inappropriate relationship." Dale had me by the figurative balls: No father could pretend not to care at a moment like this. I took a step back. "We keep a gun on hand for when I'm out of town, Dale. It's got a safety lock, and we keep the bullets separate to make sure there's no accidents. But if you ever come onto my property again, whether my wife's alone or not, what happens won't be an accident."

Dale nodded his head and turned his back, moving in the direction of the hoopty. "Oh yeah, that hits me where I live. Got me scared now, son! Suppose I'll feel safer being sheltered from you in Hotlanta." He met my stare just before climbing back in. "Take it easy, I'll tell Clay you said hi."

As Dale's car wheezed and choked its way down my street, I swallowed the lump in my throat and grabbed my cell phone from my jacket pocket.

Behind me, I heard the garage door open, then the smooth sound of Nikki's voice. "Mitchell? Who was that?"

My hands shaking with rage, my brain unable to process Nikki's question, I kept my back to her, my gaze fixed on the pavement. I punched Gina's speed-dial number and bit my lip again. I had to know what I was up against.

22

O.J.

Cherrelle's school had an open house this morning, so I skipped the first two hours of my broadcast. I wanted to meet all her teachers at Saint Andrew and flex my muscles in front of her classmates, so they'd know this little Black girl ain't from the projects. Saint Andrew is a top-rated school, and it's relatively diverse for a Chicago Catholic school, but I was worried about folks being uppity. I figured if I stayed in Chicago long-term I'd switch Cherrelle into a carefully selected city school so she'd be around more of "the people," but for now I had to err on the side of bourgeois to make sure she got a top-notch education.

After I'd made the rounds, pressing the flesh with her teachers and with the principal, a disturbingly foxy lady in her late thirties, I wrapped Cherrelle in a bear hug.

"Mmph, mmph, mmph," she tried to say, her mouth pressed up against my leather bomber jacket.

I kissed her on the forehead, held her back at arm's length. "What, baby girl?"

"Stop it, Daddy. You're making me look like a little girl."

I cocked an eyebrow. "You *are* a little girl, Cherrelle. But I feel you. I promise, no more bear hugs after today, at least not in front of your classmates. Okay?"

She smiled, shifted in place. "Okay."

"Are you ready for this? You know to call me on the phone I gave you, if anything's wrong."

"I know. I love you, Daddy."

Oh Lord. Now she was about to embarrass me. I blinked a tear out of my eye. "Love you, too. Bye now." I turned and walked out of her classroom, which still teemed with chattering parents and kids, before I was overcome.

By the time I reached the studio and slid into my chair, just in time to kick off the eight o'clock hour, I had removed the "dad" hat and was in full "O.J. Way" mode. I started out by putting Trey, who'd sat in for me with Liz, in his rightful place. "Trey, I know you want to be Black—well, let's keep it real—you want to be me." I hit a button, flooded the studio with one of my favorite lines from *The Five Heartbeats*, where the rasping, wheezing Eddie King Jr. confronts his replacement in the group: "How does it feel to be me?"

I chuckled as Liz shook her head. "You wonder that, don't ya, Trey? Well, here's what it's like to be O.J. Why was I getting hit on left and right at my daughter's school this morning?"

Trey snorted. "This sounds like a good little story."

"Well, single moms can be desperate," Liz replied. "And you never know where you might cross Mr. Right's path—the grocery store, church, a bookstore, maybe even your child's school."

I recited a litany of made-up accounts, mixing in a couple of real ones from that morning. As Liz and Trey erupted in laughter, I kept it going. "We're gonna start letting folk line up now, with your own stories of 'school love.' We wanna hear how you hooked up with someone connected to your child's school—another parent, a teacher, the janitor maybe? We all get hard up. Coming up, we'll place our charity call of the month!"

When we came back from the break, I signaled Bobby to dial up our charity target of the month. "Hope they're in this morning," I said as the phone rang over the air. "We've got an opportunity to do some good today."

Someone picked up, a female with a deep, authoritative, yet friendly voice. "Good morning, St. Paul Baptist Church."

"Good morning, this is O.J. Peters from WHOT radio. To whom am I speaking?"

The lady's tone became cautious. She'd heard of me. "This is Velma, the pastor's secretary."

"Would that be Pastor Shelby Simon?"

"Yes."

"May I speak to him this fine morning?"

A pause, then a cough. "I'm not sure he's available. May I have him call you back?"

"Well, this is really pretty urgent, Ms. Velma. We at WHOT have an opportunity to help the church raise money for some of your local at-risk kids." The church was located in Ford Heights, an area thirty minutes south of town that was one of the poorest suburbs in the country.

"Oh." Velma's voice brightened. "Let me see if I can get him."

I muted my on-air transmission and turned to Liz. "I knew the whiff of money would get him."

Pastor Simon's foggy baritone filled the airwaves. We made some quick small talk before I moved in for the kill.

"So, sir, we agree that the Boys and Girls Club in Chicago Heights could serve the families of Ford Heights, if they received some additional funding?"

"Oh yes, O.J.," the pastor said, his deep voice brimming with affirmation, "I have read where the director wants to expand into Ford Heights when he has the money."

"Well, sir, WHOT stands ready this morning to make a donation of twenty-five hundred dollars to the Boys and Girls Club, for the express purpose of expanding its mission to your community."

"Praise God, son. What would you like St. Paul to do to help implement this vision? We'd be happy to have some members volunteer their time at the center."

"That would be wonderful. In addition, how about St. Paul's matching our donation? No better way to let your light shine, sir."

The pastor sighed good-naturedly. "Great idea, and one whose time will come. Unfortunately we're a little stretched on funding right now—"

"Oh, you're too modest, sir. WHOT sent some staff over to St. Paul's property a few days ago. We noted there are three, count 'em, three reserved parking spaces for you and First Lady Simon. I understand those spaces usually hold a 2001 model Jaguar, a 2002 Cadillac DeVille, and a 2003 Mercedes. Am I correct?"

The line crackled, sounded like nobody was home.

I was grinning like a Cheshire cat now. "Hello?"

"I don't know what my cars have to do with this conversation, Mr. Peters."

Now it was Mr. Peters, huh? "Well, sir, it seems to me St. Paul has an opportunity this morning to raise the money to match WHOT's donation, if you sell off some of that excess property. I understand the Simon kids are all grown, so you don't really need three luxury cars, do you?"

"Now, now—"

"Oh, you use the extra car for missions and stuff?"

"Well, I didn't say that. It's just—"

"Pastor, I know you don't stutter and stammer that much when you're in the pulpit. I sense you're short on reasons for the third car. Don't you want to sell one, improve the lives of some local kids?"

Silence again. I had to give him credit for not hanging up already.

"Come on, Pastor, you know you want to."

"St. Paul Baptist will match your donation, Mr. Peters. Now God bless you." His line went dead.

"Okay, Pastor Simon," I chuckled, "we'll take your word and send our staff over next week to check out the car inventory. God bless *you*." I hiked a thumb into the air, signaling the next break.

The next hour flew by even faster, and before I knew it we had about a dozen minutes left for the day. As the final notes of Missy Elliott's latest jam melted into the air, I took another call on our "school love" topic. "All right, we have Marian on as our last call of the day. Marian, tell us who you hooked up with at your kid's school and why!"

A low sigh, then the caller spoke. "God forgive me for lying to your engineer, O.J." Her tone was brisk and clipped, as if she was biting the end off of each word. "I've done my share of mess, but I'm not taking part in your shameful spectacle."

I muted myself for a second, flashed an angry look through the glass at Bobby. My words shot out in a roar. "What happened to screening?"

Bobby held up his hands, shrugged his shoulders. "What you want me to do? Kill the call?"

I squared my shoulders and shook my head. "Freak it, I'll handle this my damn self. Might be fun." I released my mute button. "Marian, hey baby, calm down. Sounding kinda stressed this morning."

"Don't try to sweet-talk me, boy." It took that remark for me to pick up on the extra years in Marian's voice. This wasn't someone of my generation.

I took the sex out of my voice. "Okay, Marian, I'll behave. What's your problem with this topic of 'school love'?" I'd give her thirty seconds to vent, then have Bobby kill the call.

"I don't care about the topic, *Oscar.* I care about your irresponsible behavior. Your daughter deserves better."

I'd heard just enough to finally realize who I was dealing with, the only Marian I knew personally. The hard-edged D.C. accent, the hoarse, throaty voice attesting to her age . . . This woman was a good sixty-five years old or so, old enough to be my grandmother, but she wasn't. She was Keesa's grandmother.

"Hello, Marian," I said, keeping my tone as light as whipped cream. "You're not making much sense, but hang on the line and I'll holler at you off air." I nodded at Bobby and he put Marian on the sidelines.

When we signed off a few minutes later, I slammed my head-phones down and stormed toward the door. Liz got me as I passed her news desk, though. She shot out a hand and clasped it around my left wrist. "You know that lady, don't you? What was that about?"

I patted Liz's hand and whispered Marian's identity to her.

"Oh, she is wrong as two left shoes," Liz said, her eyes growing wide with surprise.

"I'll deal with it." I turned to face Bobby, who opened the studio door and stepped just inside the doorway. "Send that call over to my office, will ya?"

"It's already there."

I ducked into the hallway and tried to ignore the leaden sensation seeping from my thighs down to my shins. There were many people from my past I'd have been happy to hear from. Marian was not one of them.

She had never liked me, this despite the fact we'd first met when Cherrelle was one year old, by which time I had a perfect track record with regard to child support. The dislike had been mutual, though. I recalled my first encounter with Marian like it was yesterday: filtered cigarette stuck between her thin lips, arms crossed forbiddingly, a frown twisting the features of her leathery brown skin. She'd threatened fire and brimstone if Keesa didn't have Cherrelle dedicated and blessed at her home church, so I'd reluctantly spent the money to come back to D.C. for the ceremony. I've never forgotten her words the moment I walked up to them on the church's front steps. "*That's him?*"

"Marian." I tightened my grip on the phone's receiver. "I'd appreciate if you'd call me directly from now on. No one asked whether you approved of my show. How'd you get it in D.C. already?" Tony, Mitchell, and I were working on the D.C. angle, but we still had a ways to go.

"I got the Internet, boy. Now you listen here." Marian's voice was ragged around the edges but still forceful. "You wouldn't have returned my call if I'd left you a voice message. This got your attention, now didn't it?"

"You have me on the line now, Marian."

"When am I gonna see my great-grandbaby?"

I sucked my teeth, replaying years' worth of conversations with Keesa. "We can work something out. I was waiting for you to come to me."

"I told you at the funeral to call me about a good time, O.J.!"

"And I decided, based on your granddaughter's words for years, that if you wanted to see Cherrelle you'd let me know."

Silence. I imagined Marian replaying incidents from her relationship with Keesa as well as with her daughter, Keesa's mom. Something had hit home. "If nothing else, Keesa knew I loved her and Cherrelle."

"I think she did know that much," I sighed. "So when would you like to see her? I'd prefer you come here to see her first, frankly. She's still getting settled into Chicago. I'd rather not disrupt her adjustment just yet."

"I was thinking of something different. I think Cherrelle should maintain a connection with D.C.—Keesa's roots are all here."

I put a hand to my forehead. "That's not a terrible idea, for the long term. We'll just take it slow for now."

"Has it occurred to you that I could sue for custody, O.J.?"

Was she kidding? My heart started to hammer but I beat the sensation back. *Nobody's taking* my *child.* "Good-bye, Marian." I set the phone back into its station, as slowly and firmly as I could. To the phone's right, I noticed my photo of Keesa and Cherrelle, one I'd snapped on my digital Kodak the week they'd first moved here. I tugged at the wooden frame, pulled it over to me. "Just try it, Marian," I whispered, "just try it."

23

Nikki

It had been a stressful morning already, starting with a seven A.M. conference call with a promoter in Japan. It was part of my job coordinating the touring activities of 911, our top R&B act. A group of teens with run-of-the-mill talent who'd lucked into a couple of chart-topping hits, they at least knew enough to stay out of my way with respect to promotional decisions.

After a couple of additional meetings, I hunkered down in my office to review the status of several other artists' promotions. It wasn't easy, though, because every time I tried to wrap my mind around the next slate of radio ads or the details of the next event, I'd start replaying the past couple of days.

When I had seen Mitchell standing in our driveway the other morning, he'd never answered my question about who was in the car. I had figured it out pretty quickly when I heard him grab his cell phone and spit out Gina's name. She was at it again, trying to move Clay around like a chess piece, and this time I almost hoped she'd act on her bluff. I loved Clay, wanted him around more if anything, but it was hard to see a downside to a deal that moved Gina hundreds of miles away.

Of course it wasn't that simple. Mitchell's a strong man, but I'd never seen him suppress pain like he was doing now. His smiles were strained, his eyes were dimmed, and his words were few. We'd talked nonstop about ways to handle the possible move: filing for increased custody so we'd have Clay for half of each year, scouring Gina's and Dale's pasts in order to cast her as unfit, or even coming up with a way to buy her off. In the end none of the options were attractive, especially considering our own financial position. With WHOT's operational problems, there was no guarantee how long Mitchell's salary would even be there. Then there was his work on *Out of His Shadow,* for which he'd received a pile of rejection letters over the past week.

Add to this the fact that I hadn't "said hello to my little friend" just yet. Based on my charts, I was about five days late. I'd been there before, so I supposed I was getting unnecessarily anxious. As I sat in my office, though, I felt an instinctive need to mind-meld with someone. I passed on Angie, who I knew was home chasing her little ones, and Leslie, who was probably barking orders at the latest employee who'd pissed her off. I even thought about LaRae, who'd been a good sounding board about my guilt over what happened to Keesa. Finally, I went for the most natural choice and called my mother's social-work office.

Mama sang out her greeting. "Hello, this is Ebony."

"Hey."

"Hey you, been about a week since I've heard from my baby. How you?"

"I'm okay, Mama. Having a crazy day at work. They got you ready to retire over there?"

"Girl, please. I'll retire the day they carry me out of here on a stretcher. World's full of too many kids who need help."

"The world needs more like you, Mama."

"Well, once you have some babies of your own, I'm looking for you to change. I know you're brilliant, baby, but you'll get tired of making big money for no purpose."

I shook my head, used to Mama's loving but less-than-subtle hints. "Actually, it's funny you mention me having babies of my own—"

"Oh my God!" I heard Mama's phone clatter to the floor, then heard her voice off in the distance. "My baby's having a baby! I'm gonna be a grandma. Give me some!"

"Uh, Mama," I said, sighing as she picked up the phone again,

"I don't know for sure that I'm pregnant. I am a few days late, though."

"See, and you thought you'd have so much trouble. How long have you and Mitchell been trying? Since the honeymoon?"

I bit my lower lip and decided to bare all. "Officially, we never were trying."

"Huh?"

"I mean, let's just say I was hoping something would happen in another six months or so. It may have happened in a couple months."

Mama paused, her breath coming evenly over the phone. "So, you're saying Mitchell won't expect you to be expecting?"

I let it all hang out for Mama. She already knew everything about Gina and Clay and the way that had encouraged my every insecurity. What she hadn't known about was the mysterious disappearance of my birth-control pills.

"Hmm." Mama sighed, started to breathe more heavily. "How do I say this, Nikki? You've put your marriage in jeopardy, in less than a year. You need to confess this to Mitchell now, especially given the other pressures he's facing. He needs to be able to count on you."

"I'm going to tell him the truth, Mama, if it turns out I am pregnant. I'll need a few more days to know."

"No, you need to tell him regardless."

"Why? What purpose would that serve right now?"

"Nikki." She paused a second. "Do you know why I never sued your father for child support?"

The mention of my father felt like an anchor being placed onto my shoulders. I had made peace with Gene before he died, but the scars he'd left behind were still there. "Mama, please—"

"No, you may as well know because there *is* a point to your knowing now."

I sat back in my seat, shoulders tensed for a new insight into my history.

"Nikki, when I started seeing your father, I'd made up my mind to get him. I knew he was mysterious, sure, probably even suspected he was married or in a serious relationship. You know, he never let me meet his parents, his friends, etcetera. I wasn't stupid, but Gene Coleman was handsome, had a little money, and a hell of a sense of humor. My nose, and for that matter my legs, were wide open."

"I know all this."

"What you may not know is that Gene was very serious, fastidious even, about us not making a baby. I don't know if I've been with a man before or since who was more rigorous about using condoms, checking me for diaphragms, etcetera. I couldn't argue with him, of course, but it was odd at first because so many men couldn't care less.

"Anyway, the day came when I found a mutual friend of his who confirmed that Gene was married, with two daughters. It broke my heart, Nikki, but after I picked myself up off the floor I decided to *fight* for my man. He was spending more nights with me than he was with this wife anyway. We did the age-old dance, with him claiming he wanted to leave her for me but had to wait a while, and then I decided to change the game on him."

I inhaled, damn near shrieked. "You didn't."

"Oh, baby, but I did. Offered to buy Gene his next supply of condoms and poked holes in 'em. Sabotaged my diaphragms. Played enough mind games to get him to take me away for several weekends. It was just a matter of time."

My head felt fizzy. "You're saying I wasn't an 'oops' baby."

"At least not from my vantage point, no. But your father never forgave me."

I shook my head, blinked my eyes as I digested everything.

"You're not saying Gene would have eventually married you otherwise?"

"Anything's possible. His marriage to Jennifer really was bad then, and I don't doubt that he did love me. But my deception gave him the free pass he needed to turn his back on me, and by extension, you."

I couldn't speak. In our most heated arguments, Gene had never bludgeoned me with this fact. He'd held that nasty two-by-four behind his back and somehow restrained himself, no matter how much I had insulted him for failing me as a father. He'd had more character than I ever knew.

Mama got my attention back. "Don't back your husband into a corner, Nikki. Or at least let him know now if you've already done so. This is one case where preemptive action makes the best sense."

When we had said our good-byes, I clicked my phone off and stopped fighting the tears welling at the corners of my eyes. Shuddering, I dropped my head to the desk. I didn't think I'd ever been so scared.

24

Mitchell

I raced around WHOT's offices like a madman, eager to compile the last few accounting records for my latest financial analysis. It had been nearly a week since I'd done anything directly for O.J., now that we'd made our pitch to KISS, the D.C. station. They were sounding promising but were still noncommittal about making a firm syndication offer.

As such, neither O.J. nor I had any power to resist the "special projects" Tony kept creating for me. Unless we could generate some syndication revenue for the good old boys, I was especially in danger of being laid off.

Tony knocked on my door and stuck his head in. "Yo, you got it yet?"

"I'll have the presentation complete by the time we sit down with Skip and Danny tomorrow," I said. I pitched a pile of papers at him. "See how simple this is?"

"I know it's a pain in the ass, don't think I don't understand." Tony stooped to retrieve the papers, and set them back onto my desk. "Hey, look." He lowered his voice and looked over his shoulder before turning back to me. "The good old boys are going to have a special guest join the operations review tomorrow."

I raised an eyebrow. "Who would that be?"

"Well, I'm telling you now because I don't want you to sit in on the meetings he attends. His name is Rod Stark."

I reorganized my desk of papers. "Okay."

Tony retrieved an orange toothpick from his shirt pocket, started chewing it. "He's a professional entertainment manager,

Mitchell. He has experience with several actors, singers, and syndicated deejays."

Now he had my attention. I shoved back from my desk, slammed him between the eyes with a hard stare.

"Rod contacted Skip and Danny directly, I didn't have a thing to do with it. Somehow he got wind of KISS's interest in O.J.'s show. That put O.J. on his map."

"He wants to replace me?"

"He's saying that he can manage O.J.'s career on a fee-for-service basis and help position him for more syndication deals. He's also got mad industry contacts, having worked in station management, sales, and talk radio in his own right."

I grimaced. "Ah, but can he balance the books?"

Tony walked around my desk and clamped a hand onto my shoulder. "I'm going to fight for you, man. It won't be easy, given that Rod would be a contractor for us and save the station the cost of benefits and etcetera. You deserve a heads-up, though."

I shook my head. "Don't worry about it. I'm 'bout to make it big as an author anyway. See?" I pulled out a lower drawer, which by now was thick with rejection letters, unopened manuscripts, and other packages from publishers and agents who'd passed on *Out of His Shadow,* despite LaRae's support. It was starting to look like success in publishing was actually about something more than just whom you knew.

Tony clapped my shoulder and stood back from the desk. "I'll keep you posted, okay? If the signs look bad, I'll help you with referrals—"

I scowled at him, hoping the annoyance in my veins was all over my face. "I don't need your help finding another damn job. I'm a grown-ass man, husband, and father. Just get out, if you want this stupid analysis ready on time."

Tony snapped his fingers, pointed at me confidently. "Stay cool. We'll rap tomorrow morning."

*   *   *

By six-thirty that evening I had grudgingly proofed all of my analysis. I quickly adjusted some details of my PowerPoint presentation before shutting off my office lights and heading to the parking garage.

As I climbed into the car, it was hard to fight the visions of numbers running through my head: our monthly family budget. I was responsible for the mortgage, both car notes and related insurance, and my most liquid savings accounts were pretty low. Based on Tony's news, it was time to get a real job, maybe even sign with an accounting firm; hardly anyone else was hiring in this economy, and with the demise of Arthur Andersen, even that field was shrinking. The thought of pushing a red pencil full-time made my spine shudder.

I drove through the Loop and headed south of town toward Calumet City, where Gina had agreed to meet me at a Chuck E. Cheese's. A friend of Clay's was having a birthday party there, and she'd promised we could get away and talk without either Dale or Nikki around.

I pulled into the parking lot and was annoyed to find all the good spaces taken. Looked like every joker in town had brought his kid to Chuck E.'s tonight. I trudged across the faded surface of chunky, rocky asphalt and stepped inside the brightly colored, raucous lobby. Gina was standing at the end of the lobby's hallway, wearing a fluorescent windbreaker over a stylish black nylon sweat suit. Clay stood at her side, twisting anxiously in his denim jeans, white turtleneck shirt, and navy-blue vest. They were talking to another mother and little boy. I walked up to them, nodding my head and opening my arms as Clay leapt into my embrace.

I held that little man like I'd never let him go.

It took Gina to wind down the small talk and tug Clay from my arms. "You go ahead and play with little Kevin," she said, pinching his cheek playfully. "His mom will watch you guys."

I watched Clay chase little Kevin over to a large rectangular box full of multicolored plastic balls. "Hope he enjoys hanging with little Kevin tonight," I said, staring away from Gina. "He won't see him anymore if he's moving to Atlanta."

"Oh God, Mitchell. He's *two*. He'll get over it. He won't remember little Kevin or any of these other kids a year from now."

"He'll remember me."

"You're not going to be out of his life. We just have to figure out the details of how this might work."

"Is Dale really moving with you two?"

"That's still under discussion, frankly. I am sorry you had to hear this from him. He was out of line, as he often is."

I pulled lightly at Gina's arm, motioning toward a booth near the back of the restaurant. We headed that way and took a seat. "So tell me," I said, wiping some salt and dirty napkins off my side of the table, "you've made no calculation of whether this would hurt me, or how it would impact Clay?"

Gina hugged herself, looked around the restaurant briefly. "This is about me and about Clay first of all. You are not part of our family. You do understand that, don't you?"

"Is this about me choosing to marry Nikki instead of giving us a chance?"

Gina tented her hands and glanced at the table. "I didn't want you in my life, Mitchell, until I saw you had Nikki so sprung that she stayed with you, even when it meant dealing with me and Clay. It made you a challenge."

"A challenge?"

"Yeah. I wondered at first if I could get you away from her by getting you to focus on Clay first and foremost. I gave up eventually, but do I feel an obligation to make your marriage easy? No."

I smiled ruefully. "The sweet sound of honesty."

"None of that applies to this decision, though. My offer from CNN is twelve-thousand dollars higher than what I've been offered locally, twenty if you consider the cost-of-living difference. Not to mention, CNN can open crazy doors for me if I do well. Think of the life I can make for Clay if everything works out."

"Everything doesn't depend on you, Gina."

"Maybe not, but it makes a hell of a difference. How do I know you won't lose interest in Clay, once you and Nikki start having children?"

"You think that little of me? We're not even close to having kids yet."

Gina drummed the table and considered me for a moment.

"What?"

"Mmm," she said, "I've heard kids are in the very near future for you all. People around church do talk, you know."

"They're not talking to me."

"How about your sister-in-law?"

My heartbeat quickened. "Angie?"

"Yeah, Angie. Cassie Barnes, the choir director? You know she's a former gynecologist, before she quit her practice to raise her kids. Well, she told me Angie was asking her some sensitive questions about fertility, the impact of STDs, and all that. Sounded like your wife's name came up along the way. I mean hell, we can *see* that Angie doesn't need the advice for herself. How many kids she got?"

As Gina continued speaking, my brain filled with snippets from the past couple of months: the absence of Nikki's birth-control pills from the bathroom cabinet, which she said she'd moved beneath the sink; the increased frequency of our lovemaking and Nikki's sudden preoccupation with the missionary position; her visit to my office a few weeks back; and that ovulation chart of hers that I found one night. She'd explained it as a tool to make sure she'd be good and fertile when the time came. A time we had agreed was still a year or more off.

I felt my forehead crease, heard my breathing quicken. "Look,

Gina, I'm telling you Nikki and I are not working on having kids, but it really doesn't matter right now. Couch it all you want; you're about to take my only son away from me. Check yourself again before you follow through on that. You might regret it."

I slid out of my seat before she could respond and stalked over to the kids' play area. Calling Clay aside, I kissed him on the cheek and promised I'd see him in a couple of days. By that time, Gina was at our side. I tousled my son's hair and sent him back over to the other kids, keeping a steely gaze on her the whole time.

She met my stare with equal force, though there was an odd softness under the surface. "This isn't about me this time, is it?"

I let my silence, and my back, do the talking.

25

Mitchell

It was after ten when I pulled into my driveway. I'd stretched out the trip home from Chuck E. Cheese, wasting time taking the Dan Ryan back to the downtown Loop before circling back to I-290, then taking streets all the way out to our subdivision. I hadn't trusted myself to come home directly and confront Nikki.

As I let the Accord idle in the driveway, my hand hovered over my garage-door opener. Fear rimmed my heart and anger clenched my fists. For the first time, I knew Gina had succeeded at driving a wedge between Nikki and me. I didn't want to believe it, but I had a sense I'd been played for a fool at the worst possible time.

When I finally entered the house, I stepped onto the marble tile of our kitchen and spied Nikki in the family room. She was curled up on our lavender leather loveseat, in front of our brick-encased fireplace, a blanket over her shoulders. Her head hung to the side and a book on African art, which she'd been collecting since the day we moved in, dangled from her right hand. She was knocked out, unfazed by the sound of my entrance.

Turning down the volume on the television, which she'd tuned to Fox News, I hovered over Nikki. I smoothed the soft, well-pressed curls of her hair and stepped back to observe her beauty. Then I quietly walked into the foyer, heading for the stairs.

I went over every inch of our master suite: armoire, dressers, bathroom cabinets, and every last drawer in our dressing room. No evidence of any birth-control pills. No evidence in any trash can of used pads, this despite the fact she should have started her period a week ago. I could find nothing to redeem her.

When my search was exhausted, I sat at the top of the stairway, debating whether to wake her up, get this out in the open now. My blood simmered, but I wanted to believe I could keep my cool. She'd looked so peaceful, though, maybe I could wait until—

"Mitchell?" I looked down and there she stood, at the foot of the steps with her house slippers in hand, her silk blouse half open. I was too far gone to appreciate the alluring sight of her cleavage.

Nikki waved at me playfully. "How long you been here?"

"Fifteen, twenty minutes," I grunted.

"I was trying to wait up for you, what all did you do at Chuck E. Cheese?"

"I wasn't there that long."

Her smile faded a bit. "Where were you then?"

"Had to think over some things. Got some disturbing news."

"What's Gina done now?"

"Are we expecting, Nikki?"

My wife looked at me with her doe eyes and blinked twice, no words. She shifted in place. "Why would you ask me that?"

"Why don't you tell me why I'd ask that?"

She took a couple of tentative steps up the carpeted stairway, getting closer to me. "God. I don't even want to know how this got started. I stayed up because I was going to talk to you about this tonight."

"Really." I stood up and walked into the bedroom, hearing her follow me. I turned back to face her as I crossed the threshold of the doorway, my arms crossed. "Well, go."

"Okay. Before I say anything more, just know that what I did, I did because I love you and want to make a life with you."

"Are you still on the pill?"

"No. I went off them when Gina first started playing games about moving away. She has so much power over you, Mitchell. You just don't see it. *I'm* your family, dammit, and I feel like a baby of our own will symbolize that for her."

"Clay's part of our family too."

"Yes, but—God—he's attached to Gina first and foremost. And she abuses the power that gives her."

"I don't deny that, but you've always known my loyalty is with you. Haven't you?"

"Yes. But it's about more than whether you'd cheat with her. It's about whether I can give you what she's already given you." Her tone weakened. "A child."

"Nikki," I said, hearing my voice rise, "you don't have to give me anything other than you. I believe a baby will eventually grow out of our love, but it's not some transaction without which I'd end this marriage."

"There was another reason." Nikki paused, looked at her feet. "I felt like another child would encourage you to stay on the job at WHOT, or someplace else practical."

I put my hands on my hips and sucked my lower lip. "You thought you'd saddle me with another obligation, is that it? Figured I'd be flighty enough to quit my job and leave you in the lurch?" She didn't know the half of it. As miserable as aspects of the WHOT job made me, I was hanging in there. If anything, it was now clear I'd be leaving WHOT for reasons far beyond my control.

"I've encouraged your writing, haven't I? You are an excellent writer, and someday it will work out. I just don't think we should put our lives on hold while waiting for your big break."

"This is ridiculous," I said, shaking my head and pacing a circle around her. "When have I ever said we should put anything on hold for the sake of my writing?" I shook a finger in her face. "That's your insecurity projecting onto me. You never heard me say anything like that."

A tear formed in her right eye. She looked down again, her hands hanging at her side.

"Just so we're clear," I said, stopping a few inches from her and raising her chin so she met my gaze, "you have deceived me these last couple months, looking to get pregnant."

A tear bled from the same eye, rolled down into her mouth as she nodded. "Yes."

"And your period's a week late."

Another nod.

"Well, I need to know what I'm up against. You've lied to me, made me the bad guy, but I may as well know if you've succeeded in your quest. Let's go to Osco now, get one of those EPTs."

In a flash, Nikki grabbed hold of my right hand with both of hers. She looked into my eyes, her gaze now strong. "I took a test at lunch today. It was positive."

It was like she'd blasted me with a hose full of ice water. Everything in the next few seconds was new to me. My body stiffened, from brains to feet. When I'd proposed to Nikki eighteen months earlier, I had dreamed of the day we'd have our first child. Those dreams shot through my brain suddenly, warming me up again, before being overrun by white-hot blasts of betrayal and alarm. Life was about to get even more complex—on top of losing Clay to the faraway world of Atlanta, I'd soon be unemployed and likely wind up being Mr. Mom during the first few months of this new child's life. That was no way to start out.

I balled up my fists, stepped back from Nikki, and grabbed the first thing I saw: one of our gold-framed wedding portraits. Before I could question myself, I whipped the portrait off the dresser, raised it high, and slammed it to the carpet. I stabbed at it with my shoe, grinding the shattered glass one good time, and stormed into my walk-in closet. Blindly grabbing up another pair of shoes, some underwear, and a few shirts and slacks, I blurred past Nikki with arms laden.

"Mitchell," she pleaded, her voice just above a whisper, "don't leave like this, not right now." She was on the verge of tears. "We're going to have a child. Don't blame the baby for—"

I stopped at the top of the stairs, dropping the clothing and the shoes. I stormed back into the bedroom, clamped a hand over her mouth. "Stop. I can't be around you right now." I pulled my hand back.

"You're not thinking clearly," she sobbed. "Wait."

"No. Let me go." I backed away from Nikki, my eyes riveted to her frightened gaze. We were both crying, but no further words were spoken.

26

O.J.

I was on the campus of DePaul University, doing a live remote from the Chicagoland Mentoring Program kickoff rally. This was the start of the program's fifth year of operation, and they'd gathered nearly a thousand mentors, mentees, politicians, and corporate sponsors to celebrate.

I was in the university's gym, seated on a large stage and interviewing the mayor on air when Tony paged me. During the next break, I excused myself quickly from the noisy gymnasium and stepped into the pale hallway. Tony answered my call on the first ring.

"Good news, big man," he said with trademark calm. "KISS just made a formal offer to carry your show."

"Thank ya Jesus!" I felt myself leap into the air as I hiked a fist heavenward. There were a few folks at the other end of the hall, but I didn't care who caught my little act. "When do we sign the final papers? We need to get Mitchell and lock in the time to *do* this, man. WHOT needs the money."

Tony sighed. "Hey, this is a nice start, but the station still has a ways to go. As far as the signing of the contract, it'll probably be a couple more weeks. Skip and Danny want to research the D.C. market again before locking in their asking price, and we need to figure out who your business manager will be by then."

Stepping back onto the shiny floorboards of the gym, I raised my voice over the blare of Jay-Z and Beyoncé's "'03 Bonnie and Clyde." "Mitchell's my manager, Tony. What's the question?"

"Long story. You remember Rod Stark, the joker that called you a few weeks back?"

"Yeah, seemed like a pompous jerk to me. I never returned the call."

"Well, Skip and Danny seem to like him. We're in a holding pattern until they make up their mind."

"This ain't cool," I said, frowning and settling back into my chair. Liz and Trey were on either side of me, shushing me as we prepared to go live again. "Is this why Mitchell hasn't returned the messages I left at his house this morning? And why the hell ain't he at this rally?" Mitchell, who'd been a mentor in the program from day one, was the one who'd gotten me involved with this in the first place. "You need to support your boy, Tony."

I could barely hear Tony now, thanks to the gym full of parents, kids, and community volunteers. "Oh yeah, Mitchell's not at his place for the next few days. Family problems, I'm sure he'll tell you about it eventually. In the meantime, here's his parents' number."

I scribbled the number down and shut my phone just as we came back on air. I pressed forward with the afternoon's program, giving away three more Gateway laptop PCs and a mess of clothing donated by the good folks at Dillard's. All the while, my mind fast-forwarded through the afternoon, eager for my big date that evening.

For better or for worse, I like to do things big, so of course my third date with LaRae would involve a cross-country trip. Tonight was the premiere showing of *Take It All,* the film adaptation of LaRae's best-selling book to date. *Take It All* had stayed on the *New York Times* best-sellers list for six months, so the stakes for the movie were high, at least in the eyes of film critics. The week before LaRae had invited me to be her date at the premiere, the same day I'd clashed on air with Marian. I was pretty flattered, considering we hadn't done anything more than hold hands so far. The dog in me took this as an encouraging sign, of course, but O.J. the Responsible Father chose to take it all in stride.

Because my schedule was so crazy, we had agreed to meet at O'Hare Airport in order to catch our flight. I'd already arranged to have Cherrelle stay with Dr. McIntosh and his wife for the night, so I got into my Jeep and hopped onto I-94 as soon as the mentor rally wrapped. Along the way, I rang Mitchell via his parents' number, only to get the answering machine. He wasn't answering his cell phone either. I began to wonder what exactly was up with his "family problems." I'd come to view Mitchell and Nikki as having a pretty ideal setup there, but then we all wear a mask to some degree.

I arrived at the airport so late I had to do short-term parking, ensuring my bill would be out of this world. On top of that, the TSA personnel in security drew a bead on me and selected me for a full-service fondling and bag check. Then, as a cherry on top, I nearly ran over my old flame, Alison Chavis, on my way through the terminal.

She was wearing a navy blazer and matching skirt, looking like she was headed to a Saturday business meeting. As I slowed long enough to make sure it was her, she stopped cold and signaled the guy behind her to do likewise. "Hey, stranger."

"Alison, what's up, girl." I looked over my shoulder, wondering if anyone was watching. Alison and I had talked when she was in town last month, but I knew she'd been annoyed by how evasive I was. I went ahead and grabbed her in a brief hug anyway.

She smiled blankly as she pulled out of the hug. "O.J., meet my fiancé, Don Herman." The big, bulky brother at her side straightened his suit jacket and extended a hand.

I gripped his hand firmly and smiled, hoping my face wasn't too flooded with relief. "How you doing, brother? Congratulations!"

Alison got a funny look on her face, like she'd smelled sour milk. "Don and I have been friends since we were kids growing up in southwest Atlanta. You know, Jack & Jill, church activities, the whole deal. Everywhere I turned—"

"There I was," Don chimed in playfully. "It just took her a while to feel me, you know how it is, man."

"Mmm," I said, raising an eyebrow and checking my watch. I had no idea what that was like. Apparently Don wasn't much of a player-player. "I really should get going, running late for a flight to L.A."

Alison's eyes narrowed a bit. "You headed all the way there by yourself?"

"I'll be out there seeing a friend." That was true.

"Well, don't be a stranger." Alison's stare was heavy. "I'll still be swinging through Chicago for work a lot, Don's just here to keep me company this weekend."

"Okay then." I tightened my grip on my bags.

"I'm serious, O.J.," she said. "I know a lot of key people who can help your career go national. You know what I can do for you."

"Hey, you all be good," I said, deciding to ignore the undercurrent of Alison's words. "Send me a wedding invite." I turned tail and took off like the Road Runner.

By the time I reached the gate, the attendant had her hand on the door, ready to slam it shut. As I hurtled toward the door from a hundred yards or so away, I yelled a few choice words and got her attention.

When I'd huffed and puffed my way down the aisle, juggling my leather carry-on bag and a backpack full of "quiet storm" mix tapes (just in case), LaRae looked up at me playfully from her seat. We were in the last row of first class. I let the backpack slide down my shoulders as she reached for my bag. "Did you miss me?" I asked.

She gave me a twisted smile as I stuffed my bags overhead. "I was hoping I wouldn't have to miss you, Mr. Peters. You'd have owed me for this ticket!"

"It's okay," I said, sliding onto the plush cushion beneath and twisting off the stale air blowing into my face. "I had it all under control. You know I had to make an entrance."

Once we were airborne, the conversation shifted from flirty small talk to LaRae's concerns and curiosities about how the movie would play. She'd been privy to some rough cuts along the way, but this would be her first time seeing the whole enchilada, along with a selection of Hollywood elites.

"They always find some way to screw it up," she said, swirling a scotch on the rocks in a plastic cup.

"I don't know about that," I replied. "I kinda liked *The Longing* movie better than the book."

LaRae's nostrils flared as if she'd sniffed rotten cheese. "Do you have any idea how insulting that statement is?"

Whoa, seemed I'd stepped in it this time. I looked over into her glowing pupils. "Don't be mad, Twan," I said, trying to sound like Damon Wayans. "I'm a man, you know, so I liked the action scenes better on the screen than trying to visualize them. Your descriptions were so beautiful, so ornate, I got caught up more in the words than in what was happening." Surely that would help.

LaRae turned back toward the window. "Thank God you're not my target market."

I could have run with that comment, but had a feeling we'd wind up back in "battle of the sexes" territory. I tried to soften things up again. "Do you really care that much what readers think? You could never sell another copy and still retire."

She glanced back at me, considered the implications. "I think you'd have to be robotic not to care on some level. Does that mean I lose sleep over it? Hell no. Why do you think I haven't done a new book in eighteen months? Everyone wants me to do another love story, but at this point I'm empty when it comes to that type of stuff. I'll write another novel when I'm ready. And if I have to publish it online like Stephen King or something, I will.

"As far as the movies go, as long as the check is nice and they sign up a director and a lead star I'm comfortable with, I'm willing to take my chances."

I nodded. "Makes sense to me."

She cut another glance at me. "But they can never outdo my original creation. I still can't believe you said that shit. You can be a rude bastard, O.J."

I felt my forehead flush with embarrassment. "Hey, since when was I politically correct? You'd prefer me to act like Poindexter or something?" I stiffened my accent, made out like Steve Urkel. "I think everything you write is just purr-fect, Ms. Summers."

LaRae's shoulders shook with laughter, but she flashed me a middle finger. "Stay just the way you are, man. I asked you along because I knew you'd make this trip entertaining. Now will you let me get some sleep?" She reached into the webbing in front of her seat and tossed me a stack of magazines. "Knock yourself out."

I shrugged and started to flip through a *Sports Illustrated* with Alex Rodriguez on the cover. Truth be told, I was a little scared by her dismissive tone. What was I, a court jester now? The more canine side of me welcomed the challenge, though. *She may be laughing at me now, but I'll have her laughing with me tonight. All night.*

It was five P.M. Pacific time when we arrived at LAX. We caught a cab to the Ritz-Carlton, which was near the site of the premiere. I had told LaRae from the start that I'd get my own room, which she'd insisted on upgrading to a suite. That bothered my pride a little bit, but until I was syndicated outside Chicago, how often would I have the chance to stay in a place like this? I decided to make the most of it.

A little before seven I changed into my tuxedo, a wool peak-lapel DKNY I'd purchased after Tony told me it was "ghetto" to wear rentals. I straightened my bow tie one last time before heading downstairs to meet LaRae. As I strode out of the elevator and crossed

the lobby's vintage marble floor, I inhaled reverently. She was standing near the revolving glass door, her braids drawn up into a well-
coifed ball. Her leggy figure was draped in a burgundy silk velvet
corset and matching trumpet skirt. The skirt was cut just right,
leaving something to the imagination but clearly showcasing her
round, firm hips. I felt like Bob Dole with Britney Spears. *Easy, boy.*

When we rolled up to the curb in front of the theater, it was
like stepping through a TV screen into the realm of *Entertainment
Tonight.* The minute our shoes hit the sidewalk, cameras whirred,
flashed, and whizzed around us, lighting the dusky skies overhead.
Every fourth or fifth face was a reasonably familiar Black celebrity.
I even bumped into a few folks who'd been on the air with me. Of
course, most of my interviews are via phone, so it took some effort
for me to convince Bernie Mac and Vivica Fox that I wasn't just
some lying loser trying to push up.

The reception flew by, a constant string of joking over wine
with directors, actors, producers, and journalists. LaRae was too
busy being pulled around by the studio heads and producers to
mind me, so I applied my Southern charms on the various stars
and journalists. I worked it, too. I'd secured my fourth new guest
for the show, a new rapper with a CD coming out on Def Jam, when
I got distracted by a familiar face, except this one was no celebrity.

It was the same odd brother who'd been in line at LaRae's signing at Afrocentric Books. When I spied him, he was loitering near
the champagne ice sculpture, taking nips from a glass but standing
off on his own. He stood in his rented tux, scoping the crowd and
letting his growing dreadlocks cover his forehead. His mouth and
nose were partially hidden by the champagne flute. He didn't begin to look like he belonged, like he knew the first soul.

Curiosity rolled up in me and I took a step toward the brother,
just as an older gentleman with a sharp fade streaked with white
and a matching goatee stepped over, blocking my way.

"Young brother," he said, stepping dangerously close to my

personal space and locking eyes with me, "looks like you're having quite the time tonight."

I tensed, noting the brother was a couple inches taller than me but thin as a rail. I also noticed he wasn't bothering with a tux. He wore a black single-breasted wool suit with a white oxford and a fat mottled-gray tie. "Hey, just enjoying L.A., sir. You would be?"

"Oh, excuse me." He extended a firm but slightly wrinkled hand. "I'm Gray Philips, an old friend of LaRae's."

I raised an eyebrow. "Interesting. Where are you guys acquainted from?"

Philips pressed his lips together briefly. "Well," he said, eyes narrowing, "I wouldn't exactly say we're acquainted. I know everything about LaRae that there is to know." He winked. "Know what I mean?"

"O.J." LaRae sneaked up on my left side. I turned toward her voice to see her standing there with a hand on her hip. Her body was angled toward me, completely away from Philips. "We need to go take our seats."

I looked between the two of them. "That's, uh, cool. I was just meeting Mr. Philips here—"

"That's Dr. Philips." Philips was grinning now, though seemingly happy to be ignored by LaRae. "I was this young lady's mentor and graduate-school adviser."

LaRae took me by the arm but pivoted toward Philips. "Gray, you are so full of shit. You promised."

I was starting to make the connection, but by now I felt invisible. Philips stepped toward LaRae, apparently unfazed. "I promised not to force myself on you, LaRae. However, I didn't say I'd turn down an invitation to this premiere or anything else celebrating your success. Your problem should be with the studio, they sent me two invitations." He held up two fingers. "I might have given the other ticket to Jason, for all you know."

I felt LaRae freeze.

"LaRae," he said, glancing between the both of us, "you really need to lighten up. Don't worry, he won't speak to you if you don't speak to him." Philips focused on me, extended a hand again. "Mr. Peters, pleasure to meet you, sir."

I pointed toward the old man's back as he walked away. "I never told him my name." I looked back toward the ice sculpture, noted the brother from Chicago was gone. "I almost the got the impression he was blocking anyway. There was this guy I'd seen around Chicago—"

LaRae sank some of her nails into my arm.

"Ow! What are you doin'?"

"O.J., can we go take our seats please? I'll tell you why Gray knew your name, and whatever else after the movie, okay?"

My arm still throbbing, I nodded slowly and let her lead me into the cavernous movie theater. This night was getting more interesting with each moment. LaRae not only had quite a past, it didn't seem content to stay there.

Both of us being eager to lighten the mood, LaRae and I carved out a private area for ourselves. An entire row had been reserved for her and guests of her choice (not including Gray, mercifully), and there were several open seats. We hunkered down in the midst of the empty seats and prepared to pick the movie apart.

"I'm trying not to be anxious," she said, leaning over to whisper in my ear. "But I'm worried. The screenplay's already sacrificed some key characters: my leading lady's best friend, the son of the main love interest. I just don't know."

I patted her hand, trying not to linger too long. "Just remember, at the end of the day you've already been paid." We chuckled and settled in as the credits began to roll over the title track, a Maxwell number.

If audience reaction was a fair gauge, *Take It All* looked like it might be a tough sell. Laugh lines came and went with nothing but silence. Laughter cascaded from various corners during scenes meant to be serious. Worse yet were LaRae's reactions to several supporting characters. In one scene Mariah Carey walked on screen, playing the lead character's hairdresser.

"What the hell!" Her shout echoed throughout the theater. She grabbed my arm. "In the book, I specifically described Melba as having skin the color of shiny coal and a big beautiful Afro. Mariah Carey?" There were several episodes like this.

About an hour in, LaRae sank her nails into my arm again. I wasn't ready for the attack. "Damn, girl!"

"Let's go," she whispered.

I gripped my tub of popcorn tightly. This was my first dose of bad carbs in weeks, and I was going to enjoy it. "Are you crazy? There's another half-hour still, maybe more."

Even in the dark theater, I could see the fire in LaRae's eyes as she yanked me closer. "I invited you to come to L.A. with me, fool, whether that meant seeing the movie or doing what I want to do. Get up now!"

Now I was thoroughly disgusted. I held onto my precious buttery popcorn but reluctantly followed LaRae as we burst down the aisle past the curious, amused stares of the other spectators. As LaRae pushed the center doors open, her purse swinging at her shoulder, I tried to let my eyes adjust to the light.

Two journalists, a white blond girl and a bald-headed brother, charged out of the theater after us. "Ms. Summers," said the brother, who reached LaRae first, "are you leaving because something's wrong with the movie?"

I let my tub of popcorn hang loose at my side, wishing I could take LaRae away and calm her down. "Don't," I whispered.

LaRae stared back at the reporter for a second, then pushed a finger at his face. "That piece of shit on the screen has nothing to do with my book!"

I dropped my popcorn, watched the kernels collect around the tips of my black Florsheim shoes. Now she'd gone and done it.

Once she'd spewed a few more seconds' worth of invective, I took LaRae by the hand and pulled her out of harm's way. I took her cell phone from her purse and called for the limo.

As we pulled away from the curb, she looked at me, sorrow in her eyes. "You must really think I'm nuts now."

I cleared my throat and searched the car ceiling and both windows before answering. "Honest answer? You need about as much help as I do. And that's not a compliment."

Our enclosed compartment shook with laughter. "You have every right to be pissed about the movie," I said, recovering. "You couldn't have screened it earlier?"

"Oh, my agent was trying to negotiate me a full advance screening, but it got bogged down in legalese and I got caught up in some of my community projects. It just got away from me. Now I'm tied to a bomb."

I placed a hand on her knee. "It wasn't that bad. Movies ain't your line of work anyway."

"You're right." She reached toward me, exciting my heartbeat, until I realized she was grappling for the mini-fridge beneath my seat. She removed a bottle of red Merlot and two glasses. "Let's get this out of our minds, go back to the Ritz and change, and hit the fuckin' town."

"That's all good." I reached over and held the bottle of wine with both hands. "What I don't want to forget about is that Gray Philips guy. I want to know the story, LaRae. Was he your fiancé, your mentor and all? And who the hell is Jason?"

She jerked the bottle from my hands. It had already been opened, so she popped the cork and started to pour.

I stared back at her. "You can tell me. For real."

LaRae took a first swig of the Merlot. "A long, ugly story," she said, licking her lips.

"I have ugly stories of my own."

"I'll tell you this much," she said, holding out a filled glass for me. "Gray is the one, my ex-fiancé. Taught me most everything I know about literature, philosophy, even Western history. He's also the man who made me a woman."

I narrowed my eyes skeptically.

"He wasn't my first, don't be silly, but he was the first man I made love with. He taught me things about my own body, what I liked and enjoyed, as opposed to just satisfying himself."

"Not the most ethical guy, though, huh?" This from a guy who'd knocked up a member of the flock as a student preacher. This wasn't about me, though.

"We didn't become intimate until I graduated from NYU. He edited my first two manuscripts, and the rest was history."

I decided to press for more details about the past later. "If he's history, why was he here tonight?"

"Because he likes to control me. Gray's always been very adept at mind games."

"I see." Wasn't much that bothered me about an ex lurking in the shadows. I had plenty of comparable baggage. There was still one thing. "And Jason? Another ex?"

The words had barely escaped my mouth when LaRae dropped to her knees, right there on the limo floor, and smiled up into my face. "Too much talking," she said, tugging sharply at my zipper. "Open up."

"Oh jeez." I scooted back instinctively. "Look, if you don't want to reveal everything to me yet, that's your right—"

LaRae kept her hands clamped to my thighs. "O.J., I'm trying to reveal everything to you, right now." She reached behind her back, started to untie her corset.

I knew I was being played, that was the only reason I left my back pinned to the leather seat. "Look, you've had a difficult night. You don't need to do anything you'll regret."

She kept her eyes locked on mine as the corset strings popped loose and the top fell to her waist. My eyes popped at the Wonderbra and heaving bosom beneath. I twisted uncomfortably as I sprang to attention, my bulge curving into my zipper. Not the most pleasant sensation. "LaRae, please," I pleaded, squirming and shutting my eyes, "you don't know what you're in for. Once you've had it the O.J. way, you won't want any other lay."

"I'll be the judge of that." The cabin filled with the sound of my zipper as LaRae fished me out into the open.

"Ohhh, no you didn't." I opened my eyes and shifted forward in my seat. "It's on now."

As patiently and sensitively as I could, I cupped the back of LaRae's head and let her lean into every last inch of me.

27

Mitchell

For my weekly activity with Terry, my mentee in the Chicagoland Mentoring Program, I kept it simple and attended his basketball scrimmage over on the West Side. At fourteen, Terry's already sprouted into a gangly six-footer. He's got some game, but first he's got to grow into that body. I tried to encourage him as we rode to his house in my car, surrounded by the dark of night and the thumping hip-hop of passing cars.

"Just keep working on your physical conditioning, you know, push-ups, running, even during the off-season. That'll help your coordination along."

"Yeah." Terry was looking out his window, staring blankly.

"Come on, don't space out on a brother," I said, tapping his shoulder as I made a turn. "The world doesn't begin and end with basketball. Truth told, an academic scholarship is what's going to pay your way through college."

He wiped his nose on his Bulls starter jacket and briefly glanced my way. "I don't have a four-point, Mitchell. Nobody's going to pay me for college."

"You don't have to have straight As, though they're nice," I replied. "You've got to mack the standardized tests, more importantly—the SAT and ACT? Remember, we're going to start preparing for the PSAT this summer."

Terry sounded like a balloon oozing air. After two and a half years, I was used to these defensive antics.

"You're going to do fine, as long as you work at it. Those A-pluses you keep getting in English and social science? We're going to ride those talents, trust me." We turned onto Terry's block and I pulled over a few spaces away from his two-story housing project. I shut the engine off but kept my arm around the passenger seat. "You haven't forgotten we're leading next week's citywide seminar, about English and vocabulary?" There was no guarantee how many kids would show up, but the idea was to start a subgroup that would develop the kids' interest in creative writing. Anything to redirect self-destructive energy.

"I'll be there long as you come get me," Terry said, showing off the gap in his front teeth. His face darkened as he said, "By the way, can I bring a friend?"

"Sure. He just needs to bring a permission form signed by his mom. This someone from your school?"

Terry looked at his lap, twiddled his thumbs. "Yeah, he's in my homeroom, but I didn't know if you'd be cool with him coming."

I smiled, confused. "Why would you say that?"

"He was involved with the boys that killed that woman back in July. You know, the one you said you knew."

"Didn't see that one coming." I let my words hang in the car's interior for a minute. I turned, facing Terry directly. "Give me his name."

"Jackie Williams."

I filed the name and all its possible permutations away. "Let me check with my friend, see whether Jackie's up for any charges behind this. If he's been released free and clear, it might be okay."

Terry reached forward and we shook hands vigorously. "Thanks, Mitchell."

I let him climb out of the car without any more words, still digesting his question. Some nightmares just wouldn't die.

As I drove to my parents' house, I couldn't stop my thoughts from returning to Nikki. We'd been apart four days now, with two brief phone calls as our only link. It was killing me, but my pride wouldn't let me adjust course, not yet.

Nobody was home at Mom and Dad's. Walking downstairs to

my parents' finished basement, I dialed up my sister Deniece. I hadn't seen Niecy in over three months, despite the fact we talked on the phone every couple of weeks. Since she divorced her husband Willie and escaped to Madison, Wisconsin, to get a master's in nursing, Niecy has chosen to make her own separate world. My folks and I have been supportive, Marvin too, but in the end she felt the best way to flee the ghosts of her marriage was to get out of Chicago altogether.

As the phone rang, I walked back to my temporary bedroom, which used to be Niecy's. In truth it's not the room she grew up in—my parents only moved into this three-story, four-bedroom crib five years ago—but when Niecy first left Willie she stayed here for several months. As a result, she'd set up a lot of her childhood mementos—stuffed bears and rabbits, Raggedy Andy and Ann dolls, high-school yearbooks, and mid-eighties posters of singers like Christopher Williams, Kool and the Gang, New Edition, and Janet Jackson. She even had a framed blowup of me, her, and Marvin from her senior-prom night.

Niecy finally answered her phone, after at least six rings. She sounded guilty, like she was chewing her nails or something. "I've been meaning to call you." I could picture her sitting on a couch, dressed in baggy sweats, her long fine hair pulled back into a ponytail. Most guys considered my sister to be "fine," but Niecy was suppressing her beauty these days—her way of keeping the crazies at arm's length.

We made small talk for a while, until I told her the whole sordid business about me and Nikki. Not trying to counsel me too much, Niecy listened patiently.

When I was done with the account, she paused before saying, "I know she was wrong, Mitchell, but she clearly did what she did because she loves you. I know from experience, you could do worse."

I sat on top of the bed, staring at my image in the wall-length mirror across from me. I didn't question Nikki's love for me so much as her character. Never in my life had I expected she'd pull something like this, not with something as precious as the creation of life. I decided not to quibble with Niecy, though. "Speaking of experience, when can I get you to come to one of my readings from *Out of His Shadow*?"

"Come on, baby brother. I don't know if I can handle that."

"Understood. I would ask you to make an exception, though, if I ever get a publisher's interest. I want you to sign off on any decision I make."

Niecy sighed. "I guess that makes sense. I did put the bug in your mind first, I suppose."

"Exactly." I heard my phone click. "Niecy, hold on a second. I have another call."

"I hate call waiting. Look, I'll hang up and ring you later tonight or tomorrow. I love you, kid brother."

"Love you too." I clicked over. "Hello?"

"Hi, may I speak to Mitchell Stone?" The clipped, proper voice belonged to a white woman, probably someone a tad younger than me, maybe late twenties.

"This is he."

"Hi, Mitchell, this is Sharon Meredith. I'm an associate editor with Starlight Books."

My heart leapt a bit, danced a little jig. I'd heard of Starlight plenty of times, wasn't sure whether they were under Random House or Simon & Schuster. Didn't matter. From what I knew, these book people never called with something as trivial as a rejection. They had plenty of form letters for that. I tried to sound cool. "Hello, Sharon. How are you?"

"I just wanted to let you know I am reading *Out of His Shadow*. I helped edit LaRae Summers' sixth and seventh books, before Starlight hired me to help run their new line. So LaRae and I are cool, and she passed your manuscript along a few weeks ago."

I looked at my image in the mirror, mouthing "And?"

"I love it! Your writing is very succinct, lyrical even. Clearly, this is a commercial book, but in some ways it's even literary. I especially like the way that as a male, you've captured the voice of the oppressed sisters out there." Her next comment answered the question that immediately popped into my head. "Dysfunction is just so common in your community, you know? I know this will strike a chord with women from the hood to the college campus to the corporate office."

I scratched my brow. "Excuse me, Sharon, do you have a degree in African-American studies or something?"

"No," she chuckled, "just a lot of Black friends and six years' experience editing and marketing Black books. Look, I can't promise anything, but with someone like LaRae behind you, you must be getting calls from tons of publishers."

I smiled bitterly into the mirror. *If you only knew.* Apparently Sharon had no idea of my overflowing mountain of rejection letters. "I have received quite a few responses, if that's what you mean."

"Well, I just want you to know I am working hard to get my superiors, then marketing, then sales, to buy off on a contract offer for you. If you can give me a couple more weeks, we can sit down with LaRae and tell you something for sure."

I decided to push my luck. "Well, if you're able to make an offer, I trust it would be something competitive?"

"Of course. Again, no promises, but if everyone agrees with my view of the book's potential, we'll be in the six-figure neighborhood."

"Well, thank you," I replied. "I really appreciate your call, Sharon. I'll look forward to hearing from you, as soon as possible."

I clicked my phone off and sat back on the bed. Everything sounded way too good to be true, especially given the horror stories I had heard from other authors. Wasn't every day a guy got a call from a top publisher, though. I toyed first with calling Nikki to share the news, but held off. First of all any conversation would be tainted, as it had been the last two nights, by our emotional standoff. Second, the bottom line of my situation was still bleak: I was nearly certain to be fired from WHOT in a few days, and the odds of *Out of His Shadow* being unanimously ratified by Sharon's superiors was probably still pimply at best. I'd read somewhere that less than five percent of the material submitted to publishers gets purchased. Given my luck lately, I wasn't inclined to spend my Starlight advance just yet. Best to keep my trap shut for now, period.

I must have drifted off to an unplanned nap, because the next thing I knew my mother was yelling down the stairs. I awoke with a trickle of saliva running down my chin. I trudged into the basement bathroom, freshened up, and emerged upstairs in time to eat dinner with my folks.

They were seated at opposite ends of their long glass kitchen table. Dad had his head buried in a *Wall Street Journal,* and Mom was on the phone with my Aunt Rhonda. I fixed myself a plate of Mom's grilled catfish, spinach, and sweet potatoes and hovered over the table. Dad was clearly into his antisocial mode, doing nothing more than grunting at me. Mom waved and smiled, motioning for me to sit, but continued her phone conversation. I was hoping she'd kept her deal with me; given that Aunt Rhonda is a relationship expert who met Nikki back in our crazy dating days, I didn't want her being worried with our marital troubles right now.

I ate a few bites of the catfish in silence, seated near the middle of the table. Four days in and my parents and I were already tired of each other. They had peppered me with questions and advice my first two nights, but once they'd said their piece, they had let me have my own space. I wasn't complaining.

"I was thinking, Mitchell," Mom said suddenly, punching her cordless phone off.

"Thinking what?" I kept my eyes on my plate, knifed off another slice of catfish.

"If you're so concerned about the financial strain of having another child, why not sell the house? It's a beautiful place, but you all don't really need three thousand square feet. You could move into a less expensive subdivision, get something you could afford on either one of your salaries."

My father sighed, rustled his papers. "You know what I always said."

I looked at the back of the stock page, which blocked Dad's face from view. "I know, no man should let his wife out-earn him."

"Always leads to problems."

"I know, Dad," I said, my fork dropping with a clang against my plate, "I don't know why I didn't call Nikki's boss and explain that when they promoted her. Or maybe I should sue them for emotional distress?"

"Marvin," Mom hissed, "have you heard the one about spilled milk? Just read your paper, please."

"No, forget it." I whipped my plate and silverware off the table, grabbed some tartar sauce from the fridge, and took my food into the family room. I settled down in front of the twenty-six-inch boob tube and punched it to life, contenting myself with some mindless BET programming. Nothing clears the mind like the sight of shaking, quivering rumps.

A second plate and a forty-minute nap later, I looked up to see Mom standing over me with her phone. "Here," she said breathlessly, clearly annoyed.

I took the phone, looking back at her curiously. "Who is it?"

Mom waved her hands helplessly and turned back into the kitchen.

Drama, always drama. Rolling my eyes, I put the phone to my ear. "Yes?"

"I left a message on your cell phone two hours ago." It was Gina.

"I took a catnap, excuse me." I headed down the steps, back to the basement. "You come to your senses now?"

"Well, you should know I've broken up with Dale. Didn't have much choice after the son of a bitch slapped me around the room."

My heartbeat kicked up a notch. "What are you talking about, Gina?"

"I'm talking about the fact I'm in this hotel room, hoping he doesn't come back for me."

I leaned forward, ran a hand through my hair. "Is Clay with you?"

"No, he's with my mama. Are you gonna help *me* for once, Mitchell?"

I rested my head in my hands. "What do you want me to do?"

"I'm calling the police, and I know I need to stay here, at the scene of the crime. I'm through with Dale, but he's paying the price this time."

"It's probably not safe for you to stay there by yourself. Dale could come back before the cops do."

"Tell me something I don't know."

I shook my head, kicked myself again for my lack of judgment those three short years ago. "I'm headed there now. We need to talk about this moving nonsense anyway. Where are you?"

"Red Roof Inn, the one in Calumet City."

"All right, sit tight." I looked over to the dresser, reached for my car keys. I don't know why I didn't call Nikki first.

28

Mitchell

I think it was my breath that roused me from a fitful sleep. It was awful, a rank brew of morning breath spiced with the stench of pure grain alcohol. I shot forward and rubbed at my eyeballs, trying to figure when I would have tied one on. I wiped my eyes good and looked to my right, where I saw a plain white sink and wall-length mirror. A quick look around and I recognized Gina's hotel room, styled as only Red Roof knows how to do.

"What the?" I looked down, realized I was underneath the covers of the bed. Naked.

I closed my eyes, blinked several times, knowing this was some funny dream. I reopened them, took a good look around. No change. Scurrying so quickly I nearly tripped over the sheets covering me, I slid off the bed and grabbed my slacks, which were draped over a chair against the wall. I reached for my skivvies, which were tucked inside, and got myself partially decent. As I straightened up, buttoning my slacks, I caught a glimpse of myself in the mirror. Over my right eye, stretching toward my temple, was a narrow bandage. I stopped, stepped closer to the mirror, and pulled it back to find a healing, bloody scab.

I slapped the bandage back into place and hurried to the closet, yanking my jacket, turtleneck, and sweater out. Dashing them across the bed, I took a tentative seat and rifled through my jacket until I found my cell phone. I gripped it tightly and punched in Nikki's number. Our home number.

When no one answered, I checked the digital clock on the nightstand. 8:25 A.M. She was probably on her way to work. I started to dial her cell, then punched the END button. I wanted to speak to my baby, start the damage control immediately, but it occurred to me I needed to know what the story was before I outed myself. I stood to my feet, still half dressed, and tenderly lifted back the comforter and the off-white sheets. The last thing I needed to see were fresh nut stains, or any other evidence that I'd broken my vows after ten short months of marriage.

The door swung open suddenly, filling the room with a blast of fall Chicago wind. Gina stood there, her hand still on the knob. Her short hair looked freshly curled and she wore tight jeans with a form-fitting Roosevelt U. sweatshirt. "Good morning," she said, an innocent smile on her face.

"Shut the door at least." I grabbed my turtleneck, pulled it over my head, and started to fluff my sweater. "Why I am here? What the hell happened last night?"

Gina stood against the closed door, a hand massaging a bandaged spot on her neck. "That's the thanks I get for saving your life, huh?"

"What happened, Gina!"

"I ran Dale off, okay?" She took a step toward me. "It's all right, Mitchell. We won't file any police reports or anything. I pulled my thirty-eight special on Dale when he tried to finish you off. He's crazy, but his ass is scared of going back to the pen, so he stepped as soon as I flashed that barrel."

I was starting to remember some of the previous night. "So you nursed your wounds and mine? Had to strip me naked, did ya?"

A coy smile, a shrug of the shoulders. "You were bleeding pretty bad. Would you have preferred I called Nikki and your parents, told them I was rushing you to a hospital after we'd been attacked in a motel room?"

I turned away from her, sank back onto the bed. "I should be shot," I muttered to myself.

All was quiet for a minute, until I heard Gina breathing behind me. She had crawled over to my side of the bed and had her hands on my shoulders. "You uptight about whether we did anything?" She smoothed her hands over the sheets as I looked back at her. "A few things happened on this bed, I guess. I mean, after I cleaned you up and gave you something to take your mind off the pain, you got a little frisky."

I pivoted, grabbed Gina by the shoulders, and shoved her back against the bed. "You're whacked, you know that?"

"How's that? What we did last night was by mutual consent."

I backed further away from the bed, toward the TV. "*What* did we do?"

"Look, if you wanna play dumb, that's your right." She considered me closely, then rolled onto her knees. "You want to keep me and Clay in Chicago, Mitchell?"

"I want Clay here, yes."

"It's a duo or nothing."

"What's your point?"

"Now that I've gotten rid of Dale for good, maybe you could show a little appreciation."

"How can I do that when you're leaving town?"

"That's the point. Maybe if you take Dale's place, I don't have to take the CNN job. Clay and I could stay here."

I refused to let my mouth drop open.

"I'm not asking for any strings. Nikki can have the house, she can have the wedding band, hell, she can have ten babies with you. I just figure, since I've got a piece of you living with me every day, I may as well get a larger piece every now and then."

My shoulders vibrated with jaded laughter. "I'll see you in court. You're certifiable."

Gina scooted to the edge of the bed and let her legs hang off the side. "Based on whose word besides yours? You really think any court will take away my baby, when your word would be the only black mark on my record?"

I replayed what I knew about Gina's history. The bouts with depression. The restraining orders filed by an ex-boyfriend. "Are you serious?"

"My nose has been clean as a whistle since the day Clay was born. No court will hold ancient history against me."

She was right, but I couldn't leave it there. "Let's just test your theory, how about that."

"Fine. The courts will have to deal with me from Atlanta, though. I could have turned back on the CNN offer, but clearly there's no reason for me to do so. Clay and I will be gone next week."

"Don't bet on it." I grabbed my sweater, put it over my head and started to pull it down, when my cell phone rang.

"Let me help you." I heard Gina slide toward my side of the bed, reach for the phone.

"Leave it alone," I said, my words garbled by the wool of my sweater. I yanked it down over my shoulders and reached a hand toward my jacket. Too late.

Gina already had the phone in her hand and had hopped off the bed. "Hi, Nikki," she said, looking at me and flashing her middle finger from the other side of the bed, "Mitchell's right here. I'll put him on."

29

Mitchell

When I had first arrived at the hotel, my eyes bleary and my patience shot, I'd slammed my car door behind me and strode toward Room 115. I knocked mercilessly and Gina opened after a couple of minutes.

"Damn, break it down, why don't you?" She turned away, gave me a glimpse from behind of her ripped linen skirt and rumpled white blouse. I realized she'd had her spongy natural hairdo permed again.

I stood there in the doorway, suddenly wary. "I'm only here because you called me. When are the police coming?"

"They thought in another hour maybe." Gina walked back to the queen-size bed and took a seat.

I nodded in the direction of the bed, which was professionally dressed with a comforter the color of egg yolks. "You could bounce a quarter off that thing. You and Dale never got into the main event, before he smacked you?"

Gina cleared her throat, reached over to the nightstand and flashed a bottle of cognac. "You want some?"

"No." I stayed in the doorway, though I shifted so I was half in and half out, where I could see anyone approaching from behind. "I don't need to know what's happened before. Tell me this, is Dale officially out of the picture now?"

Gina rubbed at her left cheek, which was red and inflamed. "What did I say before? You can ask my mother, she's not allowing him around anymore."

My heart filled with tentative relief, if only for Clay's sake. "That's a start."

"Yes, it is." She poured herself a paper cup of the cognac, then looked back up at me. "There's no good men in Chicago, at least none who want me. The best way to make a clean break, Mitchell, is that I accept the CNN position." She paused, seemingly sensitive to my renewed heartbreak. "You may as well know they've given me an official start date, so there's no looking back now."

Despite myself, I stepped further into the room, toward the bed. "Slow it down a bit. If you really have to move, let me keep Clay for your first few months there. We'll figure out custody details after that."

Gina ignored me, tipped the cup to her lips and let the liquid travel slowly down her throat. "I hope you don't think I'm putting my career before my son," she finally said. "Clay and I are *both* moving to Atlanta."

"In time, I understand if that's the case." I was almost pleading now, still moving toward the bed. "While you get settled, though, why not let me keep him? You can take him once you've got everything in order."

Gina set her cup back onto the nightstand and let her hands rest at her sides. "We'll manage. Believe it or not, Mitchell, I'm going to respect your paternal rights through this whole process."

I couldn't stop myself. "He'll be happier with me and Nikki than alone with you in some strange city."

"Are you kidding me? Please, I know you're staying with Mommy and Daddy right now 'cause your marriage is as fucked up as my relationship with Dale was. Don't preach at me."

It was like a drill had been bored through the middle of my forehead. Ooh, the words I'd have used if this weren't my son's mother. "*My* marriage is the problem now?"

Gina stood, unfazed by my additional steps toward her. "You heard me."

"If it is, don't act like it's not what you wanted. Nikki was wrong, but you should never have poked your nose into our business."

Gina shook her head and looked at her feet. "Whatever."

"I hope you're happy, though. Now we're as miserable as you are."

"October thirteenth," Gina hissed, snapping her neck and meeting my eyes angrily. "A week from tomorrow, that's our moving day. And there's only one thing that would change my mind."

We were so close by then, she barely had to extend her arms to grab me around the shoulders. Before I could process what she was doing, Gina pulled my lips to hers and started to devour me. She pulled at my hands, maneuvered them onto her rising breasts, guided me toward the bed. For a short instant—it might have been two seconds, it might have been thirty—my body did what came naturally. Gina and I had done this many times in the days before Clay was conceived, so in some ways handling her body was like riding a bike: You never forget how to do it.

When that instant passed, though, my mind took over. I slid my hands to her sides, pushed her away from me. I released her and turned back toward the door, only to find Dale standing just inside the threshold.

"Get out of here, Dale!" I stepped back toward the bed, placed a hand in front of Gina. As much as she might deserve any beating he had planned for her, I couldn't just leave her there. "I'm not gonna say it again." I kept my right hand at my side, flexed and ready to grab the pocket knife I'd brought along.

Dale, for his part, had the look of a third-grader who'd opened his lunch box and found a dead rat. "Gina," he asked, his eyes searching her, "what the hell's goin' on?"

I stayed by Gina, at the bedside, as Dale slowly approached us, his arms at his sides and his breathing slow. As he neared, I flinched at the flashes of lamplight bouncing off his bald head.

"Stop playing dumb and get out." I stared straight into his bugged-out eyes. "Gina's only here because she's waiting for the police. You really wanna be around when they show up?"

Dale looked past me, peering at Gina again. "What's he talking about, girl? This some goddamn joke?"

"No, Dale." Gina's voice was eerily calm as she watched him stomp toward the nightstand, where he stood on the balls of his feet. "This is about me and Mitchell. What you saw," she said, suddenly grabbing my hand, "was exactly what it looked like. Mitchell still loves me, and I want him back in my life. So you and I are through."

That's when I did exactly the wrong thing. Turned my head toward Gina and bellowed, "What in God's name are you smoking?"

Dale, by comparison, needed no fact-checking. "Fuck all this." With lightning speed, he grabbed the cognac bottle off the nightstand and bashed it against a corner. "Had enough of your bourgie ass, Stone!"

He stepped toward me with the bottle's jagged remains and swung. I ducked. He swiped at Gina instead, nicking her on the neck. As she scurried to the other side of the bed, reaching for her purse, I righted myself and landed a punch to Dale's gut. He stumbled back toward the window, but held onto that damn bottle. I crouched, ready to throw another punch, but he got the jump on me. The bottle came flying toward my face, and as I felt it slice into my temple, I prayed I'd see Nikki again.

30

O.J.

I was wrapping up an interview with Kojo Ali, a reporter with the *Tribune*, when there was a knock at my office door.

I ignored the pounding, letting Kojo complete his question. "I appreciate your patience," he said. He scooted forward in his seat. "As I promised, I won't dwell on the charges around Keesa Bishop's death, but are you willing to go on record about your decision?"

I looked over Kojo's shoulder, paying attention to the knocks now. "I'm not exactly ready to preach a sermon on it. I've advocated bringing harsher charges against two kids who instigated the final attack on Keesa."

Kojo shifted in his seat, sizing me up. "And you're comfortable the other four had no hand in that night's events?"

"Based on witness accounts and testimony of the ringleading kids, yeah. They were guilty of mindless chatter and bullshitting, Kojo." I waved a hand at him. "Clean that up, but you know what I mean. As long as they accept stringent community service and mentoring, I don't think we can afford to throw them away. Maybe they'll be able to keep their younger brothers and sisters from running with bad crowds."

Kojo nodded but didn't make eye contact. "We can only hope." He looked over his shoulder before leaning in toward my desk. "One last question, if you don't mind, something to lighten the mood." He adjusted the wire-rimmed glasses on his nose. "Any truth to the rumors about you and LaRae Summers? Give me something provocative, brother."

I stood and stepped around the desk. I'd been back from my

L.A. trip for two weeks now, but LaRae and I were still the talk of the town. *Extra, Entertainment Tonight, BET Nightly News*—they and others had covered the premiere and speculated about the new face at LaRae's side. "Ah, Kojo," I said, shaking the brother's hand firmly, "a player can't kiss and tell, now. You can print the fact that LaRae and I are good buddies."

It felt funny to play coy with the press, after seeing celebs do it on my show every week. Truth be told, the foreplay in LaRae's limo had been a warmup for a very energetic night. Back at the Ritz, I'd moved into her suite, loving her first on the king-size bed, then the couch in the front room, then the marble bathroom sink. In the morning, we'd bathed and had a sensual breakfast—strawberries, kiwi, whipped cream, and a very supple quiche—before catching our flight.

I could tell LaRae was a little rusty, in fact I was guessing I was her first lover since her arrival in Chicago, but everything was second nature to her. She quickly adjusted to my rhythms and eventually took the lead. She wasn't just about getting hers, though: She'd insisted on seeing my face through every thrust, suck, and kiss. We had bonded, been truly intimate, even though she had played celibate since we'd returned home. I was lucky to get a phone call every few days.

Kojo looked down at me, his eyes full of intuition. "Uh-hum, just buddies." He continued scribbling on his notepad. "Tell me this. She as good as her love scenes?"

I winked and steered him toward the door, which was shaking again with someone's impatient bangs. I opened the door and stepped out of Kojo's way. Tony stood on the other side, looking like he'd been to hell and back. His fade was raggedy around the edges, his tie was crooked, and I wasn't sure his shoes matched his beige pinstriped slacks.

Tony looked between us, relentlessly grinding the black toothpick in his mouth. "I need to see you in my office," he said, nodding absentmindedly at Kojo.

"Let me walk Kojo out, I'll be right there."

Tony slapped Kojo on the shoulder. "He's a grown man, he'll find his way. Come on, now."

I said "Peace" to Kojo and followed the taskmaster back through the main floor, over to the other end and into his massive office. I lingered in the doorway as Tony blazed a path to his mahogany desk, which sat in front of a window that made up his entire back wall. He bent over and punched the speaker button on his phone. "Okay, Skip, Danny, I've got O.J. on the line." He looked at me, still standing and planting his hands on his hips. "Skip and Danny wanted you to hear this directly."

I slid my hands into my pockets, feeling my temples clench. Trying to ignore the hammering of my heart, I stepped closer to the desk and matched Tony's posture. "Good afternoon, gentlemen." For some reason, I couldn't find my usual rhythm: My wit well had suddenly run dry.

Skip's phlegm-filled voice rang over the speaker. "O.J., hey partner. Look, Danny and I met with our board this morning about some issues we're having with the banks. Long story short, we've had some crises at a couple other stations and cash flow has tightened. In order to get an extension on some loans, our bankers forced us to sign up for specific cost-cutting measures. These must be implemented *this month*. It won't surprise you that WHOT was first on the list."

I crossed my arms, glowering at Tony across his desk. There were times I felt like he'd sold me a bill of shit when he lured me to Chicago. Here I'd doubled the morning audience in ten months, and the station was still drowning in red ink.

Danny came onto the line, clearly playing the role of executioner. "O.J., we're taking drastic steps to get WHOT into the black. The afternoon and evening drive-time programming is going to go syndicated; we're looking at some ABC Radio Networks programming. That'll save us a ton on staff headcount, benefits, etcetera. We'll keep the nighttime 'quiet storm' deejays, but otherwise, yours is the only local programming remaining intact."

I rubbed my eyes and shook my head.

"You should be flattered, son. Bear in mind Plan B was to go ahead and switch the format to country music, starting next week."

"You're kidding." The words oozed out of me. I'd set up a life here now, not only for myself but most importantly for Cherrelle. She was loving Saint Andrew, making new friends, and progressing well with her grief therapist. I'd be damned if they'd close me down now.

Skip hopped back on the line. "Anyway, everyone has to share the pain behind this restructuring, O.J. We're going to retain your on-air talent, Liz and Trey, but the business-management deal we had, where we fully funded a full-time manager for you? Can't do it anymore."

I grabbed my class ring, toying with it to release nervous energy. "Well, maybe we can work something out where Mitchell goes to part-time."

Danny got a good laugh out of that one. "No, no, no. We'll still help you manage your career, son, but Rod Stark will now handle that for you. He'll simply charge by the hour and be a more focused advocate for you."

I frowned and stared into the speakerphone. "Who's gonna handle all the accounting analysis you've had Mitchell doing?"

Skip coughed into the phone. "This is all business, son, don't forget that. Now that we're simplifying the operation, we won't need much accounting help. We can certainly get it cheaper from Accountemps or someplace anyway."

Tony and I stared at each other, hands still on hips.

"I trust you're okay with all this," Skip said. "Again, we're telling you personally because we value your contribution. Go home and get rested for tomorrow's broadcast." He took a beat. "Tony, we need to talk off line."

Tony scratched his head and picked up the phone receiver. "One second, Skip." He mashed his mute button and looked back at me. "I'm going to tell Mitchell at the end of the day. Do you want to go with me?"

I sauntered toward the door and cracked it before stopping in my tracks. "I owe him that much," I sighed, throwing up my hands. I shut Tony's door behind me and tried to straighten my back and take the pissed look off my face. No sense encouraging rumors among the sales reps, secretaries, and clerks.

I checked my watch when I got back to the office. It was almost two-thirty, late in the day for me, but I knew I needed to wait around to speak to Mitchell with Tony. Trying not to think of the implications this would have on Mitchell's marriage, I sat at my desk and hopped onto my AOL account to get some business taken care of.

I had dealt with about twenty-five e-mails when my phone rang. I grabbed the receiver and cradled it against my ear. "Yeah?"

The voice made my heart sink. "You never returned my call." It was Marian.

I willed myself to keep calm. "Hello. I've been meaning to get back to you." She and I had been playing phone tag ever since she'd called me on my cell phone, the morning I awoke in LaRae's bed. She'd thought she was real cute then.

You sleeping with that ho you was on TV with?

I'd ignored her then and promised to call her the following week to make arrangements for her to spend time with Cherrelle, this despite the fact Cherrelle had no interest in seeing her great-grandmother.

"You're not right," she said. "You mighty hard to catch all of a sudden, now that I got proof you're a whoremonger."

"Marian," I said, continuing my typing as a form of stress release, "you're not helping anybody using those types of words. It's none of your business whom I see in my free time, as long as it doesn't impact Cherrelle."

"A leopard never loses his spots, O.J. Do you really think our family has forgotten how you treated Keesa when she was pregnant, the lengths you drove her to?"

I sat back from the keyboard, crossed my legs. "Do we want to talk about history, is that the idea? Keesa was the most honorable member of your family, as far as I can tell, and like me she was no saint. Frankly, I don't understand where this is coming from. Keesa made it sound like you hardly helped watch Cherrelle once you got remarried."

Marian's voice grew gruff. "That's not true, and you couldn't prove Keesa said that anyway. It took me a while to get Bill comfortable with us watching the baby, so maybe Keesa's feelings were hurt a couple of times. I am not my daughter, though, O.J. My record's been clean for decades."

I frowned at my image in the PC's monitor. It was true, Marian was a model citizen compared to Keesa's mother, who was still roaming the streets seeking the next crack high. Marian had retired from a secretarial position at the Department of Housing and Urban Development, and had a tidy little row house on one of the nicer streets in northwest Washington, near Catholic University. That said, she had no plausible claim to Cherrelle.

"I'm a perfectly fit father," I reminded her. "What don't you understand? My show's blowing up, just been syndicated to D.C., matter of fact. I have Cherrelle enrolled in an excellent school, and spend every minute away from work with her. Keesa moved here because she felt I was a good influence, for God's sake." I paused, then asked the question on my mind. "Is this about you

wanting a piece of my income?" If Marian got a share of legal custody, she'd get a piece of my court-ordered child support. "I know
Keesa had some concerns about your hubby's gambling debts
when you married. Things okay there?"

"You know what," Marian said, spitting her words out rapid-fire
now, "I was trying to be patient with you, O.J., but forget it. We
can handle this through the courts. I would have thought you'd
want to avoid that, seeing as how you're a minor celebrity now."

My voice rose. "What's that supposed to mean?"

"That means, your new fans in Chicago and D.C. won't care
about my family's skeletons. They may take an interest in yours."

I'd be lying to say that didn't ignite a low flame of fear in my
heart. "Oh, hell no. You're not going to blackmail me." I caught
my breath and crammed a string of banned words, reminded myself this woman was old enough to be my grandmother. "You
really are desperate, aren't you? If you need help through a financial rough patch, just tell me."

"That's the second time you've insulted me. I won't stand for
it, O.J."

"Hang up, then." She did.

I slammed the phone down and stared back at my image in the
PC monitor. I didn't know whose day would wind up worse, mine
or Mitchell's.

Nikki

I thought about taking a running leap so I could reach the passenger seat in Angie's monstrous Lincoln Navigator, but Marvin stopped me. Acting like the big brother he is, he wordlessly stepped forward and grabbed my forearm. I locked eyes with him as he lifted me up and in. Angie, who's due in a little over a month, was practically bursting, but Marvin had let his wife make her own way with a stool they kept in their garage. At the moment, he was more concerned with me and his future nephew or niece.

"Thank you, big brother." I smiled his way and closed the door. Marvin stood back, waved at us, and headed back into "South Fork Mansion," my nickname for their new house. A custom-built three-story made of burnt sienna brick, it sits on a manicured wooded lot, part of a gated community. It's a full income-tax bracket above me and Mitchell's means, that's for sure.

Angie revved the engine and reached over, patting me on the knee. "How's it feel? Today makes about six weeks, right?"

"It doesn't feel real yet, frankly." I tried to smooth my overcoat and make sure my blouse was on straight. I was starting to feel self-conscious about how well my work clothes fit. A few more weeks and it would be time to bite the bullet, hit the Motherhood store, and hope I'd one day fit back into my favorite outfits.

Angie drove down their long, winding driveway and made a left. As we came to the subdivision's gated entranceway, she looked over at me. "You'll get used to everything. It'll help having Mitchell back home."

"You're assuming I want him back." Angie was the only person

I'd told about the Gina incident. I had sworn her to secrecy, not wanting Marvin to meddle, and had decided not to tell Mama, who'd probably say it was me who drove Mitchell into her arms.

Angie kept her eyes on the road, didn't flinch. "Oh, you want him back. Whatever happened in that hotel, Nikki, I don't believe Mitchell was unfaithful."

"Maybe we should trade husbands then." I licked my lips nervously. I wanted to believe Mitchell, had been willing to hear his explanation out, but the pain of hearing Gina answer his phone was still too fresh. We were talking every couple of days, if only for a few minutes, and he had come by the house a couple times to mow the lawn, clean out the fireplace, and unplug the toilet in our master bath. He still hadn't spent the night, though. With everything going on, it was starting to feel like a reverse game of emotional chicken.

"Stop it," Angie said. "I think he's close to coming home." Angie waved at the completely unnecessary guard at her front gate and pulled into traffic. "Marvin's working on him. Your husband is still coming to grips with his role in all this. I think he finally understands he failed you with respect to Gina, you know, not shielding you from her games."

I frowned. "I think failed is a bit strong. I always loved the fact that he tolerated her for Clay's sake."

"Yeah," Angie sighed, "but Mitchell didn't stand before God with Clay and pledge his lifelong allegiance. Not to say he should literally choose you over Clay, but nothing, not even Clay, should have stood between you two."

I let my chin drop toward my chest. "I know you're not absolving me, girl."

"You're right about that, you know you were wrong. Like I said, the only reason I ever talked about your pregnancy plans with folk at church, was I assumed you were going to let Mitchell in on them."

"I know, it was my sin, and my bad."

Accelerating as we hopped on the I-57 ramp, Angie blew air between her lips. "You were wrong, but Mitchell has to forgive. Maybe getting Gina out of Illinois will help the situation, although we'll all miss seeing Clay every weekend." Despite our best legal efforts, the courts had chosen not to step in and keep Gina from moving to Atlanta. She and Clay had been there for two weeks now. She'd invited Mitchell to fly out and bring Clay back for a short stay, but after the Red Roof incident he was in no mood. He was talking about suing for full custody.

The thought of adding a legal battle to our struggles was too much for me to process right then. I let Angie's comment melt into thin air. "Girl, thanks for letting me stay over last night. I was just too exhausted to drive back home."

"Not a problem, whenever you need an ear I'm here. Especially with Marvin being off today, it's cool because I can take you into town and get you tonight. We'll have another sleepover, how's that?" She grinned. "Better take it now, I'll be out of commission any day now."

We laughed the rest of the way into town, despite the clogged highways and tight Loop traffic. I guess true friendship overrides those minor distractions. Even though I still had a headache and an anxious heart, I felt a little better as I walked through Empire's lobby.

When I got to my desk, the peaceful lift Angie gave me was erased. I had almost forgotten I had a major midmorning presentation in front of my boss, Chase Wells. All my preparation was done, of course, but butterflies mixed with the stirrings of pregnancy and I collapsed into my chair. I called my assistant, Sylvia, into my office and had her print off a fresh set of my slides. I needed to review them one last time, make sure I was ready to accentuate the key points and smoothly work in my jokes and anecdotes.

After having my morning decaf, I hurried to the little girls' room. By now it was nine-thirty and I had less than half an hour before meeting with Chase. I hopped into a stall, stripped down, and took a seat. When I felt I was finished, I inhaled anxiously and stood. Turning around, I reached for the toilet handle when the sight below stopped me cold.

The toilet water wasn't the right color. Instead of a pale yellow, it was tinted pink by a stream of red. That was when everything started to move in slow motion.

Me standing over the toilet, looking down at my panties and seeing another trail of blood, flowing from a shallow pool in their center.

My brain whirring and clicking, rejecting what I was seeing, but remembering the bouts of stomach cramping I'd fought off a couple of days before.

Desperation welling within, I hitched up my panties and slacks. Deliberately, I slid the lock on my stall open and hurriedly stepped toward the door.

The floor was slick, and my right pump went for a flight. My body followed.

When I came to, my head hurt like hell and I was turned on my side, just outside the stall. Trying to focus, I pulled my watch closer and checked the time. I'd been in here fifteen minutes and no one else had happened in?

I looked under the stall. There was more blood on the floor, by the toilet. I'd still been bleeding when I first panicked. *God.* It felt funny, but I was calling on a friend this time, not some shadowy presence good for a favor.

Please, don't let this happen, God. I know I didn't start this life the right way, but you've blessed others. Your word says children are a blessing from the Lord. I'm asking for a blessing.

My head was hurting worse now, and the strong smells of the bathroom—Pine-Sol, soap cakes, cheap perfumes, and faint whiffs of urine—weren't helping. I tried to sit up, but a new pain in my side sent me crashing back to the floor.

"Help!" My voice sounded like a little girl's. I cleared my throat, let air fill my lungs. "Help!" The massive oak bathroom door, which was fifty feet away if it was an inch, stifled and sopped up my cries like a big sponge.

My vision started to blur, and though my heart hammered with renewed anxiety, I couldn't find the energy to express it. I let my eyes close. *Think I'll nap now, God.*

I saw only pitch-black, then the silhouette of a tall man approaching me from the other end of the bathroom, which was now lit by a row of candles lining the floor.

I peered ahead. "Mitchell?"

"Not exactly." My father, Eugene Coleman himself, stepped forward from the shadows. I was oddly relieved to see Gene, especially because he was wearing the plaid flannel shirt and khaki slacks he'd worn that last night in the emergency room. It would have been too much to see him in the loud polyester suit he'd been buried in.

He stepped closer to me, bent down on one knee. "You okay, baby?"

"Don't really know, Gene."

"Still can't call me Dad, huh?"

"I tried 'Daddy' for a while, until you stood me up the tenth or twelfth time."

Gene rubbed his short 'fro. "I know, don't go there, baby. I'm here to apologize and buck you up."

"What do you mean?"

"Nikki, when you married Mitchell I thought you'd left the baggage I gave you behind. I know our, uh, problems drove you into the arms of some knuckleheads over the years, but once you and Mitchell got past his phony womanizing, you all should have been on easy street."

I stared ahead blankly.

"Apparently I did more damage than I thought. I know it's a screwy situation to be part of a blended family. When you were born, it turned my world upside down. I didn't know how to handle having two families—Jennifer and my girls, then you." Gene grimaced, switched knees. "My grandpop told me, the night he first found a sheepskin condom in my wallet, to never have kids with more than one person. 'Simplifies your life, son,' he said. Man, I didn't know how right he was."

"You simplified the situation," I shot back, surprised I didn't feel any more pain. "Just acted like I didn't exist."

"Not true. I thought about you every damn day, but Jennifer was too threatened to let me split my loyalties. No, what I did was far too common. What Mitchell's trying to do—be a father to his son while staying to loyal to you—that's one of the most courageous things a man can do."

I fought back tears.

"Mitchell is not me, Nikki. He may not be the coolest cat on the block, but he's making the best of a tough situation. Do you really think he'd cheat on you for that Gina?"

I looked down at the floor, past Gene's soiled boots. "I don't know. I mean, I don't think he would, but he is a man."

"Yeah, he's a man," Gene said, rolling his eyes, "but until he gives you reason to suspect he's doing anything more than looking out for his son, show the boy some damn trust. Sometimes I think if Jennifer had shown me that, I wouldn't have sought refuge in Red Bull, Marlboro, and Vegas. Might still be here now."

I reached forward, tears flowing now more than they had the day of my father's funeral. "Daddy, thank you. Thank you." I remembered his discretion about Mama's trickery. "You weren't perfect, but you were more of a man than I realized."

"Do this for me," he said, leaning in and nuzzling my nose with his. "You just love your husband and that little . . ."

The candles started to flicker and the room darkened. "What did you say, Daddy?"

Gene vanished, the words not making it off his lips. "That little . . ."

I grasped and groaned, waiting for him to come back. Thinking my pain was gone, I rolled onto my knees and sat up. A sharp pain ripped through me, and everything went black.

32

Mitchell

Threatened abortion. The sobering phrase rang in my ears as I drove Nikki home from the hospital. For the better part of a month now I'd held my wife at arm's length, nursing an undeniable mixture of betrayal, loss, and professional humiliation. As real as it had been, the doctor's report made my antics look increasingly self-absorbed. Playtime was over.

I had received the call from her assistant, Sylvia, in the midst of a teleconference with Sharon from Starlight Books. Now that I was days away from the unemployment line it was hard to not feel desperation for a book deal, but Sharon was playing me like a marionette. Apparently she'd switched publishers, and had started the process of advocating *Out of His Shadow* all over again. It had been over a month since she had first contacted me, and I was ready for her to put up or shut up. All that faded into background noise when Sylvia clicked my other line.

Apparently she had grown concerned when Nikki disappeared for half an hour, then finally found her in the ladies' room. Sylvia had called an ambulance and Nikki was already in the emergency room at St. Joseph, the closest hospital in her HMO network. I'd raced to the hospital, comforted Nik as best as I could, then we'd waited for Dr. Omawole, her obstetrician.

Based on the good doctor's review, Nikki had experienced enough vaginal bleeding to cause some concern. The term "threatened abortion" meant that we now had an officially at-risk pregnancy, and that news hit me like a head-butt from Warren Sapp. It took sitting in that hospital room for me to realize that with this

pregnancy, I was on uncharted ground. I'd been completely ex-
cluded from Gina's prenatal experiences with Clay. I was an experienced parent, but as an expectant parent I was as virginal as A. C.
Green on his wedding day.

Once we'd been in the car a few minutes, with distant rumbles
of thunder and the whizzing of traffic serving as our soundtrack, I
tentatively reached for the radio. We'd stayed silent since shutting
the car doors and it was bugging me out. I tuned in some gospel
on WGCI. It was a raucous choir selection, Donnie McClurkin I
think.

Nikki's voice squeaked at me from the passenger seat. "Something more laid back, please. I know God cares, but I don't need it
shouted at me right now."

I punched in some smooth jazz and placed a hand on hers.
"The doctor said twenty-five percent of pregnant women experience this. It just means you'll have to be monitored more closely."
I stroked her hand. "We'll do this together. I'll get the few things I
have from Mom and Dad's tonight."

Nikki turned toward me. I could feel the warmth of her stare.
"What if I have to go on bed rest?"

I played at being brave. "We'll cross that bridge if we come to
it. She sounded like she wouldn't know until the second trimester."

"I don't know how being out of commission for months, not
even mentioning maternity leave, might affect things for me at
Empire."

Well, that was that. I forced a peaceful smile onto my face.
There was no way I was telling her about my pink slip now. I'd
held out for a couple of weeks, feeling our tense relationship
couldn't handle it, but was ready to come clean now that I was
moving back home. I had my WHOT severance check coming
soon, but given the steady flow of bills it was already spoken for.
A few more weeks and it would be time to break open my mal-
nourished 401(k). This was not where I saw myself being at thirty,

still getting laid off jobs and staying a step ahead of the repo man. I started sweating just thinking about it.

Playtime was over, but as I heard the anxiety in Nikki's voice, I realized the ball had just moved. I would have to tell her about my "employment challenge" once I'd worked out an alternative. Revealing things now would just increase the fear, worry, and regret dotting my wife's beautiful, ashen face.

We rolled into the garage a few minutes later. I pulled Nikki from the car and carried her upstairs to the bedroom. As rain began to tap against the windows, I laid her down and looked into her warm, tired eyes. "I have something for you," I whispered, and reached into my jacket pocket. I retrieved the homemade card, a loud little thing made of orange and yellow construction paper, and laid it onto her chest.

Nikki picked up Clay's card, which he had mailed to me last week, and read the message spread across it in silvery glitter: *To Daddy and Nikki. I love you, Clay.* A baby-sitter had probably written it for him, but it was still sweet.

I wiped the new tears sprouting at the edges of her eyes. "You've been asking how I'm adjusting to Clay being in Atlanta," I whispered. "It's still not easy, but things like this help." I paused, took a deep breath. "You have to believe me when I say that nothing happened with me and Gina that night."

It still turned my stomach to think of the games Gina had played at the Red Roof Inn. I could never prove it—Dale would never cooperate with me—but my sense was she'd set both of us up that night. "She thought she could drive us apart by making me think I'd slept with her. When you kept your cool, when she answered the phone? That's what got her to admit nothing had happened." I rubbed my forehead, still replaying the night's events. "How can she be fit to keep Clay?"

Nikki didn't respond at first, just ran her fingers along my right cheek. "You really think she's unfit? I despise whatever game she was playing with you, but look at how far she's come since having Clay. I knew the girl long before you did, Mitchell, she's come through a lot of childhood trauma. She's a mess in some ways, but maybe with this CNN job she's on the road to making a good life for herself and for Clay."

I took the card from Nikki and took both of her hands in mine. "Only time will tell. I let Gina treat our marriage like a piñata these last few months, and I was wrong. I should have wedged myself between you and her, regardless of the cost. Please forgive me for that."

"Oh, Mitchell." Nikki leaned forward and pecked me on the lips. "We both let her wreak havoc, we were learning on the job. We'll get this blended-family act down yet." Her head dipped toward her chest, and she inhaled. "The important thing is that you do have Clay, regardless of what happens with this baby. With all my issues, I knew something would go wrong." Her words trailed off, choked by sorrow and guilt.

"No," I said, smiling and leaning down until my nose touched hers. "Nothing is going wrong with this pregnancy. Will it be an easy one, will it be by the book? Maybe not. That's life. I'm here with you, for every tumble down the valley, and every flight of fancy. I'm here, Nikki. I love Clay, and we'll get something worked out to keep him in our lives, but you come first. I love you."

We pressed our lips together tentatively, feeling the weight of weeks spent apart, then melded together and wiped the slate clean. I inhaled Nikki's sweet scent, her honey-tinged breath, and ran my hands down her shoulders and across her back as I gently lay on the bed next to her. In that moment, I prayed God would purge my soul of its burdens: my pending unemployment, the ever-present tease of the book deal, and today's news. I wanted my kisses to fill Nikki with every ounce of the peace, love, and comfort she deserved.

33

O.J.

I sat in the backseat of Tony's silver M3 BMW, trying to slow my pulse and enjoy the evening. It wouldn't be easy. Just before Tony, Mitchell, and Trey had picked me up, I'd completed the questionnaire that Marian's lawyers would use for the official deposition. Each question had nudged my blood pressure a little higher, increased the speed of my blood's boil. When I was done, the document had lain before me like a cold, damning portrait of the year surrounding Cherrelle's birth.

My refusal to use condoms with Keesa, once I'd had her wrapped around my finger.

The number of other bedmates I'd had during the time she became pregnant.

My constant denial that I could be the father.

My attempt to buy Keesa's silence with favors from my church's board of trustees.

Her desperate attempt to get my attention, with the help of a stiletto.

My long-distance fathering from Atlanta, and my failure since to ever get married or build a "conventional" home for my daughter.

It all stared back at me like an indictment, and as the guys' jokes and sports talk flowed around me, I couldn't do much more than ball my fists.

"O.J., everything okay?" Tony glanced at me in his rear-view mirror. "Need me to turn up the heat?"

"I'm all right," I replied, patting the leather seat beneath me. "My ass is still a little frosty though." Now that November had arrived, I was getting another taste of the Windy City's winters. They were inhumane.

"You need to lighten up," Tony said, looking over at Mitchell, who was in the passenger seat. "Remember, this is Mitchell's going-away party, and he's happy."

Mitchell tugged at his black corduroy cap. "Happy would be too strong a word. I'm just trying to blow off some steam tonight, get this stress off my back." He and Tony nearly looked like twins in their black bomber jackets. I didn't know how they stayed warm in those; I'd brought the heavy reinforcements, a padded leather trench coat, matching gray scarf, and cowhide gloves so thick the fingers looked like sausages.

"You got a point, it never pays to wallow in your stress," I said, turning and looking out the window. "You're a trouper, Mitchell." It occurred to me then that I was going to miss the guy. Not only had he come through for me professionally in recent months, but a personal bond had developed. We were even comparing notes now on our child-custody lawsuits, comparing strategy and the pros and cons of our attorneys. Mitchell had also convinced me to support the Chicagoland Mentoring Program's latest outreach efforts to at-risk kids, some of whom included the kids in Marquise's gang. He'd proven himself a friend.

In truth, between chasing ratings and rearing Cherrelle, I hadn't made many friends in Chicago. Most of them were in the car with me right then. I didn't need to lose any.

We were sending Mitchell off by supporting LaRae's poetry slam. She'd reserved the entire space at Crossroads, a Black-owned restaurant and club on the near South Side. It promised to be a good time, if only because it had LaRae's celebrity backing and entertainment including Jonathan Butler and Miki Howard. It was just us guys rolling tonight, given that Nikki wasn't feeling well, Tony was in between girlfriends, and Trey was looking to get away from his fiancée.

The main ballroom at Crossroads was lit by soft glowing candles and was dotted by low round tables draped in red cloth. We stepped inside the door and were immediately surrounded. Trey and I had to fend off some groupies, Tony and Mitchell knew half the room from high school, and of course Ms. LaRae darted over to us, bringing along an entourage.

LaRae pecked a kiss onto each of the other guys' cheeks, then sidled up along me and grabbed my ass.

I held her hand there, looked into her playful eyes. "May I help you?"

"Oh, maybe later." She kissed me on the lips, then stood back to welcome some ballers entering behind us. I watched her move through the crowd and admired her outfit: black skirt kissing the middle of her thighs, black fishnet top over a sleek silk blouse that clung to every curve. I wondered how I'd let a month pass since she'd allowed me into her private, precious little world. I was damn near celibate again, but it hit me that I'd held out for some reason. I needed to know why LaRae was playing me like a yo-yo.

After I'd hit the dance floor with the guys and a few anonymous babes, I eased over to the bar and tugged her away from a gaggle of young poets waiting to go on stage. I played at dancing with her, grabbing her around the waist and gyrating against her as I pulled her close. "Can I get some of your time?"

LaRae held me close, flooding me with her body heat and perfume. "Did you complete that deposition today?"

I frowned. She didn't need to infect things with that topic.

"I take it that means yes? You are keeping your cool, right?"

I crossed my fingers and held up my right hand. "I promise, I've only cussed Marian's lawyer out once so far."

"It's only been a couple of weeks. You've got to stay chill, O.J."

"They're already screwing with my show, you know that? Marian's got some attorney with press connections, so her accusations are getting notice. The two latest stations looking at me for syndication? They're both dragging their feet now, say they're concerned whether this suit's gonna make me look like a hypocrite." Skip and Danny had been too happy to share that bit of news with me.

LaRae rolled her eyes. "The only thing that will endanger your program is you showing your ass over this suit. Marian's not your problem, O.J." She stepped back from me but held my hands tight. "You're your own worst enemy. When are you going to forgive yourself for what you did to Keesa?"

LaRae already knew the dirty details of my past, but her question made me feel I was filling out that damn deposition again. The boiling sensation returning to my chest, I pulled her close and shouted into her ear. "Is there an empty square foot in this place, somewhere we can be alone?"

She sighed, rolled her neck, and led me through the crowd and back into the lobby. We walked past the front security table and entered a small office off the hallway. The size of a small coatroom, the windowless space had a square wooden table, a matching chair, and a scummy floor covered with boxes of T-shirts, glasses, and other giveaways for the night's event. LaRae walked to the table and hopped on top, taking a seat and pointing at the chair. "Sit, talk to me."

I made my way through the boxes, stepped around her crossed legs, and took a seat. I looked up at her and bit my lower lip. "You realize you're asking more of me than you've shared yourself."

She pivoted on the table, turned until her hips and thighs were right in front of me. "Meaning?"

"Meaning we've hardly been as intimate since L.A. as I'd expected."

"We talk every day. You were expecting more bootay?"

"Forget the sex, for the moment at least. What happened to just plain goin' out? We hang here and there, but it's starting to feel arm's-length."

"I've had some new things on my plate," she said, letting her legs kick slowly. "Between planning this poetry slam and mentoring new writers like Mitchell, my days and evenings are eaten up, Mr. Man. And you're not very accessible at nighttime."

"You're right about that," I replied with no hint of apology. "My daughter is a full-time job. I don't know if I appreciated that before we lost Keesa. You've got to work with me where I am, LaRae, that's if you really want to wade in these waters."

LaRae clasped her hands. "Look, I told you about Gray."

"I got the sense I missed a few highlights. You've mentioned your mom, the fact you never knew your dad. I still don't get it, though. What's lurking in the background, to drive you into the arms of a man old enough to be your grandfather?"

"Father would be closer to the truth. He's not that old."

I crossed my legs and leaned against the chair's stiff back. "Okay. So?"

Cornered, LaRae looked down briefly and cracked her window for me. Some of it I'd heard, most was new. Uncle T, the stern but loving uncle who had raised her, had died the year she started college. Her blossoming beauty had kicked in at the same time, just as her writing talent provided the self-esteem she'd lacked during her first few relationships, if you called having semi trains run on you a "relationship." Then there was the miscarriage, a high-school trauma she'd used as writing material but had little interest in detailing while seated in a cramped storage room.

I let LaRae's words settle, drift into the air, then took her hands in mine. "It's a wonder you even like men," I whispered. "You deserve better."

She looked over my shoulder, sighed. "You said you wanted to listen, O.J. You don't have to make it better."

I sat back in the chair, rubbed at my eyes. While we were being so open, I couldn't leave the question unasked. "You're still leaving me with one mystery. The elusive Jason, is this another ex?"

LaRae's eyes darkened and I felt her body stiffen.

"What's the story, LaRae? Come on, tell it to me as if it's one of your books."

Her hands slipped from mine. She looked past me to the chipped paint overhead. "We don't need to go there, at least not yet."

I rubbed my forehead and stood, kicking the chair away. "Never mind, then. What does a brother have to do to gain entrance behind the iron curtain?"

She kept her back to me, still staring at the wall. "I'll tell you when you've done it."

Shaking my head, I strode to the door, stepped back into the hallway, and slammed it behind me. Stalking back through the lobby and into the heart of the party, I was ready to shed LaRae like a snakeskin. Twice now she'd told me I hadn't earned full disclosure, and frankly I was out of energy. Cherrelle was spending the night at the McIntoshes'; it was time to make use of a free night, let down my shield and invite myself back to some girl's place.

I probably would have done just that, too, if not for the next cat that crossed my path. It was the same joker I'd seen at LaRae's Afrocentric signing and the one who'd been hobnobbing with Gray Philips at the *Take It All* premiere. At that moment, time, and place, it felt like one coincidence too many.

Like LaRae, he was dressed all in black: leather blazer, stretch T-shirt, straight-leg Levi's. We made brief eye contact. He blinked first and looked away. I stayed put at the bar and watched him worm his way toward a table near the back, where he sat and looked from left to right as if searching for someone. LaRae, probably.

He kept checking his watch, and when LaRae stepped back into the room I watched his eyes follow her from the dance floor to the bar, then up to the main stage. As she took the mike and began her introduction of the night's spoken-word stars, I went over to Tony and Mitchell's table. Trey, whom I'd last seen swapping spit with a big-boned sister who looked like Monique, was nowhere to be found.

I knelt down between the guys, who were seated across from a couple of girls who looked college-age. Mr. Mystery was paying for his drinks and shoving back from his table. "We need to go for a ride," I whispered. "Either that or let me have your keys, Tony."

They both turned toward me, eyes narrowed.

I nodded toward the back, pointed out homeboy. "He and I need to talk."

34

O.J.

I was afraid we'd lose the brother if he had a better parking space than we did, but as we followed him out of Crossroads he stepped quickly down the same side street on which we'd stashed Tony's coupe.

We left roughly a block between him and us, Tony and Mitchell staying a few feet in front of me and carrying on with loud, meaningless banter. I didn't want homeboy to focus on ominous footsteps in the dark, might tip him off and get him running.

We continued in calm, stealthy pursuit, glass crunching under our loafers. Homeboy walked with long, confident strides, his shoulders held high and his arms tight at his sides. Although his face had a youthful quality, his walk spelled street smarts, years spent navigating neighborhoods far tougher than this one. I was hoping he wasn't packin'.

Underneath the dim glow of a street lamp, he pivoted suddenly and stuck a key into the side of an eighties-era 300 ZX, dull red with white trim. He was several cars in front of Tony's ride, so we hopped in and waited as homeboy took his sweet time to start the ZX. When he pulled into the street, we followed dutifully.

Fifteen minutes later, we'd cruised further south when Tony started looking to his left and right, his eyes narrowing anxiously and checking street signs. The more burned-out buildings, liquor stores, and storefront churches we passed, the more anxious Tony became. "Oh hell no, O.J.," he bellowed, pausing to grab a toothpick from his change compartment. "This fool's headed toward the heart of Cabrini Green. I'm all for helping you, but I don't drive my good car into the Green."

I pointed ahead at the ZX. "He's not going into the projects, man, come on. Don't you guys mentor kids over here?"

"Yeah," Mitchell piped up from the backseat, "during daylight hours usually."

"Hey look, no shame in my game," Tony snapped, "I would never be here this time of night if O.J. didn't have us on this wild-goose chase. I'm turning around and—"

"He's stopping," I shouted, punching Tony's shoulder. The ZX had pulled into a space along a block of crumbling two-story apartment homes. "He's over there." I pointed toward a brick-faced unit a block down. "Slow down."

Tony looked to his left and right for a space, trying to park a block back from homeboy's ride. No luck. We'd have to pass the ZX and park further down, walk back to see where he was headed. Tony shifted gears and we rolled toward the ZX as the brother climbed out on the driver's side, his head down.

When he looked up suddenly, just as we rolled past, I saw the gun in his hand. No idea what caliber it was, whether it was Smith & Wesson, Glock, Magnum, or whatever. I'm one who believes the Second Amendment applies only to trained militias. I hate guns. The sight of that barrel, combined with the glint in the dude's eye, had me ready to crap my Pampers.

Tony was impressed too. He slammed his brakes instinctively. "Shit!"

Before Tony could hit the gas, which I sensed he was ready to do, Mitchell whispered into the air, slow and steady. "You drive off, you're asking for a car full of bullet holes." His eyes met mine in the rear-view mirror. "Our cover's blown, O.J. Just talk to him, let's end this peacefully."

I inhaled and let my window down, bathing the car in a bracing blast of wind chill. I made my gaze as rock-hard as possible, stared back at the dude with annoyance instead of fear. "What up?"

The brother held the gun in front of him loosely, angled more toward the BMW's engine than toward us. "You got a beef?" His Southern drawl took the edge off his words. "I don't know you brothers."

I felt my eyebrows jump. "No beef, bro. Just a question."

He gripped the pistol suddenly and flipped it into a holster beneath his jacket. "Don't you niggas know better than to trail a brother 'cross town? Good way to get yourself shot."

"It ain't that type of party, hoss," I said, shaking my head. A bubble of laughter escaped and I kept the rest down. Hell of a misunderstanding, but this was still serious business. "Tell me something."

"Who is you, for me to tell you a damn thang?"

I'm a Southerner, but this Negro's country accent was starting to work my nerves. I reached forward, extending a hand. "Name's O.J. Peters. WHOT FM, 'The O.J. Peters Way'?"

"Never heard of you," he said, taking my hand in a gruff, brief shake. "Only been in town a few months, probably headin' back to Memphis soon."

"Well anyway, I'm a radio man, uh—your name?"

"Jason."

I glanced quickly at Tony, then back at Mitchell. *Jason, from Memphis. LaRae's hometown.* I hadn't told either one the specific name I was concerned with, but they sensed instantly that the drama had just deepened.

"Jason, huh?" I looked back up at him, reminded myself he was in fact packin'. "Jason, uh, what business you got with LaRae Summers?"

The bulge of his eyes, all the more vivid against the dark night, made my stomach clench. "Who the hell is LaRae Summers?"

I glanced at Tony's dashboard, tightening my fists. "She's a friend of mine, Jason, and based on how much I've seen you around her, I'm guessing she's a friend of yours too. And ain't nothing wrong with that," I added, for the benefit of his trigger finger.

"I told you I don't know that trick."

Tony tapped my knee. "Forget it," he whispered.

I couldn't let go now. I opened the car door and shut it behind me as I stood to face Jason. The night air blasted me again and I zipped my trench up before stuffing my hands into its pockets. Jason was taller and leaner than me, and upon closer inspection was probably no more than twenty, if that. Wet behind the ears. I backed off a bit and leaned against the car. "Here's the deal, Jason. Since you don't know LaRae, I'll just tell you what she means to *me*, confidentially. I've been seeing her for a couple months now. She's beautiful, intelligent, independent, and an amazing lover." I kept my eyes on his, trying to catch a flinch of betrayal, jealousy, or rage. "I just may be in love with her. That's why I'm sweating you, 'cause you seem as interested in her as I am."

Jason laughed, placed his hands near his hips, near that gun. "You think I'm some crazy-ass stalker or somethin'?"

I held my hands up. I'd had a one-track mind: jealous lover, crazy-ass ex-boyfriend, etcetera. With LaRae being a celebrity in her own right, there was a possibility he was some kook. Why had I brought Tony and Mitchell into this? An array of numbing headlines, all of them describing our deaths, flashed across my mind. "I was guessing you were an ex-lover maybe, come back to win her over."

Jason chuckled softly and shrugged his shoulders. "Givin' me too much credit, partner."

Just behind him, on the front stoop of the nearest apartment unit, a short, slight Latina girl with a bulging belly stepped outside. She crossed her arms over a thin sundress, over which she'd draped a woolly purple sweater. She called in our direction. "Jason?" She peered our way, letting her eyes adjust to the dark. "Come in, now," she said in accented English. "Come in, now, it's cold as hell out here. You worrying me."

I didn't want him to go, not just yet. "Look, man," I said, pulling out a business card, "I'm not gonna make you defy your little woman there, especially her being in a family way and all. You wanna talk about you and LaRae, call me."

"Told you I don't know the bitch." His dry, exhausted tone took the sting out of his words. He turned away and faced his little *chica*, who was tapping a foot impatiently. "Suggest you fools get outta here while you can." As I stood watching his back, Jason marched up the icy surface of the small grassy hill. His back was ramrod straight, his pace was swift, but I swear his hands, swinging loosely at his sides, were shaking with fear.

35

Nikki

I sat up in bed, turned around, and started flipping the three fat pillows behind me, searching for the right combination and positioning. Nothing felt right, and I was getting pissed. If I had to endure another day of bed rest, I at least deserved to be comfortable. Mitchell had done his best to fluff the pillows for me before leaving for work, and had even left a breakfast tray with sliced bananas, bagels, applesauce, and orange juice on my nightstand. He was an angel, but his fluffing skills left something to be desired.

I had been all ready to go into work the morning before, when new waves of nausea and some spotty bleeding sent me back to the hospital. Mitchell had driven me, and the entire ride had been blanketed in silence. I stayed cool, and so did he, except for the small tear in his right eye. I pretended not to notice.

Dr. Omawole checked me out and assured me we were okay, but scheduled me for biweekly updates and made third-trimester bed rest official. "Barring a miracle," was how she put it. I swear, it was starting to look like I was going to fail Mitchell, myself, and most importantly, this little struggling life. I had thought that deceiving Mitchell and nearly losing his love had been my biggest scare, but in the last few weeks I'd discovered new levels of terror. Terror driven, above all, by the fear I'd set the stage for all this with every poorly chosen lover who'd crawled in and out of my bed, especially those who'd left the type of personal stamp that required medical treatment.

Once I had primped and twisted my pillows into a more effective cushion, I lay back with a copy of *Variety* magazine and let Star and her girls on *The View* play in the background. Willing my mind to go blank, I didn't look up again until I heard a door slam downstairs.

Next thing I knew, I heard feet pounding on the downstairs carpet, then heard them hit my stairwell. My heart jumped for a minute, until I remembered LaRae's call from the night before. She had wanted to come visit me, but couldn't stop by until to-day. Mitchell had hidden a key for her under the welcome mat outside.

The bedroom door burst open and Ms. LaRae stood there, draped in a bright red beret and heavy plaid overcoat. She was in her stocking feet only, having thankfully removed boots that were probably caked with snow. In her arms was a vase overflowing with bubbly, bright poinsettias. "Look at you," she said, chuckling and stepping into the room. "You look too healthy to be on bed rest already, girl."

"I'm not on long-term rest yet," I said, sitting up straight and losing my pillows' sweet spot all over again. "My doctor just wanted me to take it easy a couple days, then go on half-days un-til I'm sure there's no more damn surprises."

LaRae frowned playfully. "Nikki. You're a churchgoing woman and mother-to-be now. Clean it up."

"Oh, please. No point in my fronting with God. You know I'm gonna be on bed rest for my entire third trimester? Three months stuck in front of this mindless boob tube. Even with digital cable, I can't find anything worth watching."

"Look at it this way," LaRae replied. "You won't have to fight these crazy Christmas shopping crowds the next couple weeks. Guess where I'm headed soon as I leave here? I haven't bought the first gift yet."

I smiled despite myself. "Yeah, that'll be Mitchell's job this year."

LaRae crossed her arms and leaned against the doorway. "Hey, I have an idea for how you can spend your time on rest. *Read.* That's what we authors count on."

"I have no problem reading for three, four hours a day. After that, my eyes get tired."

"Well, however you pass the time, you do what's necessary to protect that child."

I was really glad LaRae had come by. Neither Angie nor Leslie, much as I love them, could have empathized with me at that moment. My heart fluttered as I tried to find the right words. "The idea I can literally protect this pregnancy's a joke really, right?"

LaRae looked away from me and smacked her lips. She looked back up, met my gaze, then walked to the cushioned chair in front of our dresser. She pulled it over to my side of the bed and slowly took a seat. "Talk to me, Nikki. I won't sugarcoat anything."

"It's just," I said, fiddling with my thumbs. "It's just . . ." Suddenly I was feeling self-conscious about my now-tight, rumpled silk pajamas and loud red hair wrap. LaRae, who sat a couple feet away removing her coat, made me extra-self-conscious, given her tailored maroon pantsuit and smart navy silk blouse.

"It's just," I continued, "I'm hoping you can relate to my fears of losing this baby. I never thought there'd be a question of me having kids when I wanted them, you know? I mean, I spent ages fourteen to twenty-nine *dodging* sperm. Now I'm thirty, and if this time doesn't work out . . ." I carefully looked into LaRae's eyes. The strength of her stare empowered me. "I don't know how I'd handle not being able to be a mother. I never knew how much I valued it, not until I saw it wouldn't come easy. Does that make any sense?"

LaRae inhaled, shook her head, and began wringing her hands. When she looked back up at me, her gaze had hardened. "You'll survive whatever happens, Nikki, because you're strong. I may not have known you that long, but I can read your character pretty well. I also know you'll survive, because as you know, I've survived one miscarriage myself."

I sniffed a tear out of my nostrils. "One, or two?" It had been a few months since our conversation at the concert, but I swore she'd mentioned two failed pregnancies.

Silence again. LaRae recovered quickly. "You're going to be the first person in Chicago to know this, okay? Like I said, I've been pregnant twice and I'd say both of them were failed experiences. But only one ended in miscarriage."

I nodded soberly.

"My miscarriage was around the time I graduated high school, self-inflicted almost. I had gotten pregnant for the second time, and since I'd had a hellacious first pregnancy, the father was worthless, and I'd finally discovered a love for the arts, I didn't really want to have the baby. I admit, I didn't take good care of myself, didn't take all my vitamins or get good rest, but the real cause of the miscarriage was probably my attitude. Some might say it was a mental abortion, for all I know. I carried guilt over that until Gray helped me forgive myself."

I nodded again, shifted in my seat, and reached forward to take LaRae's hands in mine.

"I know," she said, her breath coming in short gasps, "what about the baby I did have. I was fifteen when I had him, Nikki, fourteen when my gym teacher knocked me up. My Uncle T, God rest his soul, was my guardian at the time, and he was determined to have the baby put up for adoption."

I sank a little lower in the bed. "Was that what you wanted?"

"I didn't know what I wanted. I had no direction, no purpose yet. In retrospect, I think my uncle made a pretty wise decision."

"You never had any second thoughts, separation anxiety?"

"Oh, I didn't say that. Why you think I wound up pregnant again two years later? There was always regret. Professionally, would I say it was the right move? It's hard to argue with success. But the reason I never married Gray, never got close enough to anyone else to consider marriage, is that Jason always got in the way."

I gripped her hands tighter. "Was that what you named him as a baby?"

"No," she said, looking down a second, "that's his given adult name. Jason Wheeler."

"So you've met him?"

"Not directly. Gray had family who worked in Memphis's social-services office, and was able to track down the information. We couldn't contact him directly. The most we could legally do was transmit my contact information through the social-services office, so that if he or his adoptive parents chose to arrange a meeting, they'd have the option."

"And you never heard from them."

"Well," LaRae said, sniffing back a tear of her own, "his adoptive mother called me last year to say that she had shared everything with him. His reaction wasn't promising, but he didn't rule out looking me up eventually. He's eighteen now, and last I heard he had a girlfriend here in Chicago, was making a lot of trips back and forth. I knew I was moving away from New York—away from Gray—and I'd been torn between L.A. and Chicago. I guess I chose Chicago hoping Jason would look me up sooner rather than later."

I put my hands back in my lap, exhaled. My burdens were still heavy, but compared with LaRae's at least they were new. I couldn't imagine being separated from my child for eighteen years.

I wiped a tear from my eye. "LaRae, is there anything I can do? I mean, I don't know what I could do to get Jason to talk to you, but if there's anything . . ."

"Don't worry about that, girl." She was tearing up too, but her eyes were smiling. "Mr. O.J. has gotten his hands into the mix."

"I don't know how you kept this from him so long. We both know you're feeling him."

"Hmm, ugly but true. I don't know how to share my stuff with men, Nikki. Before I met Gray, every man I dated was a selfish child. Then when I committed to Gray, he built me up professionally but held me captive emotionally. When I broke the engagement, do you know he contacted Jason himself?"

My eyes grew wide. "You're tripping."

"I wish. I've never met Jason, never seen him, but for all I know, he may be following me around town. Gray told me in L.A. that he invited him to my movie premiere. You see why I wouldn't hurry to fill O.J. in?"

I shut my eyes, pictured O.J. with Cherrelle. "You really think he would abuse your trust?"

LaRae's voice caught as she replied. "Just when I thought he'd given up on me, I got a call from Gray last week. Somehow O.J. tracked him down at NYU, and has been harassing him by phone."

I frowned. "What's he doing, trying to scare Gray into leaving you alone?"

LaRae shook her head. "Gray hasn't bothered me since I moved here, he just likes to pop up every now and then to wag his finger at me. When he called me, though, he was off his game. He was in shock, said that O.J. found some guy who was following me around town and wanted help figuring out who he was. It's Jason. O.J. found Jason!"

"He's obviously looking out for you, girl."

"I just can't believe he went through all the trouble," LaRae said, her voice a whisper. "It's like he really cares, like he—"

"Loves you?" I sat back against my pillows, tried not to squirm. "I know Mitchell says you've got the boy's nose open, LaRae. Maybe now's the time to tell him about Jason, the whole story."

"That's if he doesn't beat me to the truth." LaRae scooted closer to the bed and looked up into my eyes. "I told you all this, Nikki, to remind you that at least you're doing things in the right order. There's no reason to rule out taking another shot at a baby, even if this time doesn't work out." She squeezed her hands over mine. "You have something I'd have killed for during either of my pregnancies: a man who loves you dearly."

Mitchell

Russian Tea Time is a popular, cultured lunch spot near the Loop, and I wasn't surprised when Sharon Meredith asked me to meet her there, along with Deniece. Niecy and I had been there a couple times with our parents, so we made our way downtown easily, settled for some ridiculously priced parking further down Adams Street, and walked a few chilly, icy blocks to the restaurant.

As I quizzed Niecy about her studies at Wisconsin and deftly avoided talking about my job, or lack thereof, I felt my severance check from WHOT slide back and forth in my sport coat. I'd pocketed the check, which was already spoken for, from Tony this morning, after leaving Nikki at home resting.

I had technically been off the station's payroll for three weeks now, but since the hatchet men, Skip and Danny, were hardly around, Tony had let me keep using my office space. I'd been going into "work" every day, sitting at my office PC and submitting résumés through monster.com and every other job site I could find, then blowing off steam by scouring political Web sites and writing some new short stories. A couple days each week, I was teaching creative writing to Terry and his friends, including Jackie Williams, at a library on the West Side. I'd met Jackie twice now and felt assured that this kid—short, slight, and shy, with a burning interest in poetry—had not played a part in Keesa's death. O.J. had even made a visit to the workshop last week, where he'd given a motivational speech and shaken Jackie's hand. I didn't get in the middle of their conversation, but from a distance, I saw Jackie break down in O.J.'s arms.

The free time had been nice in an odd way, but I was desperate for a Christmas miracle, something to ensure I'd have a job lined up by year-end, so I could simultaneously tell Nik about my firing and a hiring. It wasn't going to be easy, though, now that we had new legal bills coming for a potential battle with Gina. Since I had exhausted everything except my 401(k) during my last layoff from Empire Records, my back was already against the wall. I had to have a plan when I broke the news to her, even if that meant borrowing money from Marvin. It would suck out the rest of my pride, going to my brother with my hand out, but asking my folks was out of the question. I was going to handle it one way or another before telling Nikki. It wasn't her job to pick up the slack; the stress of pregnancy was plenty to bear right now.

Niecy and I stepped inside Tea Time's woody, intimate atmosphere and searched the lobby for Sharon. She had described what she'd be wearing and had e-mailed me a photo. I was counting on her to find us first, though. Given the racial makeup of the crowd, she'd have no problem picking us chocolate chips out of the cookie dough.

After we had checked our coats, I stepped to the host station. "Ms. Meredith is already here," the tall, mannered maître d' said in accented English. "This way."

Sharon stood to greet us as we stepped to the table. "Hello, Mitchell, Deniece," she said, shaking our hands vigorously and lighting the room with a hundred-watt smile. Attractive but appropriately professional, she was around Niecy's height, about five foot ten, lean, and long-legged with sandy brown hair falling just short of her shoulders. Her beige business suit was impeccably tailored, and she wore it with palpable confidence.

We took our seats, made the necessary small talk, and ordered. Uzbek vegetarian stew for Sharon, grilled quail with dried cherries for Niecy, and chicken Kiev for me. We joked about trying the vodka shots as an appetizer but settled on salads instead. Things were progressing nicely, but with each moment my severance check burned a new hole into my pocket. A few more minutes and I'd have to tell Sharon to get to the business at hand. A brother had bills to pay, and a book advance, as elusive as it still seemed, was starting to look more and more like the life raft the Stone household needed.

Once the entrees arrived and we'd each taken up silverware, Sharon smiled again and waded into the water. "Well, again, it's my honor to meet with you both today. Since I was in town for another event, it worked out great to see you in person. I have convinced my new publisher to make you an offer of one hundred and twenty-five thousand dollars for the rights to *Out of His Shadow.*"

If ours had been the only table in Russian Tea Time, you could have heard a pin drop. My mouth hung open and I heard the voice of Homer Simpson in my head: *Mmm, one hundred and twenty-five thousand dollars. Aarggh.* Seated to my left, Niecy hunched her shoulders and slammed her lips together, eyes wide with glee. Sharon, meanwhile, sat across from us, her hands clasped and her warm gaze circulating between the two of us.

I did some quick math. I'd need to hire a literary lawyer or agent, which would take a few thousand off the top. Then I'd fulfill my promise to Niecy, give her twenty-five percent since she was the catalyst for the book's material. I was already down to around seventy-five thousand gross, but in the end it would at least give me a year to nail down a job in journalism or maybe corporate communications. Time to find a vocation that would feed my passion for writing but allow me to provide properly for Nikki, Clay, and our pending little miracle.

In my mind's eye I kicked my chair back from the table, hopped on top of our plates and glasses, and belted "We'll take it!" at the top of my lungs. In reality I swallowed hard, took two drinks of water, clasped Niecy's hand, and tried not to smile too wide at Sharon. "That's certainly worth considering, thank you."

Sharon reached forward and grabbed one of my hands and one of Niecy's. "I really believe we can be the best home for *Out of His Shadow.* I wanted to let you all ask me any easy questions now, then I'll have the contract mailed to Mitchell next week. You can take time to hire an agent or lawyer, then have them get in touch with us."

Niecy chuckled, smiled. "This is wonderful. I knew my baby brother was a wonderful writer. I was honored he let me inspire his first story, too. But I never expected this."

I squeezed Niecy's hand and smiled at her. "Who knew, sis? Your story's awesome. And a lot of women can be inspired by it."

"Absolutely," Sharon said. "And when Mitchell's done with the few revisions suggested by our publishing team, the appeal will be universal."

Niecy's eyes narrowed and she let her chin rest on her palm. "What do you mean?"

"Well, just that we think the story can be made a little more vivid, a little more stark. It won't change the overall story arc or the central issues, Deniece."

I cleared my throat, insisted on happy thoughts and visions of one hundred and twenty-five thousand bucks. "Do you have a couple of examples, Sharon?"

Maybe I imagined it, but I swear Sharon rolled her eyes before shifting her gaze between us. "Well, there's a view that we should revise the main character's occupation and maybe humanize her a bit more. We were thinking, you know, instead of making her a physician, she should be more representative of the struggling African-American woman. Maybe a bus driver who was once addicted to crack? Another thought was she could be a receptionist and former welfare mom."

Niecy chewed at her top lip, gathering her thoughts before speaking. "I don't understand. White-collar women aren't sympathetic heroines?"

Sharon took another taste of her stew, savored it while we waited in silence. "Mmm, good. Deniece, I'm not saying white-collar women aren't sympathetic, it's just that we're positioning this book to have two stages of success."

I sliced into a breast of my Kiev. "How's that?"

"Two stages." Sharon held up a finger from each hand. "First, we break you big in the African-American community: the independent bookstores, book clubs, Black Expressions, radio, etcetera. Then, about two months in, while the book is still viable, we pivot and get in front of mainstream female audiences: magazines, networks, Oprah, NPR, and national women's organizations. You see? We have to think ahead about what will resonate with both audiences. I think mainstream readers will relate more to a character fighting some major obstacles."

"That's fine," Niecy said, shifting in her seat. She hadn't touched her quail since first cutting into it. "But my personal view is that the story is what it is. I understand the need to edit and improve it for craft, but beyond that, it's up to white women to respond to the story as is. What if Mitchell changes it to suit them, but it turns off African-American readers? If it flops in our community, we both know it'll never get notice in the white community." She looked over at me. "Am I right, Mitchell?"

I nearly choked on the chicken slice in my mouth. Niecy patted me on the back as I fought the spasms off and chugged some water. When I came up for air, the visions of those one hundred and twenty-five thousand bucks were still there, but they were getting pretty faint. I looked in Niecy's eyes. There was a part of me that wanted to stay silent, just keep choking.

My head felt lighter as I spoke. "Sharon," I said, feeling myself float above the room as if having an out-of-body experience, "I won't make any substantive change that Deniece is uncomfortable with. I hope these ideas of yours are suggestions, not commandments."

Sharon set her spoon down and looked back at me before responding. I felt my heart thump louder with each passing second. "All I can do is relay your reservations to my team," she said, shifting her gaze to the linen tablecloth. "It'll be a committee decision whether the offer would still stand." She looked past Niecy and directly at me. "Are you willing to take that risk? Doors in publishing only open so many times in a writer's life, Mitchell."

I took one more look at Niecy, peered into her eyes, and felt things come into focus. She'd lived the events that kick-started this book, had wiped blood from her mouth, had had two teeth replaced, had lost the ability to have children, and was carrying two literal body scars from her years with Willie. By comparison, who the hell was I?

I gave Sharon my answer and we closed the meal in a civil, if cold, fashion. Sharon scooted out before we did, claiming she'd forgotten about another appointment. She made sure to run her Diners Club card before shipping off, and ensured us we could order extra dessert or coffee on her tab. I appreciated the offer, since I probably wouldn't be receiving any other money from her publisher, but we wrapped up a few minutes after she was gone.

Niecy didn't address the obvious until we'd arrived back at my car. "I don't want you to pass on this because of me, baby brother," she said as she ducked down into my passenger seat. I had told her about my unemployment. "I'm in Wisconsin, tucked away from most of the book world anyway. You do what you have to, for you and your family."

I shook my head, held her door open long enough to respond. "What I gave her back there? That was my final answer." I shut the door and walked around to the driver's seat, the wind slamming against my neck. It was time to go home and tell Nikki what we were up against.

36

O.J.

I had to be straight rude in order to catch my flight home from New York. I'd taken Cherrelle to see Manhattan for the weekend, as celebration for her midterm report card (three As, a B-plus, and two Bs). And yes, while I was there I'd sneaked in a visit to LaRae's old friend, Gray Philips.

When our cab dropped us at LaGuardia we were snared in the web of the latest security changes. The inside check-in lanes spilled onto the sidewalk, including the self-service lanes. We tried the curbside check-in instead, and still waited half an hour in the freezing temperatures before I grabbed Cherrelle with one hand and our two bags in the other, and bustled my way to the front of the line.

The guy at the closest station gave me a fleeting look as I stepped in front of the next person. "Uh sir, we have to take people in order. You'll need to go to the back of the line."

"My flight leaves in forty minutes, and I got here ninety minutes early," I said, stepping up to him. "If I was inside, they'd let me come to the front. Y'all need to do the same."

"Sir, we have a different policy out here—"

"You got a choice," I replied, holding Cherrelle at my side and plopping my bags into the holding space in front of his station. "Process my stuff now or waste my time and everyone else's to call security. You choose." We were processed and moving through security in minutes.

On the plane, Cherrelle and I traded stories about our favorite parts of the trip: seeing *The Lion King*, ice skating at Rockefeller Center, taking the ferry to the Statue of Liberty, walking the bustling, historic streets of Harlem. The one thing we agreed on was the need to come back ASAP, when we could stay longer and get a more complete taste. When Cherrelle's eyelids grew heavy and her speech slurred, I placed a blanket over her chest and thighs and let her sleep the rest of the way.

With my baby's peaceful snores as a soundtrack, I turned and looked out the window into the cloudy gray sky. You could have picked me up off the floor when Gray Philips told me the truth about LaRae's son. I'd arranged a half-hour meeting with him in the lobby of our hotel, while I'd left Cherrelle upstairs playing video games on the TV. The old dude had rocked my world, sharing not only his history with LaRae, some of which I'd known, but answering my every question about this Jason kid. I'd figured out that something was there, something disturbing and nearly unthinkable, but even now the truth was a vapor to me. I was in love with a woman with an adult son, a soon-to-be grandmother even. I didn't know what scared me more: the idea of blending my little family with LaRae's fractured one, or the fact that she'd hidden something so profound from me.

"She's so precious." The light, airy voice startled me. I looked up to see a flight attendant, a twenty-something sister with a short, tight bob, lusciously thick lips, and cocoa-brown skin, leaning over Cherrelle. She was looking at me, showing every last one of her pearly whites.

"Thank you," I said, hesitantly. Every time I met a beautiful woman, I became increasingly convinced that LaRae had broken me. I could look at this sister, admire her voluptuous figure, but the usual canine instincts that once followed? They were as faint as the radar on a busted submarine.

"My name's Charlotte. I just wanted to say I love your show." She extended her hand, and I shook it softly. "I've followed you since your days in Atlanta. I used to be based there."

"Cool," I replied.

"I heard you're on the air in D.C. too. When will you be picked up in Atlanta?"

I shook my head. "These things are unpredictable, Charlotte. Politics, you know." Politics and the fact I was damaged goods as long as my custody battle with Marian raged on.

"I read on the Web about your little girl's great-grandmother suing you," Charlotte said, her eyes going soft. "She can't be telling the truth."

"That's nice of you to say." I cleared my throat, hoping she wouldn't make me chase her off.

"Well, if you need anything, don't hesitate to let me know." She flashed a smile, hesitated. The words I'd have said a few months ago flashed across my mind. *Look me up next time you're in town,* followed closely by my business card. Gestures from the old me, the one who'd have had Charlotte joining the mile-high club before this flight was over. Today, though, the new, neutered O.J. just waved, letting Charlotte get back to work.

I drifted off for a catnap, which ended abruptly with a jolting landing at O'Hare. I roused Cherrelle, who's the heaviest sleeper I've ever known, and we scooted off the plane before the aisle got too clogged.

My cell phone vibrated against my hip as we stepped into the terminal. I had Cherrelle walk just ahead of me and snapped the phone open. It was Mitchell. I beat him to the punch. "What's up man? You in line for that government cheese yet?"

"Well, my severance check is gone, if that's what you mean. Look, my phone's been ringing off the hook thanks to you."

"What's up?"

"It's your attorney. He's been trying to track you down all weekend."

"Oh yeah." I had ignored my lawyer and my new business manager, Rod Stark, since Friday. "Why's he bothering you? He knows Stark is the man to bug now."

"Yeah, well, I guess he's trying everyone possible at this point. They're trying to get you to fly to D.C. this week, to complete the depositions and get in front of a judge before year-end."

"Jesus," I whispered. It really was a prayer this time. I didn't have the strength for this, not on top of everything else. Cherrelle was staying with me, it was as simple as that. God was just going to have to make it happen.

"Anyway, give him a call," Mitchell repeated. "I know from experience, man. Custody disputes don't just magically go away. I've got Gina flying into town next week to finalize arrangements for our situation with Clay."

"You're right," I said, gripping Cherrelle's hand as we stepped into a people-mover train, headed for baggage claim. "Thanks, bro. We'll have to get together sometime soon. I'll have Tony set it up."

"Don't treat me to lunch," Mitchell teased. "Just do like your boy Doug Banks: Pay a major bill for me. Say we start with my mortgage?"

"Hey, my brother," I replied, laughing, "you gots to get your own."

"Whatever. Look, you may as well know one other thing."

"What?" The people-mover slowed to a stop and I nudged Cherrelle through the crowd and toward the opening doors.

"Somebody asked me what you were doing in New York this weekend."

"What? Nobody was supposed to know where I was, you knew that." I'd mentioned it to him and Tony in passing but had sworn them to secrecy. "Was this my attorney or somebody from Marian's camp? They'd love nothing better than to say I went away to fool around with hookers or somethin'."

"Just trust my judgment, okay? Let's just say you may have someone waiting for you in baggage claim."

Cherrelle and I were on an escalator now, creeping toward the baggage area. I rubbed the back of my neck, annoyed at folk getting into my business. "You're fired, Mitchell."

His laughter danced across the line. "God loves you too. Peace."

I flipped the phone shut and stepped off the escalator behind Cherrelle. As usual, there was a Chinese wall of the young, old, Black, Latino, Asian, and Caucasian, amassed in anticipation of the latest arrivals. I decided not to bother scouring the crowd for familiar faces; anyone waiting for me was probably a subpoena server.

Cherrelle held my hand and led the way through the crowds toward the Delta baggage stations. She'd traveled this route enough with Keesa to be an old pro. "This way, Daddy. I'll get the bags."

I chuckled at her eight-year-old optimism. My bag weighed more than she did. "You can try, baby."

We paused and surveyed the electronic screen listing every flight and its associated baggage station. Just as I located our flight number, I felt a tap on my shoulder. Time for battle? I turned, ready to kick some ass—or kiss some, if it was a pleasant surprise like a fan or something.

When I came face to face with LaRae, all the melanin drained out of my face and dripped down into my shoes. Too soon, too sudden. It had been a week since I'd seen her, and in the month since our confrontation at the poetry slam our relationship had been a grab bag. I had stayed out of touch for two complete weeks, following up on information about Jason and harassing Gray, but leaving her alone. Then she'd invited me to a late lunch on a Monday, which turned into an unplanned rendezvous at her condo. We'd followed that a few days later with a picnic lunch along Lake Shore, then kept some distance until going to a Bulls game last week. We were together, bonding physically but skirting emotional intimacy.

Standing there facing LaRae in the airport now, my uneasy stomach told me the time had come to stop fighting. For both of us. The floor moved beneath me as I stared into the straight line of her lips and the peaceful look in her eyes. My mouth wouldn't move.

Cherrelle was quicker on the draw. She squealed with delight and clapped her hands. "Hi, Ms. LaRae." She stood between us, her hand still clasped to mine. She looked up at LaRae. "Where did you go for the weekend?"

"Nowhere, honey." LaRae softly placed a gloved hand atop Cherrelle's curls and let it rest there. "I thought you and your daddy might want a ride home."

I gripped Cherrelle's hand and pulled her against me, causing LaRae's hand to slip off her head. "That's too kind of you. We drove my car here, though."

Cherrelle looked up at me, a judgmental frown on her face. "We took a *cab*, Daddy."

I pretended not to hear, continued the stare game with LaRae. "Strange that you came all this way to give us a ride. Sure you weren't meeting anyone else here?"

LaRae closed the distance between us, got close enough that her boots skimmed the front of my Timberlands. She placed a hand on Cherrelle's shoulder. "I talked to Gray," she said, smiling now. "He said you guys had a productive talk."

I kept my gaze hard, pulled Cherrelle away from her reach. "It was very informative, yes. I felt much safer talking with Gray. Unlike Jason, he didn't greet me with an Uzi."

LaRae was struggling to keep her cool. "You couldn't wait until I was ready to tell you, could you? You had to be the typical man about it." Volumes more insults rested beneath the surface, content she was clearly withholding for Cherrelle's benefit.

"I told you *everything*." The airport might as well have been empty now. I held her stare as closely as I held my daughter's hand. "You told me nothing by comparison."

"Some of us need more time than others."

We were speaking our own code now, and I was tired of it. I reached forward with my free hand and pressed LaRae to me. Our lips found each other's instantly, and we fell into a long, deep kiss. As our lips meshed and brushed with increasing rhythm, Cherrelle's hand slipped from mine. I reached around LaRae's waist and plunged deeper into the kiss, ignoring the snickers surrounding us. When we came up for air, we pressed foreheads, laughing as Cherrelle cut her way between us.

"Can we go home now? You guys are so embarrassing. Everybody's looking at us."

37

Mitchell

I was stopped at Fifty-fifth and Garfield, talking with my dad on my cell phone. I had two passengers, LaRae in front and O.J. in back. It was a sunny, brutally cold Saturday, just a few days before Christmas, and we were all sacrificing some precious last-minute shopping time. We were headed to the last Chicagoland Mentoring seminar of the year, one that happened to be focused on careers in communications. O.J. and I were going to talk about WHOT's operations, and LaRae would give an insider's account of how her books had been adapted to cable TV and film.

The seminar was being held in Hyde Park, but I'd picked O.J. and LaRae up so they could come home with me afterward and help make a grand lunch for Nikki. She'd had a rough week, and Lord knows she needs the extra company to keep from going stir-crazy. I wrapped up my conversation with Dad and punched my phone off. I looked over at LaRae, who was still flipping through the business plan I had mailed her last week. "So what do you think?"

"Well," she said, smiling wickedly, "it's a good thing Nikki can keep working from home, while she's on rest. This is an ambitious plan you've got, Mr. Stone. It won't happen overnight."

From the back seat, O.J. dipped into the conversation. "You don't think he knows that? My boy's holding it down, or didn't you hear he has a new job?"

LaRae looked at me, taking care to ignore her man. "Accounting, right?"

I sucked my teeth. "I like to call it financial analysis. Basically, I'll be a contractor for the Robert Half agency, a temp for hire. I don't want to be on anyone's career plan, nothing that will tempt me to settle. But a lot of companies, given these economic times, are happy to hire analysts to fill in for workers who are ill, on maternity leave, etcetera. Then there's others who prefer to hire someone like me to do a specific project or two, then step off before I become a long-term expense."

LaRae began thumbing through the business plan again. "Well, that should give you some time getting this off the ground. Or should I say, us."

O.J. leaned forward, sticking his head between the driver and passenger seats. "Don't toy with my boy, LaRae. He's got enough stress, what with those custody negotiations on Monday."

"Thank you for feeling my pain." I knocked fists with O.J. before pulling into a parking space on University Row. I was anxious about my meeting with Gina tomorrow, but for now each day had enough trouble of its own. "I was trying not to rush Ms. Summers here, but you know . . ."

"First of all, ignore him." Laughing gently, LaRae placed a delicate hand over O.J.'s face, shoving him further into the back seat. It was still hard not to see them together and remember their battle in the WHOT studio months ago, but I was getting used to them as a couple. At this point Nikki and I were hanging out with them almost every other weekend. I didn't know all their business, but between what O.J. had shared with me and what LaRae had told Nikki (all of which I knew, of course), I knew they were standing firm. If I didn't know any better, I'd think Brother O.J. was in love.

LaRae tapped her watch as I parked the car. "We have a few minutes, right? Just give me your formal verbal pitch, like we were sitting across a conference table or something."

I nodded, squared my shoulders, and went into the spiel I'd memorized over the last couple weeks. "Well, the story starts with my decision to forego that book deal for *Out of His Shadow*." It still hurt to speak of the deal out loud; that money would have saved me from at least a year of debits, credits, and spreadsheets.

LaRae sat forward in her seat, her eyes growing serious. "Oh, we're going to find you the right publisher, believe that. Like I told you before, I really respected your decision, once you explained everything. Took me years of success to develop that type of backbone."

"I didn't really have a choice," I said. "I knew I still needed to put my writing skills to work, though. That's what got me thinking about teaching, some way to stir up the latent writing skills in our youth and the community in general. The Community Writer's Clinic will have that as its main purpose. A one-stop resource center that channels the writing gifts of potential poets, novelists, and memoirists throughout urban Chicago."

LaRae flipped through a few pages in my business plan. "Yes, now you're saying the clinic will provide services to adults and to students beginning in the sixth grade. Services to include training in creative writing, self-publishing, commercial publishing, on-line marketing, and publicity and promotion."

I nodded in affirmation. "Yes, in addition we'll host monthly writing workshops, competitions, and poetry slams."

"Beautiful idea," LaRae said, "but I've had some of these myself. What makes this one different?"

"For one," I replied, "this would be a private enterprise. We would raise money to support the services for children and maybe for college students, but the adult programs would be fee-based. We could employ a sliding scale to make it affordable for single mothers or people who are between jobs, but in general the adult side could be profit-making."

LaRae scrunched her little nose skeptically. "How many adults in the hood have time to worry about writing a book?"

"We wouldn't just focus on the hood. My suggestion would be to set up somewhere toward the Loop, so we're accessible to the

South Side, West Side, and more upscale areas. Middle-class folk would be the bread and butter of the adult side. How many signings have you attended where at least one fan mentioned a book they have in them, but have never gotten around to writing?"

LaRae nodded, smiled. "If I had a dime for every time I hear that, I'd be twice as wealthy. You have a point, Mr. Stone. Tell me, who would oversee this little enterprise?"

I held up my hands. "Well, I do have an MBA and plenty of business experience. I'd be the point man for getting everything off the ground—fund-raising, seeking any bank financing, hiring architects if we build a facility, hiring real-estate brokers if we buy an existing building, and so forth."

LaRae crooked her neck, turning to look at O.J., who by now was sprawled across my back seat. "I am amazed you have muzzled yourself this long. You don't have anything to add?"

O.J. barely stirred. "Sounds to me like my boy's handling himself well. You're already money in the bank, woman."

"Shut up." LaRae let a smile crack her lips before turning back to me. "You willing to do this for free, Mitchell? I'll sign up right now to make a major donation and I'll even recruit loudmouth here to help raise funds. We'll have to raise a lot of money before we could get you a salary, though."

I turned and fully faced LaRae. "I'll do this free of charge for two to three years, if that's what it takes to get it off the ground. I spent eight years doing finance just because it was there; I can certainly spend three doing something I'll love, something with meaning. With my temping income and Nikki's income, we'll be okay."

"Even with a new baby and with little Clay to provide for?"

"Nikki and I have discussed this," I replied. "She supports me and trusts that we'll work it out. With my schedule being more flexible, I'll be able to shepherd the baby to and from day care and our parents' homes, then in the evenings I'll be able to do a lot of the clinic business from home. I'll never get rich doing this, but I think my kids will respect me someday."

"Well, I am scared of y'all." LaRae waved the business plan at me. "E-mail me a copy of this. I'll start recruiting some author friends and other VIPs to help fund-raise. We'll go from there."

"Well," O.J. said, piping up suddenly, "what say we get the hell on over to the auditorium? You all gonna have us on C.P. time before we know it."

"Calm down," I said, admitting to myself he was being a good sport. I climbed out of the car and looked over at O.J. as he exited and went to open LaRae's door. "We've still got half an hour before the program starts and fifteen minutes before Terry and Jackie meet us."

O.J.'s face grew stern as LaRae stepped from the car. "Jackie, huh?" A little cloud of steam punctuated his question. "You think he's really bringing all those little punks with him?"

Following closely behind him, LaRae rubbed at the back of O.J.'s leather trench coat as we crossed the street, headed toward the center of campus. The temperature was in the mid-twenties, but the blue skies were beautiful and the streets were icy but clear of traffic, so our pace was leisurely. "I thought we agreed we wouldn't call them punks," she said, still rubbing his back. "Remember, these are the ones that can still be saved."

After several months of investigation, the police had determined that Marquise and two other kids, one of them the one that Nikki picked out of the lineup, were the only ones truly responsible for Keesa's death. Neither Jackie, Terry's friend, nor any of the three other boys they'd invited today had any prior record whatsoever. In fact, discussions with their neighbors and a community policeman revealed that most of the boys were known only for harmless pranks and the occasional shoplifting. Even the boy Nikki picked out of the lineup had admitted that he, Marquise, and the third boy were the only ones who'd intended to rob anyone that night. The others had been caught by surprise by Marquise's first approach on Keesa and Nikki, and then thought everything was over once Keesa disarmed the boy.

O.J. had digested this evidence slowly and deliberately, balancing his desire to make everyone pay for taking away Cherrelle's mother with a duty to salvage any souls that might have been in the wrong place at the wrong time. I greatly admired his response, one he was testing fully by meeting these boys today. I placed a hand on his shoulder as we continued walking, O.J. flanked by LaRae and me. "You know what you're going to say to them?"

"That there's no happy ending for my daughter," O.J. replied, his eyes focused on the clear skies. "That, if they'd had the character to knock Marquise out or otherwise check him, none of this would have happened. They need to know that much."

We continued toward the auditorium, our boots clop-clopping on the stone sidewalk.

O.J. wasn't finished. "After that," he sighed, "I'm gonna tell 'em about God's grace, about the fact he brought me from a mighty long way and can do the same for them. They're getting a better shot at life than a lot of kids in their situation would, and if they'll take advantage of it, I'll help them out. I can't work miracles, but I can help. Simple as that."

Nikki

"Girl, you're doing me proud." My mama was finally giving me her blessing, even if it was just over the phone. "You and Mitchell have had a sister stressing for months. I think you're going to be okay now, though."

Stretched out on the leather sectional sofa in our family room, I tugged at my wool blanket. "I know I started this out wrong, Mama, but we're getting it together now."

"That is such a blessing. Now you've just got to get the legal arrangements complete with that silly Gina."

My front doorbell rang. "Speak of the devil," I said. "I love you, Mama, but I have to go. Got company."

"Company? Girl, what are you doing with company when you haven't been feeling well?"

"I'm not dead, Mama. I can entertain people while laying up on the couch. Even Gina."

"Why on God's earth do you have her there, especially with Mitchell away? Couldn't this have waited until he gets back from that mentoring thing?"

"Oh, that would be a good idea," I said, lumbering toward the foyer. "A nice way to start World War Three, I think. I love you, Mama."

"Oh Lord, I'm getting palpitations again. . . ."

I clicked the phone off, leaned against the door for strength, and popped both locks. I swung the door open and stared at Gina, who stood on the other side of the wrought-iron security door. She had her arms crossed, her hair perfectly coifed, and a straight line for a mouth.

I forced a smile, then let it go slack. "Come in," I said, keeping my tone light. I took her red wool overcoat and complimented her Ann Taylor business suit and lacy blouse. I knew I wouldn't get much in return; I was keeping it real, rocking a white cotton maternity top and a roomy pair of matching pants, fuzzy house slippers, all of it topped off by a hastily tied ponytail.

I let Gina lead the way back into the family room, preferring to minimize any opportunities for her to "accidentally" bump me or shove me down the basement steps. "Have a seat over here," I said, motioning to the loveseat nearest my little perch on the couch.

"I kept asking myself why I accepted your invitation," Gina said stonily as she sat down.

"I'm glad that didn't stop you." I lay back against the cushions, closed my eyes for a second. "Gina, I'm barely into my second trimester of pregnancy, and I'm already tired. Tired physically, emotionally, and spiritually."

Gina sat with her knees touching, her shoulders high and tight. "And that's all my fault."

"Oh no," I said, waving a hand, "that's not what this is about. This is about me learning to accept certain facts, facts that won't change even if I have ten kids by Mitchell. Those facts are simple: First of all, you will always be in his life, until Clay turns eighteen and even afterward. Anything Clay achieves in life—college graduation, grad school, military commendations, whatever God has for him—he will always want his mother and father there to celebrate with him. So like it or not, you will always have some claim on my husband.

"There's a second truth, though, one that I overlooked for months. Mitchell loves me, and not you. I know in my heart that he didn't sleep with you in that hotel. He may have been naïve to get drawn in with you and Dale that night, God bless him, but he definitely didn't go there looking for some booty call."

Gina crossed her legs, settled back against the loveseat a bit. "You may as well know, you're right. I did strip Mitchell naked that night, once he'd gone to sleep. I got him good and drunk. . . ." She trailed off, looking at me warily.

"Go on," I said, my voice shaking. I held my breath and bit my tongue.

"I guess I wanted one last challenge, to see if I could win Mitchell over from you. I was scared about moving away, I was sick of Dale. I set that whole night up, okay? Dale did hit me, but we were at his place, in his bed, when it happened. I went to the hotel that night, called Mitchell over, then called Dale and told him to meet me so we could make up."

Hot air whistled through my nostrils, but I was still calm. "Let's stick with the point where you stripped Mitchell naked."

"I ran my hands over him, okay? But that was it. I couldn't do any more. You surprised?"

I shook my head. "No. It just confirms my faith in Mitchell. Do you realize you could have gotten him or Dale killed, Gina?"

"Nikki, please. You wanna press charges now?"

"Forget it."

"You don't need to worry about Dale anyway. I left his ass just in time. That fool's in jail already, helped one of his boys break into a bunch of cars near Malcolm X College."

"No offense," I said, searching her eyes with care, "but Dale is beside the point. You may go through a couple of Dales in Atlanta, but you know what? I honestly believe you're on the right track now. You got sick of Dale because you want someone who will treat you right and be a positive presence for Clay. If you didn't, you wouldn't have taken the courageous step of moving away and going to CNN. I've been so blinded by my possessiveness of Mitchell, I haven't appreciated that."

Gina uncrossed and then crossed her legs again, her eyes bouncing all over the room. "What do you want then?"

"It's not about what I want. It's about what you and Mitchell want, and about what Clay needs. Mitchell's income has taken a dive recently, and mine will drop for a while next year when I go on maternity leave. We're going to go into debt if we have to take you on over custody rights, and I'm guessing you will too. We'll do it if that's our only option, don't get me wrong, but I know in your heart you don't want that any more than we do."

Gina tented her hands in her lap, trained a stare in my direction. "Since when did you know me so well?"

"You think I've forgotten?" I held her gaze, fought the urge to reach out a hand. "Gina, I know what your stepfather did to you back when we were kids." I started talking faster, trying to get it out before she got offended. "I haven't told anyone, not even Mitchell, okay? But I know that's why our friendship didn't last past junior high, because my mama told me your secret. And I know that plays into some of your behavior today."

"You been using me as a case study in a psych course, Nikki?"

"Nothing like that. I'm just tired of so much going unspoken between us. You were never really my type, and you'd probably say the same for me. If our mothers hadn't been cool, we'd have never hung out, but you're not a bad person. For a few weeks, I was blessed with a friend who had a lot in common with you. Keesa said most babies' mamas, hell, most single moms, are just mothers trying to survive.

"You're no different from Keesa, you're a sister playing the cards she was dealt. And I think you've been playing them a hell of a lot better since Clay was born."

Gina bit her lower lip so hard it flushed beet red. She rubbed her neck, looked at the carpet for a minute. "You don't mean that."

"I do. Do I sound like I'm kissing your ass right now? I already told you there's no way you'll ever steal Mitchell's heart, that I know you lied about sleeping with him. Are those the words of an ass-kisser?"

Gina inhaled sharply and wiped something from her left eye. "I have to go."

Fighting my instincts, I shrugged and slowly stood. We walked back out to the foyer and I retrieved Gina's coat and hat. She dressed wordlessly and didn't meet my stare until I had opened the front door. I caught her by the hand and slipped something into it. "Something to think on? I'm reading it now."

She took the book, *The Blended Family*, from me and surveyed it grimly before stepping outside. "See you later," she said, turning just long enough for me to see the blankness of her expression.

I stood in the doorway, shivering from the blast of cold, and watched Gina storm to her car. Maybe I'd pushed too hard, but I had a feeling I'd sleep better that night.

38

O.J.

It was a quarter before seven on this Monday morning, time for me to put my lil' bit of money where my big fat mouth was. LaRae stood outside my studio, perched on the other side of the glass for moral support. Trey was on my right, Liz to my left. I was about to try something none of my radio heroes had ever dared, at least not to my knowledge. I was about to unmask myself on air. Live and unscripted, no safety net.

As the studio rocked with the bass of Kirk Franklin's "Revolution," I cherished each moment and every little feature of this studio that had been home for the past year. I'd had some good times, experienced new heights of professional success, all while weathering tragedy and growing into a surprisingly good father, if I do say so myself. I tapped my microphone nervously as Kirk's last notes faded into the distance. With my next words, I'd be as good as dangling my career over a ledge.

"Coming up on seven o'clock, folks," I drawled, aiming for a voice of calm. "As we've discussed this first hour, we're taking confessions this week. Anything you need to get off your chest, any admissions that will cleanse your soul, why not do it here? Besides, as my pops says in his most popular sermon, scripture reminds us that what's done in the dark will eventually come to light. Why not shed light on your wrongs voluntarily? It's the start of a new year now, what better way to start it off?

"Well, you all know me, Brother O.J. ain't gonna ask you to do anything I won't do myself. You won't hear Trey talking about his harem and you won't hear Liz cop to those electronically powered devices she keeps under the bed, but I'm kicking the year off with my own confessions." I turned to my news ace. "Liz, will you read that news account about me?"

Liz had the deadpan thing down. "Could you be a little more specific? You're quite the talk of the town these days."

I blew hot air into my mike. "The *Tribune* article, please."

I perched on the edge of my seat and stared at LaRae through the glass as Liz read the story over the air. It was an update on Marian's custody suit, complete with quotes from her attorneys about my "irresponsible" record as a father and my allegedly "abusive" treatment of Keesa. Thank God I'd read it over a cup of coffee earlier, otherwise I'd have spewed so many F-words the FCC would have put me out to pasture.

When Liz was done reading the little character-assassination piece, I shook my head. "Yeah, pretty messed up, huh?"

Trey's tone was muted, almost solemn. "You a better man than that, O.J. Everybody who's heard your show, worked alongside you this past year, they know that."

I looked at Liz, who had stayed quiet. She shrugged. "What're you looking at me for? I just read the story."

"That's okay, Liz, don't defend a brother." I took a deep breath. "I love you for taking up for me, Trey, but I don't deserve it. Chicago, you've been good to me this past year and I love you. I mean that. I've lost a precious woman here, but I've also gained a hell of a lot. You've earned the right to hear the truth about these stories calling me a deadbeat dad.

"I was a rogue in high school and college, you've probably figured that out. Played at being a preacher, was pretty good at it too. It was all a game, though. You think Jesse Jackson and Henry Lyons are bad? If I'd stayed on track in ministry, I'd have made them look like choirboys. I was seeing my pastor's daughter, the leader of the youth choir, a divorcée in her early thirties, and the woman who eventually bore my child. And this was just at my church, this isn't even getting into the girls on my college campus.

I was something else. You players out there, just trust me, couldn't none of y'all have hung."

"So you was a dog," Trey chimed in. "You're human, man, that don't mean you ain't redeemed yourself since."

I sat back from the mike, ran a hand through my hair before continuing. "Well, my fair-skinned brother, it doesn't stop there. A key test of a man's character is how he reacts when a woman he doesn't love tells him she's pregnant. I failed that test with a capital F. I told the young lady she must be mistaken, that even though we'd had plenty of unsafe sex, there was no way I was the father. I ridiculed her claim of being faithful to me, insisted she'd gone back to being promiscuous. When that didn't work, when she still pursued me, I tried to buy her off. Offered to use my influence at our church to get her extra help with her college tuition." I had to pause at that one, trying to believe that had been me at one point.

Trey, who'd heard some of this before, smiled faintly. "You came around, right man?"

"Oh yeah. When the young lady—Keesa Bishop was her name, may she rest in peace—when Keesa snapped under the pressure of rejection and disrespect, she attacked me." I had decided to go vague here for Cherrelle's sake. We'd have an appropriate talk about all this tonight, before it could get back to her through friends or any of their ignorant parents. "It was a knock-down, drag-out fight, boy, but it took the aftermath of that to convince me this woman was sure I was the daddy.

"So I graduated college, moved back home to Atlanta, and waited for the birth so I could confirm the truth with a blood test. In the meantime, I swore I'd never abuse the institution of the church again, so I revoked my self-imposed 'call to preach' and became a junior-high teacher, in English. After about a year, I'm kicking it at a club one night and meet this fine woman. One thing leads to another, ya know, and next thing I know she's getting me airtime on her family's radio station, speaking out about local education issues. From there, my winning personality took over. I got a late-night radio show interviewing singers and musicians, then got bumped up to afternoon, then finally morning drive time. But what kept things going? The fact that I kept this young lady going, if ya know what I mean."

Liz jumped in. "By this time, you knew that Cherrelle was your daughter?"

"Oh yeah," I replied. "But that was in the background by then. I sent some child support, don't get me wrong, and started going back to D.C. a couple times a year to see my daughter, but that was about it. I was living the high life in Hotlanta, man. It took the death of my last grandparent, my paternal grandfather, who passed when Cherrelle was about four, to get me serious about being in her life. It's hard to attend a funeral, see a man's children honor him, and not wonder whether your kids will care when your time comes."

"So," Liz said, "you've been daddy on the spot ever since?"

"I'm not perfect," I said, my voice softening. "When Keesa moved here with Cherrelle, I was anxious about becoming a full-time father. I was still too focused on my career. Well, despite the hell we caused each other, Keesa probably saved my life by moving here. The chain of events that followed were painful, but I'd be lying to say I'm not better for it. Bottom line, I am a full-time father now, and nothing will change that. So you all excuse me while I speak to a certain listener in D.C.: I've just spilled my dirty laundry, just yanked my worst skeletons out of the closet. Either my audience is with me or not. Maybe I won't get any more syndications, maybe WHOT will go country overnight. Not my problem. Cherrelle, you come first. This is for you." I cued up a cut of Stevie Wonder's "You Are the Sunshine of My Life" and let it rip.

As the joyful music blasted, Tony met me at the studio door, his arms crossed and his brow stitched with stress. "I couldn't stop you," he said, as LaRae hovered behind him, her eyes wide and a big smile on her face. "I had to let you finish, O.J., but we're gonna hear about this from the good old boys. Especially the part about the station possibly going country."

I clapped a hand onto Tony's shoulder. "You did the right thing by waiting, man."

"Today is it, though," he said, slapping a hand of his over mine. "I start playing censor again tomorrow."

"Appreciate it." I stepped around him, grabbed LaRae's hand. "Hey, beautiful. Thanks for being here."

She reached for my chin and began to stroke the skin slowly but forcefully. "You were brilliant, just like I knew you would be. I can't believe you're going to repeat that every hour today."

"I have to," I said, guiding her further down the hallway, beyond Tony's earshot. "The average listener only catches between fifteen and thirty minutes of me a day. I need to hit as many folk as possible."

LaRae tightened her grip on my hand as we arrived at my office door. She leaned into me, more out of fatigue than lust. "Some day when she's a little older, Cherrelle will love you for what you've just done. Nothing's more healthy than a clean airing of the truth." Her neck slumped over my shoulder and her voice became a whisper. "That's all I want to do for Jason."

I held her to me and ran a hand over her braids. "I'm working on him," I whispered, trying not to feel powerless. Nearly a month of telephone diplomacy had failed so far. I'd reached out and touched Jason five or six times, moving from slow, tortured conversations of two or three minutes to our most recent call a week ago, when he'd opened up on me with the resentments he felt toward LaRae. The boy was an emotional pretzel, so captivated by the thought of his biological mom that he'd basically stalked her for six months, but so damaged by abandonment that he couldn't approach her.

I'd pleaded with Jason, pulled out every stop. Tried to put myself in his shoes, asked him to trade with me. If God gave me a choice between lunch with my late mama or lunch with Jesus, it would be a nail-biter; I miss her that much. I couldn't fathom that any young man wouldn't want to know his biological mother, especially when she'd entrusted him to others only because she'd been a baby herself.

There was no reasoning with this one, though. Society and years of viewing himself as a victim had hardened Jason's heart to a point that was nearly hopeless. I wanted a happy ending for him and LaRae, but it was starting to look like we'd have to settle for the knowledge that we'd tried to make it happen.

Still holding LaRae against me, I looked down the hallway to see Tony charging straight toward us. He yanked a thumb over his shoulder, gesturing wildly. "We need you in the studio, sooner than later. Trey and Liz can only fill your shoes for so long."

I brushed my lips lightly against LaRae's and let her into my office. I hustled back into the studio. Liz was completing her news update. Before I could take my seat, Bobby motioned me over to his switchboard. "Take a look at what you've done, O.J. And if you think this is heavy, you should hear what the KISS callers are saying in D.C."

I followed Bobby's frantic finger-pointing and looked at the board. The phone lines were jammed, for better or for worse.

39

Nikki

There are moments you know your life is about to change forever. My biggest moment came this morning around three A.M., when a series of what felt like contractions jolted me from sleep. I endured the first one, closing my eyes and counting until the grinding stopped. The most intense pressure subsided in less than a minute, but when that was gone I still didn't feel right.

With my swollen stomach throbbing in pain, I looked over at Mitchell, who was still snoozing peacefully, his right arm draped over my chest. Deciding to wait a few minutes before alarming him, I grabbed the remote and clicked on the TV. *The Cosby Show* was on Nick at Nite, just perfect. No point trying to sleep while awaiting the next hit, so why not watch Black America's first family while preparing to start my own.

After another fifteen minutes, another contraction barraged my poor battered uterus. This time the grinding was like salt in the wounds of my aching abdomen. "Oh Lord Jesus," I moaned into the dark as Dr. Huxtable bounced that fat white boy, Peter, on his knee. I'd hit Mitchell with plenty of false alarms these last couple of months, not to mention the extra maintenance I'd required as my emotions grew increasingly unpredictable. Then there was the wild swing in my libido a couple months back, when everything down south had swelled just right. He'd been a trouper, but between his daytime temping, his evening meetings for the writer's clinic, and our monthly visits from little Clay, I had felt guilty jumping Mitchell's bones twice a day. That had ended before Easter, though.

I had fought the pull of my bladder since first waking up. Trying to stay cool, I gently rolled back the comforter and sheet covering me and gingerly took steps into the bathroom. I reached down around my swollen belly, hitched up my maternity shirt, slid down my panties, and did my business. Fearing another contraction or more abdominal pain, I slumped forward, dropping my forehead into my palms and wondering if I should wake Mitchell. That's when I looked into the toilet bowl and felt my heartbeat stutter. It was like the Red Sea in there, worse than the day I blacked out at work.

I could taste the fear on my tongue as I hopped off the toilet. As much trouble as I had put Mitchell through, his trials were just beginning. Gripping my side in agony, I rushed to the bed and sank my nails into his arm. Mitchell's eyes popped open suddenly and he shot upright in the bed. "What? What?"

Leaning over him awkwardly, I looked him in the eyes, realizing my nails were still embedded in his arm. "We have to go, now." I anticipated his response. "I know we're supposed to have another four weeks. Just trust me."

We erupted into a mutual flurry of activity. I climbed out of bed and ran to my closet for our pre-packed overnight bag. Mitchell nearly tripped over the comforter, he hopped out of bed so fast. He bolted into the bathroom, washed his pit areas, and was dressed in five minutes. Then he was at my side as I tied my hair back in a bun and threw on a wool maternity outfit.

Another contraction hit as we pulled the Infiniti out of the driveway. Mitchell drove like a man possessed, racing through the streets like the baby was already hanging out of me. I gripped the leather armrests, to block out the pains shooting through my stomach and to keep from sliding back and forth as Mitchell barreled toward the hospital.

I had paged Dr. Omawole from the car, and she called in shortly after we were checked into a room. She was concerned that I was already experiencing labor pain, and even more troubled by my abdominal aches. "I'm coming right in, lady," she said, sounding hurried.

Sitting at my bedside, Mitchell played at being brave when I replayed the conversation for him. He scooted closer to the bed and took my hand. "She knows what she's doing. We'll wait for her, patiently."

We considered calling Mama, Angie and Marvin, and my in-laws, but decided to wait until we knew where things were headed. No sense putting everyone else though extra hell. We'd call them and others like Leslie, Tony, and O.J. when we were in the clear.

When Dr. Omawole arrived, around four-thirty, she gave me a physical exam, hooked me up to an electronic fetal monitor, and ordered an ultrasound and a blood test. Mitchell stewed in the waiting room as time stretched endlessly before me. The labor and the abdominal pain had worn me down so much, I was ready for a hit from the anesthesiologist.

When Dr. Omawole awoke me from a fitful sleep, I felt like I had slept for hours. Leaning over me, she smiled weakly. "You've been out for half an hour," she whispered. "Some of your family is on the way." By description, I realized it was Mama, my in-laws, and Marvin and Angie. I wondered who was watching their kids, especially little Leah, their six-month-old. "They are all nice people. Except for your husband, I told them they cannot see you for a while.

"We need to talk about next steps," she continued, her voice crisp but empathetic. "We have some challenges, Nikki."

I felt my body flush with every fear and anxiety that had stalked me these recent months. "I want Mitchell," I replied coldly. "I don't want to hear anything else without him here."

Almost on cue, Mitchell opened the door and walked over to me. Our eyes locked, and I knew instantly that he already had some clue about what was coming. "What is it, Doctor?" he said.

Dr. Omawole's eyes glowed sympathetically as she stood and looked directly at me. "Based on your abdominal pain and the bleeding, I believe you are presenting with a mild to moderate placental abruption." She quickly explained the term to us. Long story short, my placenta had separated from the uterine wall, meaning the baby was at risk and my blood loss might continue until I went into shock. Concerns for my own health went out the window, though, when the doctor pointed out that the electronic monitor showed evidence of "fetal compromise."

"We can't just sit and wait," she continued. "I try to avoid this as much as possible, I already told you that, but we will have to perform a cesarean delivery."

Mitchell dipped his head before peering up at the doctor from his seat. His eyes darkening and his mouth set in a line, he looked like he had been slapped. "A C-section?"

The doctor blinked once as she responded. "Yes."

Mitchell opened his mouth and shut it as if trying to censor himself, then met the doctor's eyes again. "Are you sure we've waited long enough for the labor? Why did we take all those Lamaze classes?"

The doctor put her hands into the pockets of her white coat. "There is a possibility that with another two to four hours, Nikki's labor might progress. However, due to the baby's condition and her bleeding, that route poses extreme risks."

I bit my lower lip and started chewing. The thought of a C-section scared the hell out of me. I knew it was a major operation and would raise the stakes.

Dr. Omawole picked up her clipboard and held it to her chest. "I will come back as soon as I secure an operating room, okay? I will give you a few minutes to let this sink in." She turned back toward us as she stepped to the door. "This is our only option, trust me."

I looked forlornly at the door as it closed behind her. Why

couldn't anything be simple with this pregnancy? I looked at my husband, felt my grip on his hand going limp. "You don't want them to cut me open, huh?"

Mitchell inhaled deeply, looked down at me. "I knew this might be necessary, but it's not natural."

"I'm tired, baby," I said. "We have to do what's best for this child, nothing else."

We sat there in silence for a minute, our eyes locked together. I wasn't sure, but I had the feeling that like me, Mitchell was flashing back through the highlights of our four years together—the early dates, our first hookup, our wedding day, the nights spent arguing, fighting, and loving. We were putting all that on the line today, but I was seized now by a sudden blanket of peace. I had been blessed in my thirty years to make peace with a father who had spurned me, to fall in love with a wonderful man who treasured me, and now I had spent eight months carrying his child. There were millions of women throughout time who'd never experienced any of that. I was through complaining.

Mitchell

I was banished to the waiting room with my family while they prepped Nikki and got ready to transport her to an operating room. Just after six, they wheeled her upstairs.

The waiting space outside the operating room was small, so Angie stayed downstairs and began calling other family and friends to ask for prayer. I rode up in the elevator with Nikki and the doctor.

All three of our parents met me in the upstairs hallway, where we spoke in hushed, reassuring tones. Finally, I heard the door to Nikki's room open behind me. I turned and saw Dr. Omawole point a smooth ebony finger at me. I nodded grimly and placed a hand on Mom's shoulder. "Keep us in your prayers."

Mom took my hand and covered it with both of hers. "Are you sure you don't want to pray too, from out here?" She was searching my eyes, pressing gently.

"I need to be in there, Mom."

"Your father stayed in the hallway during all of my births. And Marvin, well, you know what happened with Sarah, right?"

My big brother was fair game, especially since he had left to swing through his office. I had his moral support, but as a high-powered attorney he couldn't afford to drop everything over what was still just a potential crisis. "I know Marvin fell out in the operating room, Mom." I gave a weak smile. "That doesn't mean I'll do the same."

Mom frowned but removed her hands, letting mine fall back at my side. "His was a natural delivery, even. I'm just saying, there's no shame if you stay out here."

I pulled her close, hugged her. "Thanks, Mom. Love you."

"I love you and Nikki, son."

When I stepped inside the room, Dr. Omawole and her staff already had Nikki surrounded. Nikki had received her regional anesthetic, so she was still awake and with it. The nurses on either side of the bed smoothed a powder-blue drape over her midsection. The covering had a ready-made hole, which fit snugly over Nikki's exposed tummy. I walked to the right side of the bed as one nurse began to clean Nik's belly with some type of sponge on a stick soaked in yellowish-brown liquid. Our eyes met, and I filled mine with the most loving, fearless smile I could muster.

Standing near Nikki's head, I steadied myself and placed my hands on my hips. I'd seen a couple of birth videos to prepare for today, but unfortunately none had included a C-section. I assured myself it couldn't be that bad and continued to stand watch.

Once the cleaning was complete, the nurse on the other side of the bed looked up at the doctor. All too suddenly she said, "We're ready."

That's when Dr. Omawole did it, held out her hand and accepted a short, sharp steel scalpel. The reality of what they were doing hit me. They were going to cut Nikki open? How could they, when she'd already lost excessive amounts of blood throughout this pregnancy and during the past day's labor? I wiped my brow, cleared my throat. I was staying up, I had to see everything. Nikki deserved to have me at her side.

I held my breath as the doctor raised that scalpel with confidence and precision, first making an incision through her skin, then taking deeper cuts through additional layers. I had lost count of the number of incisions when I heard a loud, "No, stop!" The words escaped before I realized they'd come out of me.

The doctor was good. Though the head nurse turned full around and glared at me like I'd spit in her face, Dr. Omawole continued right through her latest downward stroke. This time blood spurted and sprayed, and a mild shower of fireworks bloomed across my vision. I felt my knees knock, then weaken. *Oh no. You kidding me?* "This isn't happening," I said, stumbling back from the bed and crashing into the wall, which I slammed with my head. All the lights in the room went out, at least for me. I heard the whirring of the equipment, heard a nurse say something like "I knew it," then things were quiet.

When I opened my eyes, I found myself locked outside of the operating room, banging on the doors. This time the doors were made entirely of clear glass. I could see everything but couldn't do a thing about it. The doctor and staff huddled over Nikki, working feverishly. All I could see were streams of blood and weary looks on the faces of everyone in there. The one face I couldn't see was Nikki's. I banged on the door, screamed at the top of my lungs, to no avail. I turned around to search the hallways for help, only to find my family had left. I returned to the door, and saw that everyone had stepped back from Nikki's bed. Blood all over the place. Heads hung low, shoulders slumped. No sign of movement from Nikki. No baby.

"Mr. Stone? Mr. Stone, snap to." The words were accompanied by a blast of smelling salts to my nostrils, and I shot forward, found myself back in the hallway. Dr. Omawole was seated next to me.

I looked at her and steadied myself, gripping the sides of the plastic chair. "Where is my wife?"

The doctor blinked twice before responding. "Your wife is resting after the surgery, still very groggy, but wants you both to hold the baby at the same time."

"H-he's already born? No one woke me up."

"I had a nurse check you and assure you had just fainted. We had the orderlies place you here, so you could rest during the procedure. It's a tense time for any father. We kept your family apprised in the meantime."

My heart did a new flip of joy. "Thank you, Doctor." *And thank you, God.*

"Just get in there, now. Your parents and mother-in-law are antsy to see this child too. For a preemie, he is surprisingly healthy."

As I stood with wobbly knees and hurried into the preemie ward, I was reminded this was still a fresh experience for me. Everything was so new. I went to Nikki, who'd been wheeled in, and kissed her. The attending nurse opened our baby's unit and slowly lifted him out. I took the wrinkled, caramel-colored boy into my arms first, then held him over Nikki and lowered him into her grasp.

"He's perfect," she gasped, counting off his ten fingers, ten toes, and four little limbs. "Five pounds, fourteen ounces, they said. Not bad, considering."

I was speechless by comparison. "A boy." I was still processing, my senses being flooded with both pleasant surprise and immediately torn loyalties. I always wanted to have a son with Nikki, one I could name Mitchell Jr. maybe and raise with my full influence. But already?

It still seemed like yesterday that we'd worked out a new custody arrangement for Clay, back around Christmas. Gina had proposed something surprisingly reasonable: monthly visits to Chicago for him, for up to a week each time until he started kindergarten. It had been hard to argue with that. I had put my attorney on hold for a couple more years.

As peaceful as that front was now, the little creation in my arms would soon test it. How would I raise him to be Clay's brother, keep them as equals without this new arrival playing Isaac to Clay's Ishmael? I looked at the floor and sighed. "Each day has enough trouble of its own."

Nikki, still patting the baby's back, looked up at me. "What?"

"Nothing, just reminding myself to stay in the moment." I reached over, grabbed one of her hands and rested my other hand on the little one's mushy head. "I love you, Mrs. Stone."

"I love you, too. I want you to name him."

I stared at her, confused. "Baby, you've been working on name ideas for six months. You know my preference, but I'll let you choose."

Nikki's lips spread in a mixture of smile and grimace. "I want it to be your choice. I know this didn't start out right, me having my own agenda and all. Now that he's here, you should make the call."

"Well," I said, bending over so I could reach her face, "there'll be time for that later." I leaned around my son and kissed Nikki with more passion than on our wedding day.

We rotated people's access to come by and observe the baby, especially given that extra folks had shown up by then. Our parents came first, of course, then Marvin, Angie, and Deniece, who'd just arrived from Madison, and Nikki's girl Leslie. Once we were back in Nikki's room, the WHOT crew came knocking.

Tony, Trey, O.J., and LaRae burst into the room, instantly shattering the sedate atmosphere I was trying to maintain for Nikki. "You fools are the last guests of the day," I warned, pointing my finger, "so behave."

"We won't be long," Tony chuckled, stepping up to the bedside. "We saw the little guy," he said, referring to the child we'd eventually name Mitchell Eugene Stone. He'd be saddled with Daddy's first name and Mommy's Daddy's first name, but he wouldn't be a "Junior."

Tony winked playfully as he stood by the bed. "Yes, you and Nikki did some beautiful work during your time at WHOT, Mitchell. Sure you don't wanna come back now?" The good times were rolling at the station nowadays. If I was right, the station was about to sign O.J. to his fourth syndication deal that week, Denver this time. Since his on-air confessional, not only had Ms. Marian dropped her custody lawsuit for Cherrelle, but O.J.'s ratings had shot through the roof in Chicago, D.C., and the recently added Houston. Apparently a whole lot of listeners saw themselves, past and present, in O.J.'s words.

When Tony and Trey were done arguing over who the baby most resembled, LaRae nudged through the crowd and kissed Nikki on the cheek. "I can't wait to hold him in a few weeks, girl. He is too cute."

"Check her out." O.J. rolled his eyes and elbowed me in the side. "She damn near dropped her grandbaby on his head last week, and now she's an expert."

"Oh, LaRae," Nikki moaned in elation for her girl. "Jason finally came around?"

LaRae pursed her lips. "Well, *he* still has a way to go, but his girlfriend started returning O.J.'s messages last month. She invited us over one day while Jason was at work last week."

Nikki smiled. "So he's actually relocated here?"

"Looks like it, girl. I'll break him down someday, right? He can't hold out forever."

O.J. sidled up and placed an arm around her waist. "No," he said, stroking a stray braid away from LaRae's face, "he can't."

As LaRae's eyes filled with gratitude, I took Nikki's hand in mine. The room went silent except for Trey's and Tony's banter, as they sat in front of the TV. For Nikki and me as well as O.J. and LaRae, it was time to reflect on the unique blessings and challenges of our common mission: the age-old, baffling, ever-present search for that perfect blend. If they were anything like us, they probably had no idea how to get there.

One thing was certain, though. We were going to make the most of the journey.

ACKNOWLEDGMENTS

After God, I owe thanks to more people than I could accurately name in this space, so let me lead with a blanket "good lookin' out" to everyone who has been a help to me in any way. There are thousands of books published every year, and you chose to support mine. I sincerely appreciate it.

I am blessed with a family that is the best support system one could have. Mrs. Kyra Robinson, Mom, Dad, Russ, and Barrett, you keep me going when life tries to stop me in my tracks. Shelli, I love you. Little Miss Alexis, you will always be my favorite niece! To my "VP of Sales" and cousin Tony Alford Jr., you serve as Aaron to my Moses in those difficult bookselling situations. To the entire Robinson and Alford families (that's about half the city of Dayton, with sprinklings in Atlanta and D.C.), you are supporters, role models, and encouragers. I'm also indebted to my father, my brother Barrett, and my friend Valerie for ensuring that the account of Nikki's pregnancy was medically sound.

Thank you to the industry professionals behind this book: Audrey LaFehr and the New American Library team, Elaine Koster, and Peggy Hicks.

To the booksellers who helped expose readers to *No More Mr. Nice Guy* and *Between Brothers,* may we meet again this year! Emma Rodgers and Black Images, Jokae's African-American Books and the Pettus family, Hue-Man Bookstore, Sacred Thoughts Bookstore, Medu Books, Atlanta Southwest Regional Library, Nubian Bookstore, the Atlanta, Detroit, and Houston branches of the Shrine of the Black Madonna, Howard University Bookstore, Reprint Bookshop, Karibu, Mitchie's Fine Black Art & Gallery,

Cush City, Tricia's Books and Things, Nu World Books, Zahra's Books 'n Things, Truth Bookstore, Books for Thought, Heritage Bookstore and More, Black Facts, Montsho Books, and those I've not yet visited, let's do it again. I also appreciate the growing number of managers at Borders and Barnes & Noble who supported my signings and are encouraging the formation of more African-American book clubs.

I have many friends who have been supportive, but two couples get a special mention: Moise and Andrea Cummings (you can pay us later for match-making you guys) and Mayon and Nicole Neal. When I was a self-published author stuttering his way through readings, you guys were there, cheerleading all the way. Another subset of supportive friends would be my fellow authors. At this point there's too many of you to name, but I do thank Timm Mc-Cann and William July for being the first established authors to give me a hand up. Every author who has looked out for and encouraged me in any way, this sentence is for you. Let's keep feeding the readers while elevating our respective crafts.

Finally, to every book club and individual reader, your praise, encouragement, and constructive criticism remind me of the privilege it is to be a writer. Keep cracking those book covers.

About the Author

C. Kelly Robinson is a graduate of Howard University and Washington University in St. Louis. A former corporate financial analyst, he is a 2001 recipient of the Individual Award for Achievement, a recognition from the National Council on Communicative Disorders. He lives outside his hometown of Dayton, Ohio, where he is working on his next novel and authoring freelance articles. In addition, he continues to speak to high school, college, and community groups, sharing his experiences as a self-published and bestselling author. Visit his Web site at www.ckellyrobinson.com or send him an e-mail at ckrob7071@aol.com.